HAZARDOUS MATERIAL

KURT KAMM

Published by MCM Publishing, a division of Monkey C Media
www.MCMPublishing.com

Book Cover & Interior Design by Monkey C Media
www.MonkeyCMedia.com

Edited by Denise Middlebrooks

Printed in the United States of America

Kamm, Kurt L.

Hazardous Material / Kurt Kamm. -- San Diego, CA :
MCM Publishing, c2013.
      p. ; cm.

ISBN: 978-0-9888882-0-3 (print) ; 978-0-9888882-1-0 (ebk)
Summary: A firefighter battles his painkiller addiction and the
infamous Vagos outlaw motorcycle gang. He joins the Sheriff's
Department in a drone search for a meth lab in the Mojave Desert north
of Los Angeles. An enigmatic aerospace scientist joins the intrigue.
Hazardous Materials, illicit drugs and aerospace technology are brought
together in the author's fourth firefighter mystery. --Publisher.

    1. Fire fighters--California--Fiction. 2. Medication abuse--Fiction.
3. Motorcycle gangs--California--Fiction. 4. Methamphetamine--
Fiction. 5. Hazardous substances--California--Fiction. 6. Aerospace
engineers--Fiction. 7. Drone aircraft--Fiction. 8. Mojave Desert-
-Fiction. 9. California--Fiction. 10. Mystery fiction. I. Title.

PS3611.A4686 H39 2013
813/.6--dc23   1304

ALSO BY KURT KAMM

ONE FOOT IN THE BLACK – A Wildland Firefighter's Story

"Kurt Kamm has been there with the firefighters, step by step, and you will feel in the pages of this book that you are right there in the middle of a firestorm as well."
—Dennis Smith, author of *Report From Engine Co. 82* and *A Decade of Hope*

"With **One Foot in the Black**, Kurt Kamm has used the tools of popular fiction to shine a light on the inner workings of the wildland fire service. The tortured main character, who tries to pull a brutalized life together by joining Cal Fire, the Golden State's fire protection agency, takes us on a journey from training ground to fire ground that vividly captures the sense of family, of pulling together, of physical challenge and mortal danger that go with this increasingly vital occupation."
—John N. Maclean, author of *Fire on the Mountain* and other fire books

CODE BLOOD

An edgy L.A. Noir thriller! Kamm takes the reader into the world of emergency medicine, the science of stem cell research, and the unsettling world of blood fetishism and body parts.

Code Blood is the winner of three FIRST PLACE national literary competitions:
• 2012 International Book Awards, Fiction: Cross Genre category
• National Indie Excellent Book Awards® – Faction (fiction based on fact)
• The 2012 USA Best Book Awards Fiction: Horror

RED FLAG WARNING – A Serial Arson Mystery

"NiteHeat is memorable—another lunatic out setting fires."
—Mike Cole, CalFire Battalion Chief, Law Enforcement

Red Flag Warning has won two FIRST PLACE national mystery competitions:
• The Written Art Awards – Mystery/Thriller 2010
• Royal Dragonfly – Mystery Category 2011

Visit Kurt Kamm's author/firefighter website at **www.KurtKamm.com**

HAZARDOUS MATERIAL

This is a work of fiction. The characters, names and events in this novel are entirely the product of the author's imagination. Many of the fictional events are portrayed in actual locations in and around the County of Los Angeles.

TOXIC WASTE CONSISTS OF WORDS, thoughts, sounds, images, and emotions that are harmful. They damage your heart and mind and make it more difficult to live as a positive person. Toxic waste never makes your life better, and always makes it worse. It creates inner pollution, and if you let it accumulate, you experience an inner holocaust that annihilates your dreams. There is no limit to how bad your life can become when toxic waste fills your heart and mind.

Zero Tolerance to Negative Thinking Website

INTRODUCTION

THE STORY YOU ARE ABOUT to read is fiction, but the methamphetamine and outlaw motorcycle gang subcultures described in this novel are real. The darkness and violence they create touch every community, large and small, across the country.

I have spent 19 years in law enforcement, dealing directly with the members of outlaw motorcycle gangs and with the clandestine world of methamphetamine. I have personally seen the toll that both have taken. We have all heard the stories, watched the newscasts, and seen the highway billboards depicting the havoc that methamphetamine wreaks on both individual users and the environment. Most of us will never experience the drug's devastating effect on users' families, who have to live with it every day.

Methamphetamine and outlaw motorcycle gangs have always been dark partners. Nowhere in the United States has their relationship been more prevalent than in California, a state that has spawned some of the most violent gangs in the world which, in some cases, have become global threats. The dangers posed by outlaw motorcycle gangs should never be understated; they are among the most dangerous criminals on the planet.

If you are looking for a vanilla picture of drug use and the biker world, then stick to T.V. dramas with loveable and conflicted characters. If you want a true picture, you should read HAZARDOUS MATERIAL. Kurt Kamm has conducted painstaking research to provide the reader with an inside look at the bikers, the meth, and the men and women in red hats and blue uniforms who have dedicated their lives to fighting the plague of violence and broken lives.

I know that you will enjoy reading HAZARDOUS MATERIAL as much as I have, and I hope that the next time you see that fire engine, hazmat unit, or police car pass you, you will have a greater appreciation for what "Americas Heroes" are up against. Facing this danger is what we accept when we pin on the badge.

Steve Cook
Midwest Outlaw Motorcycle Gang Investigators Association

ONE

THEY SPENT ALL DAY SMURFING, trying to buy pills with pseudoephedrine at every convenience store and gas station between Valencia and Acton. It didn't work; everyone wanted to see an ID. Then they hit the grocery stores. She stood at the checkout counter and shouted obscenities while Davey and Sky went to the medicine aisle and stuffed their pockets. At Ralphs supermarket, the manager chased Davey out into the parking lot. It got late and they started to sweat and get cramps. The recipe said you needed 10,000 pills to make a pound of meth. They had collected less than 400. It would just have to do. They drove back to the trailer to cook what they had.

The doublewide was filthy. Half-empty containers of Mexican food, candy-bar wrappers and soda cans covered the floor, along with a box of week-old chocolate donuts and a small mountain of torn blister packs. She saw cockroaches going for the food. Maybe they were lizards, or huge ants or spiders. She wasn't sure. She sat on the stained green couch and pulled pieces of stuffing from one of the cushions. Nausea seized her. She was compacting and hadn't shit in a week. Sweat drenched her body. Her skin itched and she thought she felt bugs crawling over her scalp. She twirled her greasy black hair around filthy fingers. Her hands shook as she picked at the scabs on her face and neck.

Sky told her to keep watch outside through the spot he left uncovered on the window. Sky warned her to keep her eyes open and pay attention. She tried, but it was boring and it was hard to concentrate. There was nothing to see. A half-moon hung in the sky and the desert was empty. Sky said the police were out there hiding, watching, waiting. Sky said you never knew when they might come. Sky said this. Sky said that. Talk. Talk. Talk. Sky was a pain in the ass, only good for one thing—helping her get off when she couldn't find a vein.

Her mind drifted. How long had she been here? The time passed so quickly, or did it drag on minute by minute? The bikers had left a pile of stolen laptops, cell phones, iPads, a guitar, power tools and a microwave oven near the door. Snakes slithered out of the guitar. Her heart hammered in her chest. She reached in her pocket and pulled out the cheap Indian amethyst earring she sometimes wore on a chain around her neck. Sometimes she put it on Schare. Where was her daughter Schare? Had she left her somewhere? It was hard to remember anything. It was so hot inside the trailer. She was suffocating. Her fingers were raw from popping pills out of the blister wrap. She put the earring and chain back into her jeans pocket.

Davey turned the old Waring blender to HI, and the whine filled the trailer as diet pills, cold pills and antihistamines were pulverized into a cloud of white dust. "Sweet," he sang out over the noise. "*In*tense. *In*tense." He couldn't stand still. He danced around the counter, his head bobbing. "I'm a chemist." He waved his hands. "I'm a kick*ass* chemist."

Sky came out of the tiny bathroom and pulled his belt tight around his waist. His jeans hung down on his skinny hips. "Fuuuck, how long is this gonna take?" He was desperate for a hit.

"We gotta follow the recipe," Davey said. He stopped fidgeting long enough to turn on the heating coil and place a large aluminum pot on the counter. "I'm the kickass chemist," he repeated, and bent over to study the instructions again. "Hey, we need the denatured alcohol. Where's the denatured alcohol?" He rapped his knuckles against the pot. "Denatured alcohol," Davey screamed.

"Zip it," Sky said. "They could be listening. They have devices."

"Get the alcohol, dude," Davey said. His face twitched. He bobbed his head and danced around.

Sky looked up at the ceiling of the trailer. "They could be coming in on a stealth helicopter, like they used on that Bin Laden guy." Sky had sealed the mobile home tight. He went to one of the small windows covered with black garbage bags and masking tape and looked out into the darkness through a peephole. "They could be outside right now." He smoothed the tape. "You never know. FBI. DEA. ATF. CIA. The Marines. They could have attack dogs. They could be working with the fuckin' bikers. It's a conspiracy. They want our stuff. They could be pointing a death ray at the trailer right now."

"Alcohol!" Davey screamed.

Sky reached under the metal table and pulled out the plastic bucket filled with denatured alcohol. Sky was jittery and his hands shook as he wrestled with the pail. When he yanked the top off, alcohol spilled on the floor. Fumes drifted through the trailer.

She gagged at the odor, twisted her hair around her finger and felt the squish coming on. Nothing mattered now but getting some crank into her body. "Where's the rig?" she asked. "I need the rig. I need a hit." The monster inside chewed on her guts. It was insatiable; it demanded a humping, ginormous hit. It wanted it *now.*

"Keep quiet—I'm reading," Davey said. "I'm studying the recipe. I'm the cook." His head bobbed. "I'm the kickass cook. I'm studying the recipe."

"Where's the…" She found the syringe between the cushions of the couch. The monster told her to dissolve a bump of meth in a teaspoon, suck it into the needle, find a vein and slam it home. Her body required it. Her brain craved it. It was all she could think about. She couldn't do anything without it. She longed for the lovely rush and the waves of calm when the drug swept through her bloodstream. She wanted the snakes, lizards and cockroaches to disappear. She wanted the world to return to its bright, exciting colors. She hated her skinny, filthy body. Once she was beautiful. She was only twenty-seven, but now she had the body of an old woman. Men had once admired her breasts. Now they hung wilted and shrunken like lemons left in the sunlight. Her neck was withered. She weighed less than one hundred pounds. Her teeth were rotting and her breath smelled. A chemical odor oozed from her body. She had bruises and splotches on her arms, between her toes and every other spot where she had shot up whatever drug she could find. Most of her veins had collapsed. Earlier in the day, she had found one on her wrist, but now it too had disappeared under her skin, hiding from another spike.

She picked at her scalp and tried to remember why she was here. Right now, there was nothing but the stinking fumes, the peephole showing the blackness outside and Sky inside, bitching, bitching, bitching.

As soon as Davey finished cooking, they'd be fat with their own crank. That's why she was here—to get her share, find a vein and bang it.

"We're cookin." Davey dialed up the heat on the electric coil. "Can you believe it? We're making our own meth. *Our own meth.* Nobody's gonna rip us off with fake stuff. We're makin' our own Tina."

Sky placed the bucket of denatured alcohol on the counter next to the aluminum pot. "They could be breakin' through the door any minute." More fumes rose into the confined air of the trailer. "Any fuckin' minute, they could be comin' in." He tried not to inhale, but that was impossible.

"Whooeee," Davey said. He held up the ragged sheet of paper and read aloud. "To separate the ephedrine from the binder, mix the powder in the bowl with the alcohol. This is called 'pill pulling.'" He slapped Sky on the back. "We're pros, dude. We're pill pulling. How d'ya like that? We are awesome. We're pill pulling. Tina's coming to our house."

Sky poured denatured alcohol into the pot and managed to spill half of it on the floor, spreading more vapor.

"Now we gotta get rid of the sediment," Davey said. "We're supposed to use Martha Stewart sheets to filter it out."

"Martha fuckin' Stewart sheets?" Sky said.

"It says here they have the smallest weave," Davey said. "Do we have a problem?"

"We'll use what we've got." Sky ripped off a piece of a soiled bed sheet lying on the floor and handed it to Davey.

She watched the snakes continue to glide out of the guitar. Some had two heads; some had a head at each end. She was sweating. Her scalp itched. She dug her fingernails into the places where she had already torn off the scabs. She was dizzy from the vapor. Shit. She needed a cigarette. She stood up and started for the door.

"Hey," Sky demanded, "where you goin?"

"Out to smoke." She reached for the cigarettes in her jeans.

"No you're not." Sky put the bucket of alcohol down and came toward her. She looked into his dead eyes. His pupils were wide open, hollow.

"Keep your eye on the fuckin' window."

Before she could tell him there was nothing to watch, Sky shoved her hard and she stumbled backward onto the torn cushions of the couch.

TWO

*E*NGINES *129, 329* AND HAZMAT *Squad 129 ....*
When the tones sounded, Bucky Dawson lay in the shadows between sleep and wakefulness in his bunk at Station 129. His brain echoed the sadness of the recurring dream about searching for his father, a contract firefighter killed by a land mine in the burning oilfields of Kuwait. When he opened his eyes, Bucky saw the flashing orange light in the hall indicating a HazMat incident. He checked his watch. It was 1:45 a.m. A HazMat call at 1:45 in the morning? It had to be a meth lab.

The disembodied voice from dispatch continued to echo over the speaker: *... respond to Lancaster Narcotics call. Meet sheriff's escort at La Tijera Road exit off Highway 14.*

Bucky was fully conscious now and smelled the scents and odors of the station. Last night's green peppers hung in the air. The ammonia solution used to swab down the floors released its distinctive tang. The hydrocarbons from the lubes and diesel fuel in the apparatus bay seeped into his nostrils. He got out of bed, pulled on his jeans and stepped out into the hall. While the three men from the Air Squad—a helicopter pilot and two paramedics—rolled over in their bunks and pulled pillows over their heads to block out the light and noise, nine men from the Los Angeles County Fire Department Hazardous Materials Task Force 129, some only half awake, gathered in front of their lockers and began to pull on their gear.

Randy Farrell, the team leader, yawned and looked at his watch. "Ten to two. Must be a Tweaker call."

"Why do they have to cook meth at this hour?" Bucky said. He didn't expect a response. Everyone knew the answer—tweakers never slept.

"Those freaks have no respect for a person's sleep," AJ, the safety officer, said.

"No respect, period," Farrell added. He yawned again.

"Let's grab a bunch of the meth-heads and bring them back to the station," AJ said.

"Then what?" Bucky said.

"And then beat some respect into them." AJ shook a ham-sized fist in the air. "We'll keep 'em here for detox. They can sweep the station, polish the apparatus and clean the toilets."

"Then we wouldn't have anything to do." Bucky said.

"Not tonight, Rambo," Farrell said to AJ. "Let's go."

The crew moved through the doors from the sleeping quarters directly into the cavernous two-story equipment bay where cold blue-white fluorescent lights reflected off the polished, deep-red paint of the vehicles. The outer doors rumbled up into the ceiling and the high desert wind blew dust in their faces. The men hoisted themselves into their engines, slipped on their headphones and hit the ignition switches. Diesel engines rumbled, Farrell blasted his air horn once and HazMat Task Force 129 rolled out into the darkness of the Mojave Desert.

They travelled down Highway 14, which bisected the south end of the desert. The road was empty and they went with red lights but no sirens. Bucky sat on one of the jump seats in the back compartment of the massive HazMat Squad, the vehicle they called the Box. His entry partner Jason, as well as AJ, sat with him. Bucky smelled the Red Hot cinnamon candies on AJ's breath and wondered if he ate them in his sleep. The air conditioning kicked in and blew frigid air at their backs. Through the glass partition, they could see Farrell and Baxter in the front cab. The dashboard reflected tiny pools of red, orange and green light from dozens of gauges, switches and instruments.

The diesel gave off a deep-throated rumble and created a vibration that climbed Bucky's spine. The jump seats were hard, with upright back supports and he felt a faint pain in his lower back. He had taken a Percocet before he went to sleep several hours earlier. Now he wanted another, but would wait until they returned to the station. The agonizing sting from his pinched nerve had subsided to an occasional twinge almost two months ago, but he still took the painkillers. Bucky knew it was time to quit, but the Percs made everything a little better—he felt more energetic, happier, and best of all, the nightmares didn't come as often.

Just before the Kern County line, Task Force 129 turned off onto La Tijera Road, a strip of cratered old blacktop that ran for a couple of miles before it turned into dirt. A deputy wearing a reflective SHERIFF'S DEPARTMENT vest stood by the door of his black and white at the end of the pavement. As they approached, he waved them over with a high-powered halogen flashlight and spoke into the radio on his shoulder. The two engines stopped behind the HazMat Squad and the firefighters climbed out to hear what the deputy had to say.

"We've got a major meth lab out there," the deputy told them. "Mexican nationals in a doublewide. They're probably armed. We've got an entry team going in as soon as you get into position."

"Where's 'out there'?" Bucky asked.

"East—Jesus," the officer said. "About twelve miles southwest. Dirt road all the way."

"Why are we doing this now?" Baxter asked.

"We got the tip around midnight," the deputy said. "We've been waiting for weeks for this. It's a big takedown. We're going in non-code, no lights, and no sirens. You follow me. We have to hurry, but keep your RPMs down. We can't have a lot of noise."

"Fuckin-A," AJ said. "We'll be so quiet you can hear a lizard fart."

Bucky doubted that two 21-ton fire engines and an 18-ton HazMat Squad the size of a tour bus could be quiet at any speed.

"As soon as you get there," the deputy said, "our team will take out their cameras, lights and motion detectors. Once we do that, we have to make an immediate entry, before they realize what's going on."

"Can you describe the layout?" Farrell asked.

"You'll be downwind," the deputy said. "Is that what you wanted to know?"

"*Down*wind?" Farrell said. "You're kidding. We're not coming in downwind of a meth lab."

"We can't help it," the deputy said. "The road runs on the south side of the trailer. There's no way you can drive across the sand to the other side. There's a stand of Joshua trees, about 250 yards from the trailer. You'll be behind that." He handed Farrell two King radios.

"Monitor the tactical blue channel, but do not, repeat, *do not* break radio silence."

"Are we going in?" Bucky asked. "Or just standing around?"

"You're on standby," the deputy said. "We have a forensics van. They should be able to handle the lab. OK? C'mon, we've gotta roll."

Bucky knew what "standby" meant. It meant their entire team had to set up as though it were a full-blown hazardous materials incident and then just wait, do nothing, and finally pack up and return to the station. He had already been through the meth lab drill in the middle of the night a few times.

Long before Bucky joined the fire department, Lancaster had become the U.S. capital for methamphetamine production. The remote areas of the vast Mojave Desert were perfect for the Mexican gangs and the bikers who moved in to set up big, dangerous drug labs. Skinheads and outlaw bikers, using the "Nazi" manufacturing method, fought for dominance with the illegals using the "Mexican National" method. They set booby traps to protect their own operations and blew up each other's labs. Sometimes the chemical vapors from the cooking ignited, creating powerful explosions that added to the mayhem. There were countless stories from old-timers in the fire department about drug raids. In the beginning, law enforcement relied on County Fire to deal with the toxic liquids and fumes and the first HazMat teams suffered burns from corrosive chemicals, inhalation injuries from toxic vapors and one firefighter died in an explosion. Things were different now. The narcs had their own multi-agency response team called IMPACT, experienced hazardous materials handlers trained by the Department of Justice to work a meth-lab crime scene. Law enforcement no longer wanted firefighters stomping around destroying evidence, but occasionally they still called out a HazMat team in the middle of the night and when the tone sounded, the response team rolled out, set up and did nothing for several hours while the Narcotics Squad took down bikers, Mexicans, or paranoid speed freaks.

"Why call us at all?" Bucky once asked his lifelong friend, Miguel "Mike" Ortiz, a detective on the North County Narcotics Squad. "You won't let us near the scene anyway. Why not use IMPACT?"

Mike, a tough little guy who looked like he lifted weights all day, said, "It's all about timing. Sometimes we have to move fast and there's no time to get a warrant and mobilize IMPACT. The first thing defense attorneys do is try to get the evidence thrown out by proving that an illegal search occurred. We have to show it's a volatile situation—you know, imminent danger to life and property, escape of suspects, that kind of stuff. We have to establish the need for an immediate response, which is called 'exigent circumstances.' We bring you out and that indicates we think there's imminent danger and no time to get a warrant."

Bucky looked into the darkness of the desert as the Box bounced along over the dirt road. The stars sparkled and a half moon hung in the sky. When they approached the stand of Joshua trees, he made out two sheriff's vans that belonged to the assault team and the assessment team—a criminalist and scientific support personnel. He reached into his pack for the night vision glasses he had purchased on eBay. This was a perfect time to try them out.

The HazMat vehicles stopped next to the sheriff's vans and Bucky was the first one out of the Box. He was surprised because there was no telltale odor in the air. He expected a thick, sweet stench drifting downwind from the meth lab. Instead, his exceptional, almost preternatural sense of smell picked up only faint alcohol vapors.

Farrell joined him in the dark. "Smell anything, Buck?" he asked.

"Not much," Bucky said. "Alcohol fumes." He checked the scene with his night vision glasses and saw the doublewide outlined in glowing green. The windows were masked from the inside, but light poured out from a few spots left uncovered. More illumination leaked from under the front door and through a few small holes in the side of the trailer.

Bucky's entry partner, Jason, joined him outside, rolled up a door on the side of the Box and pulled out the large drawer containing their SCBA air tanks and masks. The men from the engines joined them and slid out other drawers that contained protective suits, measuring devices and decontamination equipment. They began to bump test—warm up—the meters they would use to test the air if they had to make entry. AJ pointed the temperature gun at the trailer, but was too far away to get a reading. Bucky let his night vision glasses hang around his neck and helped begin the setup.

Bucky knew the routine: At a cost of thousands of dollars, the nine men from the HazMat task force would spend the rest of the night staging in the desert. They assumed nothing and followed a strict safety procedure. Two

21

HazMat entry men, one of whom was Bucky, and a backup team, would be in full protective gear, ready to move forward if needed. They would test for toxic vapors as they proceeded, and if they got unusual meter readings, would stop or pull back until they determined what they were dealing with. Decontamination equipment would be set up to wash them off when they returned. The tech ref—the technical reference man—would remain in the Box and boot up the electronic gear. He would connect to various databases and to the weather bureau, analyze the readouts sent by the entry team's meters, track airborne contaminants and report the findings.

Bucky left his turnout coat unbuttoned. Tonight, the early morning September temperature was warmer than usual, hovering in the upper fifties. He slung his breathing apparatus onto his back and let the mask hang at his side. He leaned against the side of the Squad and focused his night glasses again on the doublewide. They were the old first-generation binoculars, but they still provided adequate light intensification and a decent image. Bucky followed two green bodies, men from the sheriff's assault team, crawling on the ground around the trailer. He thought they might be cutting wires or disarming booby traps. Three other figures edged forward. Two carried assault rifles and one held the ram that would pulverize the thin metal trailer door on the first impact. Bucky couldn't determine whether his friend Mike, from the sheriff's department, was part of the group.

Bucky was still looking through his night vision glasses when the door to the trailer suddenly opened, flooding the sand with a bright rectangle of light. The assault team pulled back and melted into the darkness. A thin woman wearing a white T-shirt and jeans came to the doorway with a cigarette between her lips. She stood for a moment, twisted her hair around her index finger and then pulled a lighter from her pocket. As she struck a flame, it illuminated part of her face and Bucky was astounded. It looked like it was his sister Brandy standing in the doorway of the trailer. He couldn't be certain, but his sister had the distinctive habit of twisting her hair around her finger—something she had done since she was a child. Bucky played with the focus on his glasses and tried to get a better look at her face.

The sound of the explosion hit his eardrums a split second after the flash of light from the 2,000-degree ignition. The woman's body disappeared in an expanding ball of orange fire and the doublewide disintegrated in the blast that blew the roof off and the walls outward. The powerful odor of combustion was the last thing to reach Bucky's senses as burning pieces of debris fell to the ground.

Bucky heard the frantic chatter from the sheriff's assault team coming from the radios. He and the other men from HazMat Task Force 129 watched the light from the explosion subside as flames consumed the remains of what had been a clandestine methamphetamine laboratory.

THREE

"THAT WAS SOME EXPLOSION."

In the early morning hour, every light was on in Station 129. The returning men, high on adrenaline, stood in front of their lockers, taking off their turnouts and talking about what had happened. The air-rescue flight crew, awakened by the loud, excited voices, crawled out of their bunks and stood in their underwear listening.

"Just after I was deployed," Farrell continued, "an incoming shell hit a half-empty munitions trailer. Same kind of fireball. You never forget the concussion from an explosion like that."

"Explosion?" someone from the flight crew asked.

"Meth lab," Baxter said.

"We were back maybe 250 yards," Farrell said. "There's a doublewide, and the Sheriff's Department is all over the place. They're about to take the door down with a ram when a woman comes out and lights a cigarette. Can you believe it? She lights a cigarette."

"Boom," AJ said. He looked up at the ceiling. "It's raining aluminum and tweakers."

"It was a little close for comfort," Baxter said. "It almost took out a couple of narcs."

"They're gonna be picking up body parts with tweezers," AJ said.

Bucky sat on the bench, still wearing his gear, and stared at the floor. His night vision glasses hung from his neck, the smell of the blast etched into his memory along with the image of the woman consumed by the ball of fire. "I think that was my sister," he said in a low voice.

The conversation stopped. Everyone turned to look at him.

AJ was the first to speak. "What? Your sister?"

Bucky nodded.

Farrell sat down on the bench and put his hand on Bucky's back. "Oh man, that's terrible. I thought you said she was ... uh ... in prison." Farrell realized his remark didn't help and looked at the other men for support.

"How do you know it was your sister?" Jason asked.

"I was watching her with my night vision glasses."

"No way," Jason said.

"I'm not certain, but my sister is small, thin, the same body type." Bucky rubbed his eyes and took off his turnout jacket. "And she has this habit of twisting her hair around her finger...."

"C'mon, Buck," AJ said. "We were pretty far away. It could have been anyone."

Bucky stood up, pushed his Nomex pants down onto his boots, slipped them off and stuffed everything into his locker. He held his head in his hands for a moment and then looked at his watch. It was 6:00 a.m., two hours before his shift was over. He wanted a pill.

As soon as he arrived home, Bucky popped a Percocet. He chased it down with a glass of orange juice and walked out onto his tiny wood deck, sandblasted by the wind. He lived in the smallest house in a neighborhood of small houses, on the flats below Quartz Hill, the only decent residential area in Lancaster. Somewhere a dog barked. The sky began to turn to a pale blue as the sun rose in the September sky. Within minutes, the Perc began to take effect and created the mild opiate haze he had come to depend on. Hours before, he thought he had seen his sister blown apart in a meth lab explosion, but now, with the drug in his bloodstream, his pain and sadness were muffled.

The last time he had seen Brandy was several years ago, in a federal prison in Colorado. When had she been released and why hadn't she contacted him? He knew he was at fault for Brandy's path in life—he was her older brother and she had been his responsibility. Once again, Bucky wondered how the little sister he had tried to protect and nurture grew up to be a biker chick and a drug addict.

He went inside and called the Lancaster Sheriff's Station. He didn't expect Mike to be in his office, but he answered on the second ring.

"Detective Ortiz."

"Mike? It's Bucky."

"Hey Buck. Were you out on that meth lab response last night?"

"Yeah, you?"

"I almost got my fucking head blown off. That was too close for comfort. Been sitting here for the last two hours writing a report. What's up?

"Mike, I think Brandy might have been the one who came to the door and lit the cigarette."

"Brandy? Out at the trailer?"

"Did you get a look?" Bucky asked.

"Hell no, I had my face in the sand."

"I'm not really sure, but—"

"That's hard to believe, but let me put a call in to the coroner's office. I'll talk to you later—I'm swamped and I haven't slept in twenty-four hours."

By mid-morning, the effect of the Percocet had come and gone and Bucky was exhausted. He went into his bedroom, took off his T-shirt and scratched his shoulder and chest. Recently, he had developed an itching sensation that wouldn't go away. Small patches of his skin were red and irritated and he wondered if it might be from the Percs. He lay down on the bed and as soon as he closed his eyes, he fell into a troubled sleep.

Bucky dreamed of a long line of bikers roaring down Highway 14. His sister stood on the bitch pad of one of the Harleys and as they wove back and forth, she leaped from one bike to another, never losing her balance. The bikers watched her, yelled obscenities and pumped their fists in the air as a salute each time she jumped. She shouted something to him. He knew she was angry but she was speaking a strange language he couldn't understand.

He awoke hours later to the voice of a woman from the County Coroner's Office leaving a message on his answering machine. She said they were trying to identify the persons killed in the trailer explosion and had received a call from Detective Ortiz. In the morning, she was sending an investigator to Bucky's home to get a swab of his DNA.

The remainder of the day was a blur. In the late afternoon, Bucky went out to the garage and pumped iron for an hour and a half. Lifting weights was a ritual. The whisper of the cables running through the pulleys, the clank of the iron plates dropping into place and his own heavy breathing—all were sounds that soothed him. He liked the way his heart pounded and the feeling of blood surging through his veins. He did repetitions until his muscles were exhausted. When he finished, his body was drenched with sweat.

When he came inside, Bucky stopped to look at Zoll, the lizard he had recently picked up after the HazMat team responded to a woman's frantic 9-1-1 call about an alligator in her garage. The owner of Critter Corner in Lancaster had identified it as a Savannah Monitor lizard, indigenous to Ethiopia. He said it had to be someone's pet that had escaped. Bucky named it after the Zoll monitor, the cardiac device the fire paramedics carried. He was fascinated with the reptile because he had learned that lizards smell with their tongues, picking up scent particles in the air from half a mile away. When he first brought the lizard home, he had spent hours waving onions, hot dogs, sprigs of mint and other items above the glass tank, watching the lizard for a response. The foot-long reptile flicked its tongue, but otherwise remained immobile, hiding with only its head protruding from a cave of small rocks inside its glass tank.

Bucky went to the refrigerator and extracted two of the live worms he had purchased at the pet store. When he held them inside the tank, Zoll's tongue struck like lightning, taking the worms in an instant. "Good girl," Bucky said, although he had no idea of the lizard's gender.

In the evening, he took another P, upping the daily ante for the first time from three to four pills. He floated along for a couple of hours until he sank back into the swamp of his thoughts. Bucky had worried for some time that addiction would take his sister, but it was always a vague anxiety about something that might occur in the distant future, not anything that would happen now, and certainly not because of a meth lab explosion. He lay awake in bed and replayed the events in the desert, culminating in the scene of the woman's body enveloped by orange flames. He watched the film in slow motion, viewing each frame carefully, trying to see the figure at the door of the double-wide more clearly. He watched as she twirled hair around her finger and he tried to persuade himself it wasn't Brandy.

Perhaps he was mistaken. The night vision glasses could have played tricks on his eyes. Maybe Farrell was right—he was too far away to see clearly. Bucky thought of every reason why he could be wrong, but in his heart, he knew otherwise.

He thrashed around on his bed in the dark and the memories started coming back. Bucky was nineteen when he found their mother in bed, dead from liver failure. It was 1999, and Brandy was only fifteen at the time. They had been fending for themselves since their father was killed in Kuwait eight years earlier. Now they were truly alone.

Named after her mother's favorite drink, Brandy never had an interest in alcohol, but she couldn't pass up a pill or a powder. Bucky knew she had sampled painkillers, muscle relaxants, stimulants and whatever else her friends stole from their parents' medicine cabinets. As she grew older, Brandy began to smoke marijuana regularly and when she started asking him for money, he found out she was buying Ecstasy and Ketamine on the street. She was usually high when she came home, giving him a sullen stare and locking herself in her bedroom. The silences began to last longer and her anger became more explosive.

Brandy had a short childhood. She grew up too soon, staying out late at night partying and missing school. She became a stunning teenager and looked several years older than her real age. Bucky wondered where her beauty came from. He saw traces of both their mother and father in her face, but Brandy's looks were unique. Her only real interest was men—not boys. She had an intense need to be desired, and gloried in their attention. Bucky wondered why she always chose the ones who were the worst of the worst.

Brandy found her own replacement family of bikers, addicts and other lowlifes. She began to disappear for days at a time and when Bucky refused to give her money, she stopped coming home at all. One afternoon, after a two-month absence, she returned on the back of a Harley. She was with a man at least twice her age who looked like trouble. He waited outside on his hog while Brandy came in and told Bucky, "I'm going to Burning Man for a week. I need some cash."

"In Nevada? How do you plan to get there?"

"We're going on Kenny's motorcycle." Brandy looked out toward the driveway. "Can I have some money?"

"You're going with that guy?"

"Yeah, with *that guy*. He said it'll be a learning experience. Every year they have a theme. This year it's The Body. It's all about self-expression."

"A learning experience?" Bucky was furious. "It's a weeklong drug orgy. Anything could happen to you. Bikers share their women. You could get raped."

Brandy snorted and said, "Get real, Bucky. Are you going to give me some money or not?"

"No way."

"Then fuck you."

Bucky remembered that incident as the moment when he no longer recognized the person who had once been his little sister. When she went upstairs to pack up a few of her belongings, he confronted Kenny the biker, who sat astride his Harley in the middle of the driveway. The engine was running and each time he gunned it, a deep roar reverberated through the straight drag pipes.

"Aren't you robbing the cradle?" Bucky shouted over the noise.

The biker looked at Bucky through dark glasses, smiled and said nothing.

After Brandy left for Nevada, Bucky didn't hear from her for three years, until she called him collect from the Colorado Women's Correctional Facility.

Bucky was still awake when the first light of morning came. He glanced at the clock and wondered what time the investigator from the coroner's office would arrive. He willed his exhausted body out of bed and went into the bathroom. A splash of cold water on his face roused him, and when he saw his reflection in the mirror, he was shocked at his haggard image. He reached for the Percocet bottle and dumped the contents into the palm of his hand. Twenty-eight of the oblong, pale yellow 10-milligram pills remained. Even if he limited himself to three Percs a day, Bucky realized he would need a refill in less than ten days. The previous week, he had called his doctor's office twice and left a message requesting a prescription renewal. When he got no response, he sent an email. The following day, a nurse wrote back, "Dr. Randall has received your messages for renewal of the Percocet prescription. To prevent abuse of leftover painkillers, telephone and e-mail requests for prescription refills will not be honored. If you are experiencing pain, please come in for a consultation."

Three years earlier, when Bucky struggled to move a 250-pound compressed gas cylinder, he strained his back and the pain had been so bad he could barely move. He tried over-the-counter pain relievers, maximum strength Tylenol, NSAIDs and even muscle relaxants, but nothing helped. He was off work for almost two weeks before Dr. Randall, a workers' comp orthopedist, wrote a prescription for sixty Percocet tablets and told him to take one pill four times a day for seven to ten days. The pills were a miracle—the pain diminished, and as a side effect, Bucky discovered his mood had improved and he was sleeping better. He was back working regular shifts in a week.

On several subsequent occasions, he twisted or strained his back and the agony returned. Each time, Bucky went to Dr. Randall and took home another prescription. "Percocet is Oxycontin's ugly little sister," the doctor warned. "Use it only when you need it." Bucky listened and used the painkiller sparingly. In the process, he accumulated a supply of extra pills. When he tweaked his back in July, he went to the doctor and received yet another prescription. Now, it was mid-September, weeks after the pain had subsided, and Bucky hadn't stopped; he was still taking the pills. When it was in his bloodstream, he was still Bucky, just a happier, more energetic version of himself.

Bucky paused before swallowing his morning Perc and wondered if he was an "abuser." His mother and sister were addicts; what did that make him? He concluded he had no reason to worry. The difference was that he didn't need Percocet, except maybe right now during this rough patch in his life. He knew he had to stop taking the pills, but he could do it anytime—tomorrow, next week, or whenever—it was no big deal, this just wasn't the right time.

He looked at himself in the mirror again and this time saw a healthy thirty-one-year-old firefighter, a man who lifted weights, who was in good condition and who took care of himself. Bucky Dawson couldn't be a drug addict. He made a decision—he would continue using the Percocet over the weekend and would definitely stop on Monday. No problem.

A white car with a Los Angeles County logo parked on the driveway. When Bucky opened the front door, a heavy-set woman carrying a black briefcase extended her hand. "Mr. Dawson?" she said. "Samantha Dudley. I'm an investigator with the Coroner's Office." She held up the ID in the plastic pouch hanging around her neck.

Bucky shook her hand and said, "Come in."

A faint medicinal smell came from the investigator. Bucky wondered if she spent time in the depths of the morgue, handling bodies.

"I'm sorry," she said, "I understand your sister may be one of the deceased."

"That's what we're going to find out, I guess."

"Normally a relative can do a visual of the … uh … body, or look at something identifiable. In this case—"

"I know. I saw the explosion." Bucky rolled up his sleeve. "You want a blood sample, right? Should we do this in the kitchen?" He wondered if the Percocet would show up.

"Actually all we need is a buccal swab."

"A what?"

"A swab of your cheek cells. We can do it right here." The investigator put her briefcase down on the small table in the entranceway and removed a glass tube with a long Q-tip inside. "All I have to do is rub the inside of your mouth. It's real simple."

"How long does this take?" Bucky asked, and opened his mouth.

"We should have results in two or three days. We run 24/7, but we're understaffed and there's a huge backlog." The investigator rubbed the inside of his cheek with the swab.

Bucky remembered AJ's comment about picking up the body parts with tweezers and imagined the coroner somehow comparing the remains to the cells from his mouth. Would there be a match? Would a technology he didn't even comprehend confirm that Brandy was killed in the explosion?

Samantha Dudley removed the swab, inserted it into a glass tube and sealed it.

Bucky had a wild thought. Could this woman send his DNA somewhere to create new family members? Maybe some research center could conceive another Brandy, and maybe a new mother and father as well. Bucky would have a complete family again and this time things would be different. He would make sure his new father stayed home and helped raise them. He would confront his new mother and make her stop drinking. He would take better care of Brandy and not let her get involved with bikers and drugs. Would the cloned versions of his mother and sister still be prone to addiction? Was there some sort of overriding pattern in the genes that would send everyone down the same path even if they all started over?

"What did you do before all the fancy DNA stuff," Bucky asked. "How did you identify a corpse?"

"Dental records, usually. We used whatever part of the jaw we could get. Sometimes it took forever." She took a clipboard out of her briefcase. "Just a few questions and we're done."

"Go ahead."

"Full name?"

"Bucky Dawson. Bucky Richard Dawson."

"Bucky is your actual first name, not a nickname?"

"Real name."

"Date of birth?"

"2-18-80."

"And your Social?"

"Social Security number?"

"Yes."

"952-56-3670."

"I need the same info for your sister."

"Brandy Michelle Dawson. Birthday…" Bucky paused to think. "6-1-84. I don't know her Social Security number."

"That's OK, we can get it," the woman smiled and said. "That's it. Thanks, Mr. Dawson." She closed her briefcase and extended her hand again.

He stood at the door and watched the investigator back off the driveway, then went back into the kitchen. He washed his coffee cup, looked at the lizard, turned on the television, turned it off and wandered out onto the back deck. The wind blew in his face and he went back inside. A long, empty day loomed ahead like a stretch of the Mojave. He sat at the kitchen table and tried desperately to think of something to do. He could go to the grocery; his refrigerator was almost empty. He could change the oil in the Bronco; the warning light was flashing on the dashboard. He could get another tattoo. He had a double strand of barbwire on his biceps and had intended for months to add something to it. Bucky couldn't sit still for an ink needle right now; he was too restless and it was the wrong time to make a decision about something as permanent as a tattoo. He just had to get through the day. Tomorrow he would be back on duty and busy, unless the coroner confirmed Brandy's death and the department insisted on bereavement leave. If he had to mourn his sister's death, he wanted to do it without taking time off. A week away from work was a frightening prospect.

The feeling of his morning Perc began to fade. The effect of the pills seemed to be diminishing and Bucky wondered if he could be building up a tolerance to the drug. If so, that would be the first step to addiction. It was probably time to stop. He would do it soon, but not today. To prove to himself that he could control his drug use, he decided to wait until after lunch to take another pill.

Bucky went to the refrigerator and took out a pear—one of two resting on the bottom shelf. Pears were Bucky's favorite fruit because of their fragrance. He never tired of the gentle aroma of a pear and the Bosc was the best, with the sweetest of scents. He sliced the fruit, put the pieces on a plate and pulled up a chair in front of the lizard's tank, which rested on a kitchen counter. "What's up, Zoll?" he asked. The lizard was on top of a rock, soaking up the warmth from the heat lamp. It was immobile, except for its tongue, which moved constantly. Bucky leaned in toward the tank and said, "Not much of a talker, are you?" The lizard retreated into its cave. Christ, Bucky thought, I'm sitting here alone, talking to a *lizard*.

He finished his pear and tried to imagine what had gone on in the trailer the night of the raid. Was Brandy there? Was she strung-out, learning to cook meth with one of her biker boyfriends? Bucky tried to visualize the last hours of her life, but all he could see was the image of the explosion.

Fifteen minutes later, Bucky was thinking about taking another Perc and worried about his supply. He booted up his computer, googled online pharmacies and scrolled through the websites for prescription drugs. Some required a brief telephone call with a "doctor." *Endlessmeds.com* promised it had "great relations with many understanding and compassionate physicians who will write you a prescription over the phone." *Noprescriptions.com* advertised, "Buy Direct." *BuyDrugs.com* offered "an anonymous handle so no one knows your identity but you."

BuyDrugs looked like the best bet. The site offered Endocet, Magnacet, Narvox, Roxicet, Tylox and Bp Percocet. Bucky had no idea the drug had so many variations. He placed two 30-tablet bottles of Bp Percocet in his online shopping cart. Including a $35 membership fee and $15 for second-day priority mail delivery, the total was $735, a staggering amount. He had no idea how much Percocet was supposed to cost because his insurance had always covered prescriptions from his doctor. This was a big expenditure, actually a huge expenditure, but right now, he wanted to have the extra Percs *just in case.* He charged everything on his credit card and tried not to think of the cost.

Bucky scratched his chest. The itching was getting worse. Before he logged off, he searched "Percocet Side Effects" and saw that one of the first signs of overuse was itching. He also read about the difference between abuse and addiction—addiction was a biological disorder and abuse was "inappropriate" use. Neither definition applied to him because he was only using the pills during this emergency, until he knew whether his sister was dead or alive. He read further about a Percocet addict who was taking twenty pills a day and was found in bed lying in his own waste. That was awful, but had nothing to do with him. He didn't have any of the side effects listed on the website like nausea, vomiting, convulsions, confusion, constipation, sweating or itching. Well, he did have the beginning of a skin rash, and the irritation was getting worse, but maybe it was from the heat. Bucky concluded he had nothing to worry about. Next week, he planned to begin to wind down his usage, and that would be the end of it.

He surfed the Internet for a few more minutes, became bored and logged off. The walls of the house were closing in on him; he had to get out and do something. It was almost time for lunch and he decided to head for the station. He hoped the companionship of the men on B Shift would lift his spirits.

FOUR

"A CESSPOOL OF UNDESIRABLES." That was the description of Lancaster in an *Antelope Valley News* article.

On his way to Station 129, Bucky looked at the gang graffiti scrawled on signs and walls across the city. His hometown had changed so much that he hardly recognized it. When he was growing up, Lancaster was a nice, safe, middle-class city. Now it was a ghetto of marginal people, lifted from the inner city and spilled out onto the high desert. The transformation began when the state created "affordable housing" in the Antelope Valley and filled Lancaster with low-income subdivisions. Later, a prison opened and then Immigration and Customs Enforcement—ICE—built a detention center to hold criminals awaiting deportation. Lancaster became the scrapheap for all the things no one wanted in their own towns. Bucky's childhood community was now home to Crips, Bloods, and other gang members, their friends and relations. At the same time the gangs were moving in, the methamphetamine craze attracted bikers, Mexican illegals, drug dealers and meth freaks. The empty spaces of the high desert became a magnet for anyone who wanted to be a meth chef. Crime became rampant and decent people were afraid to go out after dark. The Sheriff's Department helicopters—"ghetto birds"—orbited nightly, shining their spotlights on streets where semi-automatic gunfire was a regular occurrence. Anyone who could afford to move away did so. When the financial crisis hit, families who were upside down on their mortgages walked away, leaving their homes to meth chemists and drug addicts. The decent people who remained in Lancaster were prisoners in their own hometown.

When Bucky turned onto Avenue M and crossed over Highway 14, he passed the Valero carwash and made a U-turn. His old Bronco was dusty on the outside and filthy on the inside. Bucky thought it might cheer him up if he stopped to have it washed.

The carwash had been renovated since he was a child and the storefront church next door, where his mother had attended AA meetings, was torn down years ago. As Bucky walked along the narrow corridor, watching the rotating brushes and soap wash the Mojave grit from his Bronco, he inhaled the smell of the detergent and remembered the times he and Brandy had waited in the air-conditioned cashier's area while their mother shared her problems with other addicts next door. He remembered how Brandy, seven years old, clutched Schare, her doll, and cried whenever they were left at the Valero station. Brandy was terrified, thinking each time that their mother had abandoned them. Bucky tried to distract his little sister by pulling greeting cards from the racks and making up stories about the pictures. Sometimes people paying for their carwash paused to ask if they were lost or needed help, which made Brandy even more frightened.

Bucky watched through the glass windows as his Bronco worked its way to the end of the carwash. While a crew of kids dried it off with dirty rags, he stood on the sidewalk and looked at the spot where the church had been.

After the AA meeting, their mother came outside and spoke in a loud gravel voice to another AA member, a skinny man with a sunken chest. "I'm supposed to feel like I'm never alone? Give me a break."

Bucky stood with Brandy and listened to their mother. "Who do they think they're kidding? I just lost my husband in Kuwait and I got two kids. What am I supposed to do with them, huh? We're tryin' to live on his miserable fireman's pension. Hah—that's a joke. You bet I'm alone and I don't see anybody rushin' in to help me." She subsided into a fit of coughing and hacking.

The man with the sunken chest nodded his head as she pointed to her children. "How am I supposed to raise these two? Huh?" She fished a cigarette out of her purse, lit it and inhaled. "Am I supposed to work and take care of my kids and stay clean? How am I supposed to do all that? Huh?"

The man with the sunken chest turned away and started across the street.

Their mother approached them. Her eyes were bloodshot, her face bloated and her pasty skin the color of the Mojave sand. Bucky was only eleven, but already understood that the family had no money because his mother spent it on alcohol and repeated visits to rehab clinics. Brandy, four years younger, had terror in her eyes as their mother reached down and tried to take her hand. Brandy clutched Schare and moved closer to her older brother.

As the years passed, their mother sank deeper into her addiction. She often remained in her bedroom all day, and if she did manage to get out of bed, sat in the kitchen or out on the deck, drank Bloody Marys, smoked and coughed. Later in the day, if she could function, she might make an effort to clean the house or prepare dinner. By the evening, she was back in oblivion.

Bucky learned to ignore the turmoil of his life and concentrate on getting through one day at a time. He did his best to take care of his younger sister, but he wasn't a mother or a father, he was just Bucky, her older brother.

Bucky watched several teenagers make a halfhearted effort to dry the Bronco. It was still dripping when they finished. He gave them a couple of bucks and the remaining water evaporated in the late morning desert heat as he continued across Avenue M toward the station. The brief high desert transition from 115-degree summer days to 15-degree winter nights was underway and for a couple of weeks the weather would be tolerable.

Station 129 was located on a nowhere street between two junk yards. In addition to the resident fire and HazMat crews, the station had a landing pad where Air Ops stationed one of its Blackhawk helicopters, the Bird, for fire and medical emergency response in the North county. It rested with its enormous rotor blades hanging down, resembling an insect dying in the heat of the desert sun. At the front of the station, the American and State of California flags flapped, edges frayed from the continual wind. On the far side, the two-story apparatus bay doors opened onto 6th Street.

Bucky drove around to the back of the station and saw that Engine 329 and the Box had just pulled in. He parked in the shade and walked across the cement into the bay. The first man out of the Squad was Walter Browne, Captain of the B Shift. "Hey Buck," he said. "What's this I hear about your sis'?" Browne stepped forward and clapped Bucky on the back. "What're you doing here?"

"I thought I might join you for lunch. Were you out on a call?"

"Yeah, a natural gas line ruptured out near Plant 42 early this morning. There was a huge gas cloud blowing toward one of the facilities. They evacuated half the buildings and set up a security perimeter. The federal police were all over. Closed down Avenue M."

"Full security alert?"

"Of course, but it was just a corroded valve. SoCal Gas was out there almost as fast as we were. We tracked the gas while they shut down the line and did the repair. At least we got some good practice at modeling a toxic air cloud." Browne looked at his watch. "I can't believe it took five hours."

Bucky had been on a few HazMat calls that took him into the restricted zone around Air Force Plant 42. It was more than a "plant." There were actually several groups of huge buildings spread out over an area of more than ten square miles. Some of the facilities were big enough to hold the largest aircraft and had what the Air Force called "fly away" capability from a shared runway that ran down the center of the area. An Air Force Colonel was in charge of Plant 42 and Bucky had responded to one incident where the HazMat team had to wait outside a building until the Air Force decided whether to allow them inside. Many of the operations conducted top-secret defense work and had a let-it-burn policy rather than admit outsiders, even firefighters.

The men from the B Shift saw Bucky and gathered around him.

"Hey, Bucky, I heard about the other night."

"Any word about your sister?"

"You think it was her?"

"Sorry, man."

Suddenly Bucky felt claustrophobic, even in the enormous equipment bay, and was sorry he had come to the station.

"What was she doing out there?"

"She hanging with bikers?"

Bucky felt he couldn't bear to stand around again describing the explosion and answering questions about his sister. He wanted to be outside, away from all the same men whose company he had just sought. "Thanks, guys," he said, and backed away. "I guess I do need some time off." He retreated to his Bronco and sat for a moment, watching the men connect the Squad and engines to the overhead exhaust vents, and then disappear into the station to prepare lunch.

As he was about to leave, Bucky was startled by the roar of a jet overhead. He looked up through the windshield to see an unfamiliar aircraft with short stubby wings, less than a thousand feet above the station. He watched while it rolled ninety degrees, rolled farther to fly upside down, and finally completed the circle and righted itself. It climbed higher, looped around and the thunder of its engine trailed it back toward the runway at Plant 42.

None of the men inside the station even bothered to come out to see the flyover. Everyone in Lancaster was accustomed to seeing strange aircraft thundering overhead at low altitude, landing and taking off from Plant 42. As long as Bucky could remember, the Lancaster-Palmdale area had produced some of America's most advanced aircraft. A few miles beyond Plant 42 was Plant 51, better known as the famous Lockheed Skunk Works. The CIA tested Predator Drones nearby at the El Mirage Flight Test Facility and the West Coast home of the Space Shuttle was a few miles north, at Edwards Air Force Base. It was common knowledge that a large part of America's billion-dollar "black" Air Force and space defense projects went on in the Antelope Valley. Bucky often wondered about the disconnect. How could Lancaster be such a wasteland when the facilities around it spent huge amounts of money and were filled with real rocket scientists?

FIVE

"**D**AWSON, I NEED TO SEE YOU!"
Battalion Chief Vlasic, in charge of North Region Hazardous Materials Task Force, leaned over the second-floor balcony of the station and waved Bucky up.

Bucky removed the key from the ignition, got out and climbed the stairs to Vlasic's office. During the two years Bucky had been a HazMat specialist, he had been in the chief's office several times and it was never a pleasant experience. Vlasic always wore his black battalion chief's uniform, a perfectly pressed shirt, trousers that had sharp creases and black shoes with a high polish. He always looked as though he had just shaved and had ten hours of sleep. He never seemed to sweat, even in the extreme heat of the Antelope Valley, and Bucky wondered what he had looked like when he was a firefighter in the field. Was he spotless in his turnout gear or covered with soot? Had he ever been out in the field?

When he reached the chief's office, Vlasic was already behind his desk. "Come in, Dawson," he said. "Close the door." He pointed to a chair.

Bucky sat down and looked across the well-organized desk. The chief had a reputation for being a control freak. Fire officers' desks were usually a sea of charts, reports, radios, telephones and empty coffee cups. Vlasic's desk was a pond of calm. Papers were organized in neat piles. Pens and sharpened pencils, all points up, were stuck in an Edwards Air Force Base ceramic coffee cup at the side of his desk. Folded maps were stacked under a fire engine paperweight. Blue operations binders filled a small bookcase, portable radios stood at attention in their chargers and his rough service laptop rested in the center of his desk, flanked by two telephones. A dozen citations and certificates of training decorated the wall behind the desk. Chief Vlasic also managed to control the air in his office—he ran a small filter and ionizer in the corner and Bucky detected no odor print. He couldn't see Vlasic's foot under the desk, but the slight movement of his body indicated he was tapping out some unknown beat. Sitting or standing, the chief always tapped his right foot.

Vlasic pressed the fingers of both hands together in the form of a church steeple and said, "Farrell tells me your sister might have been killed in the meth lab explosion. What a terrible thing to see —"

"It's not confirmed yet," Bucky said, "but I'm pretty sure I saw her before it went off. The coroner sent someone out this morning to get my DNA sample."

"Well," Vlasic said, his voice shifting into command tone, "if it turns out to be true, you'll have a week's bereavement leave." He paused and looked out the window, then looked directly at Bucky. "How are you feeling? Physically, I mean. How's the back and neck?"

"I'm good—no problems."

"Working regular shifts, right? No disability, right?"

Bucky wondered what the chief was getting at. "Yeah, I'm good."

"I'm asking because I got a copy of the e-mail response sent to you from Doctor Randall's office. I don't know if I was supposed to receive it, but it's too late now. The question is, if you're not hurting, why are you trying so hard to renew a Percocet prescription?"

"I—"

Vlasic held up his hand. "If you're injured, you should be on leave. If you're not, you know the department's drug policy is zero tolerance. Do you realize what could happen if we're out on a critical situation and you make a mistake because you're not thinking clearly? We take enough risks without adding mental confusion from painkillers. What if you injure yourself or someone on your crew gets hurt because you do something stupid? What if it's a civilian? I will not permit anything like that to happen on my watch." Vlasic sat back. His eyes bored into Bucky's skull.

"I'm not—"

The BC held up his hand again. "I can't take a chance. I will not have a drug incident on my HazMat team." Vlasic pulled his cup of pencils and pens across his desk and began to turn them point down. "I've notified the union rep about this. A week from Monday, I want you here in my office at 9:00 a.m.

There'll be a guy from a testing laboratory with a cup and you're gonna pee in it. I hope you'll be clean." Vlasic centered the pencil holder on his desk. "No, you will be clean. Got it? If not, you're gone. Understand?" Vlasic paused. He forced a smile, and as an afterthought, said, "We want you on the team. I'm sure you'll pass the test and that'll be the end of it." He stuck out his hand, shifted back into his empathetic voice, and said, "I hope that wasn't your sister."

"Thanks, Chief." Bucky shook his hand, which was dry and cold.

"But if it was, you've got a week of bereavement leave. Take it."

SIX

"THE DEPARTMENT'S DRUG POLICY IS zero tolerance."

Bucky sped down Highway 14 on his way to see the spot where his sister died. Had his doctor intentionally sent a copy of the e-mail to Vlasic, even though it would have been a violation of the HIPPA confidentiality rules? Bucky knew his battalion chief was right. He couldn't risk being on a Percocet high while on duty. When the package from *BuyDrugs* arrived, he wouldn't even open it; he'd just toss $735 worth of drugs in the trash and go cold turkey. At the La Tijera exit, he took the turn too fast and skidded partway off the road before he regained control and headed out into the desert. The Bronco rattled and bounced as Bucky sped over the dirt road. He needed new shock absorbers. Actually, he needed a new SUV.

Bucky passed clumps of Joshua trees, named by Mormon settlers who likened the plant to Joshua, arms raised to heaven in prayer. When he reached the spot where the Squad and engines had stopped, the isolation was striking. The remote and sparsely populated Mojave was a magnet for meth cookers for the same reason it was attractive to the Air Force—there weren't any neighbors to spy on your covert activities. Bucky parked and walked across the sand toward the site of the explosion. At the edge of the debris field, he stopped at the yellow tape marked: SHERIFF'S DEPARTMENT CRIME SCENE in black letters, tied to stakes surrounding the area. White signs, waving in the wind, hung from the tape, warning: CONTAMINATED AREA, TOXIC HAZARD. The Sheriff's Department had come—sifted through the wreckage, scooped up chemical samples and collected whatever other evidence they needed—and gone. The site was ready for the toxic waste handlers to cart away the rubble that remained and bulldoze the sand.

Bucky stepped over the tape and walked across the debris and litter to the black crater that had once been the doublewide. The early afternoon sun felt hot on the back of his neck. He smelled the charred remains of the trailer, reduced to bits of scorched metal, wood, plastic and Styrofoam. Ragged pieces of the aluminum walls and roof were scattered across the sand. A small refrigerator, now black with soot, lay on its side several feet from the center of the blast. Bucky saw twisted parts of metal chairs and the remains of a table and a microwave. A blackened skeleton of springs and wire was all that was left of a couch. A car, color unknown, had been burned and gutted, the windows blown out by the blast, the tires a pool of melted rubber.

Bucky walked around aimlessly, looking at the debris and kicking at the wreckage with the toe of his boot. He almost walked past a small purple stone lying on the sand. He stopped to pick it up and held it in his hand. It took him a moment to realize it was an earring. The clip on its backside was bent around the remains of a blackened metal chain. Standing under a hot sun, Bucky felt a cold tremor ripple through his body when he understood he was holding one of the earrings he had purchased for Brandy years ago on his visit to Canyon City. Could she have been wearing it around her neck? It was unmistakable. It was her earring, and if there had been any doubt, this was as good as a DNA test—his sister had perished in the explosion.

He tried again to imagine the last minutes of Brandy's life and saw her again at the door of the trailer, holding the lighter, a cigarette in her mouth. A sense of sadness washed over him. "Brandy," he murmured, "you deserved better than this." He slipped the earring and chain into the pocket of his jeans, sat down and closed his eyes. In a few months, blowing sand would cover everything and there would be no trace left of the explosion. Whatever remained of his sister would disappear in this desolate spot in the Mojave.

Bucky caught a scent, the smell of a male human body upwind. When he opened his eyes, someone was standing several yards in front of him. He saw black biker boots in the sand. As he raised his gaze, he saw jeans, a wide black leather belt and a silver metal chain extending from a belt loop into a pocket. A soiled white T-shirt covered a muscular chest. Thick arms and a neck decorated with tattoos completed the torso. The man had two days' growth of hair on his face. His head was shaved except for a single long braid of hair growing out of the back. The biker seemed focused on something behind Bucky.

He nodded slightly and Bucky felt the impact on the side of his head an instant before he lost consciousness and pitched forward.

SEVEN

"WE CAN'T LEAVE HIM HERE. Dump him somewhere."

The voice roused Bucky. He opened his eyes and pain surged through his head. He was lying on the floor of the desert, his cheek pressed against the sand. It was late afternoon, and the rays of the sun were almost horizontal. The wind was blowing, as it always did, and dust and grit had created little walls around his face.

Bucky weighed 185 pounds, but someone picked him up like a sack of potatoes and dropped him on something hard. He was barely conscious, but his nose didn't fail him. The body scent was from the biker who was standing in front of him just before he was knocked unconscious. Bucky stored the aroma away with all the other important odor prints he had encountered throughout his life.

The sound of the engine revived him. He was lying in the back of a pickup truck. Bucky tried to move, but the pain in his head was too great. He felt the bump, bump, bump as the vehicle bounced over a dirt road with a washboard surface. He sank back into darkness.

Everything around him was black, but the unrelenting high desert wind convinced him he was awake. No longer in the back of the pickup, Bucky was lying on the sand. When he sat up, pain shot through his head, down his neck and into his body. Lightning flashed behind his eyeballs. He looked up at the icy, glittering diamonds in the sky. A meteorite burned through the heavens. Bucky sat in the emptiness, steadying himself, palms pressed against the sand. He began to shake—partly because of the blow to his head and partly because the scalding heat of daylight was gone and the temperature in the 2,000-foot high desert had dropped fifty degrees.

Bucky tried to clear his head. He stood slowly and a wave of dizziness and nausea overtook him. He sank to his knees, retched and waited for his head to clear. He was thirsty and the taste of vomit was bitter in his mouth. Pain throbbed in his skull and when he touched the side of his head, he felt blood, still wet and sticky, mixed with sand. He reached into his jeans pocket for one of the three Percs he had folded into a piece of paper. They were gone, along with his phone, wallet and the keys to his Bronco. His fire department identification card and the blackened chain wrapped around the amethyst earring were still in another pocket.

He scanned the horizon and saw nothing but a weak glow from the illumination of Los Angeles, 100 miles to the southwest. He managed to stand again on weak legs and turned slowly to search the space around him. A half-moon illuminated the lonely, remote emptiness and reflected just enough light to outline Joshua trees with spike-leaved arms. Bucky sat down again. The voice of the Mojave, the wind, moaned. He sank into a black pit.

The ball of fire rose up from the eastern horizon and began to heat the cool night air. The desert inhabitants had already disappeared underground in anticipation of the sun, leaving Bucky to face the new day and millions of harsh, empty acres alone. The arid scrubland stretched out in all directions, saying nothing and offering little more than vistas of sand, creosote bush and Joshua trees. Bucky struggled to his feet. The ache in his head had subsided from a blinding pain to an insistent, throbbing pulse behind his eyes. Dried blood and sand created a crust in the hair on the left side of his head.

Bucky began to walk, using the sunrise as his only point of reference. He headed south, hoping to see the San Gabriel Mountains, which marked the southern end of the Mojave and the gateway to Los Angeles. If they—whoever they were—had taken him north and dumped him in Kern County, then he might eventually see the Tehachapi Mountains off to his left. Perhaps he would see Highway 14 or the Southern Pacific tracks, both of which ran north-south through the center of the Antelope Valley. Even if he couldn't find a landmark, he was confident he could orient himself and find his way back to civilization—he had lived on the edge of the desert his entire life. Bucky scanned the desolation again, looked up at the empty sky and searched for a trace of life. A few hawks glided on the air currents and a flock of ravens crossed the sky. Anxiety tugged at him. He took a step forward and heard an unmistakable sound. He stopped and watched a large rattler slither into a tuft of desert grass. Bucky inhaled. The dry wind carried no scents, no odors, and no information. It wasn't often that he could take a deep breath and not smell anything.

Bucky had never needed a Percocet as much as he needed one now. His mouth was bone dry, but if he had a pill, he would hold it under his tongue, suffer the bitter taste and wait until it dissolved. Relief would follow the metallic flavor, push away the anxiety and give him the energy and clarity to save himself. He checked his pockets again, hoping to find a stray painkiller. All he found was lint and sand.

Waves of heat rose from the desert floor. In a few hours, the temperature would rise to over 110 degrees. His body would soon give up its water and begin to wither. If he died in the desert, the dust of his bones would mix with the sand. Perhaps some of the particles from his body would someday rub against remains of his sister's body. The heat pressed down on him. He hadn't had anything to drink for a day and needed water. The throbbing behind his eyes was unrelenting and he was afraid he had a concussion. His watch said 8:20 a.m.

He tried to track the path of the sun and walk a straight line south, but it was impossible. As the sun rose in the sky, Bucky soon lost all sense of direction. Everything looked the same. South was north, north was south. He shaded his eyes and looked up, hoping to see a black and yellow Los Angeles County Firehawk hanging in the sky, searching for him. The first rule of survival was to remain in one place and let someone find you, but that was not an option. How could they search for him if they didn't know he was missing? Bucky continued to walk for what seemed like several hours. When he checked his watch again, it was 8:42 a.m. How could it be so hot so early in the day?

Bucky felt dizzy and disoriented. Which direction was he headed? He looked back and saw the zigzag of prints he had made. The arid wind blew a blizzard of fine particles in his face. He wondered where the Mojave sand came from. Was it once part of the surrounding mountains, ground into dust from centuries of erosion? The desert soil might have taken centuries to accumulate, but Bucky feared his own time might be measured in hours. His throat was parched. He thought he might drown in the heat and light. He scratched his chest and imagined plunging into a cool mountain lake.

Something reflected the bright sunlight and he headed toward it. When Bucky reached the top of a sand dune, he looked down at a 40-foot long, 9,000-gallon polished aluminum semi-trailer tank truck lying on its side. County firefighters had already responded to the rollover. Bucky approached the Incident Commander, a man he didn't recognize, standing off to the side.

"Is the tank damaged?" Bucky asked. "Anything leaking from the relief vents?"

"All secure," the IC responded.

The other men were standing around, doing nothing; watching him. Bucky jumped into action. "We need a charged hose," Bucky shouted, and pointed toward the tanker. " We don't want a spill. Get a ground wire on the tank. Have you requested vacuum trucks?" They wouldn't be able to upright the 80,000-pound trailer until the contents were off-loaded.

"We were waiting for you," the IC said. "We don't know what we're off-loading,"

"Waiting for me?" Bucky looked at him again. Who was this guy? What station was he from? "What's the matter with you?" Bucky shouted. All the IC had to do was check the red diamond-shaped placard on the tank. One of the first things any firefighter learned was how to read the NFPA symbols. A tanker like this had to be carrying some type of Class 3 flammable liquid. "What's on the diamond?" Bucky said.

"Look for yourself," the IC responded. "There is no diamond. No placard. Nothing."

"Impossible. Where's the driver?"

"There is no driver."

Bucky went to the overturned trailer and walked around it. The IC was right. There were no placards. There were no signs, stencils, markings, letters or anything else. How did the tanker get here? What happened to it? Spotless pipes and valves lined the underside of the gleaming aluminum tank. He looked at the tires—they had never touched asphalt. In fact, the entire rig looked brand new.

Bucky knew what he had to do. He ran to get the air drill. He should have been wearing his proximity suit and breathing apparatus, but he wore a T-shirt and jeans. He should have used the meters to find out if any vapors were leaking. Rather than climb to the top of the tank and drill through the thin aluminum into the dead air space above the liquid, Bucky stood on the sand and began to cut a four-inch hole at eye level. "C'mon, c'mon," he shouted over the sound of the drill.

The drill finally broke into the tank, and when Bucky yanked it out, cool crystal-clear water gushed out onto the sand. Bucky stepped into the middle of the stream and let it wash over him. He opened his mouth and it cascaded down his throat. The water was pure and it tasted wonderful. Bucky thought he could never get enough of it, but the gusher turned to a trickle and then stopped.

Bucky turned to talk to the IC. He was gone. Bucky looked back at the overturned tanker. It shimmered in the hot air and evaporated. He was still thirsty.

9:18 a.m. The haze on the horizon cleared and Bucky thought he could make out the blue and brown profile of hills in the distance. They were too low for mountains. Perhaps it was Lumen Ridge, where they tested rocket engines at Edwards Air Force base. He searched the sky, but no search and rescue aircraft appeared. Would anyone come?

10:05 a.m. Bucky spotted a lake in the distance. He dragged himself toward it until he saw the rock-hard clay of the lakebed, and, floating above it, the water that was only a reflection of a blue sky.

The sun was directly overhead. He heard a distant rumble and saw two tiny silver fighter jets streaking overhead. Were they headed toward Edwards? There was no way to tell. They were far too high to see him, and in a moment, disappeared into the blue-white haze. The sound of their engines faded until all Bucky heard was the silence of the hot desert day. He longed for a Percocet.

Dust devils and whirlwinds spun in the distance. The sun was relentless and Bucky wanted to shrink inside himself. Moisture escaped from every pore and his body temperature was rising. His sweat evaporated as soon as it collected on his skin. His blood began to thicken, forcing his heart to work harder. His blood vessels started to constrict to maintain pressure. Dehydration hovered over him like a vulture. The wind assaulted him. The voice of the desert called to Bucky, "Come with me." He stopped to stare at the small, sun-bleached carcass of a rodent and realized he might die.

The late afternoon sun beat down on his back and the scalding, dry heat was like the inside of an oven. Bucky lay on his stomach, his chin resting in the sand. Nearby, a steel-blue dragonfly with threadlike legs stood motionless. It stared back at him with large, multifaceted eyes, regarding Bucky as a strange intruder in its desert world. Suddenly, four gossamer wings vibrated and it disappeared into the air with a faint buzz. Bucky desperately needed water. His lips were cracked. His skin was red. His head throbbed. The heat pressed him into the sand. Tiny insects with silver wings crawled inches from his face. If he had wings, he could fly. If he were a desert tortoise, he could dig into the sand and hide from the sun, burrow down until he found water. He closed his eyes and imagined washing down a pill with a pitcher of ice-cold water.

Bucky's father had told him stories about local people who spent too much time in the desert sun. "The heat did something to their brains," his father said. "They began to have crazy thoughts. They thought they were receiving telepathic messages from saucer people." As a child, Bucky loved hearing the stories about the saucer creatures with strange names like Ashtar and Elcar. One was called Luu, and Bucky took it for his own secret name. Brandy named her favorite doll Schare, the saucer people's name for Earth. Bucky wanted to know if the tales could be true and pressed his father for more details. "Don't be stupid," his father had said. "There's no little people coming from outer space."

He shivered with cold in the darkness and curled into the fetal position. Behind him, Bucky heard a faint sound and something moved. He took a deep breath but the wind was in his face, and he smelled nothing. He listened more carefully and thought a coyote might be creeping up on him. Bucky rolled over, and in the light of the half moon, saw a dark, round shape a few inches away. He reached out, touched it and felt a hard, rough piece of armor. It moved and

Bucky let out an involuntary gasp. It answered back with a hissing sound and he suddenly felt a warm liquid run down his arm, soaking through his T-shirt and burning the raw skin of his chest. He was overwhelmed with the odor of uric acid as the pungent smell of urine passed fully into his nose. It was so strong he gagged and wanted to vomit, but his stomach was empty. The dark shape of a desert tortoise turned and slowly receded.

The growl of a distant engine roused him from a feverish sleep. Out in the darkness, Bucky saw two tiny blue eyes of light. The eyes grew larger and became halogen headlights. The growl became the sound of an OHV—an off highway vehicle—used by the recreational riders who came to tear up the floor of the desert with their souped-up buggies. If he was near the El Mirage Recreation Area, then he was much farther east than he had imagined. Bucky watched the headlights of the vehicle. It turned and moved parallel to him. No one rode around in an OHV in the middle of the night, even in a recreational vehicle area, unless on a search and rescue mission. At last, he thought, they're coming to get me. The vehicle stopped with the engine still running. Bucky stood up and called out in a hoarse voice. The strong desert wind was at his back and he was certain his voice would carry: "Over here. Over here." Bucky's parched throat barely worked and his shouts were drowned out by the sound of the OHV. "Turn off the motor," he cried out until his voice became a whisper. He staggered toward the OHV, but only covered a few yards before it turned and headed back in the direction from which it had come. Bucky had no voice left to call out, no strength left to pursue the vehicle. Bucky collapsed on the sand. He still smelled the tortoise piss.

A lone coyote howled in the distance. Bucky suffered through his second night on the sand. He shivered. His tongue was stuck to the roof of his mouth. He felt nauseated and wondered whether he was suffering from heat stroke and dehydration, or whether he might have withdrawal symptoms. He hadn't gone this long without a Perc in months. The moon cast a blue light over the floor of the desert. Bucky gazed up at the stars and watched the white and orange lights dart back and forth in the night sky. They came together and circled overhead, then coalesced into disc-shaped objects with flashing lights. Bright beams of light shone from their undersides, crisscrossing the desert.

Now Bucky understood. The rescue party in the OHV had contacted the saucer people. They were coming to save him.

The chirping sound of a cactus wren woke Bucky. The sun told him it was early morning. A gust of wind brought a face full of tiny sand articles and a scent. Someone was frying bacon and making coffee. He struggled to his feet and tilted his head back. His nose captured the faint but delicious aroma of food and he walked toward it.

The saucer beings, Ashtar and Elcar, came riding over a sand berm on OHVs. Bucky must have been on the right frequency, because they spoke perfect English. The last thing he remembered was Elcar shouting, "Hey look, there's a guy out here."

EIGHT

"**I** THINK HE'S WAKING UP."

The aroma of bacon and coffee disappeared and a strong, bitter antiseptic smell filled Bucky's nostrils. He knew he was in a hospital before he opened his eyes. The first thing he saw was an IV bag suspended from a thin aluminum pole. His gaze followed the clear tubing down the side of the bed to his elbow where a patch of tape held a needle in his vein. He turned his head slightly and saw a second IV hanging from another pole on the other side of the bed. He tried to focus on the clock on the wall, but it was a blur. His head hurt. His brain was in pieces. Bits of dreams came back to him—memories with jagged edges. He saw an overturned water tanker and an OHV racing across the sand. He heard the saucer people.

He opened his eyes again and this time things came into focus. The smell of the hospital was the same and the IVs were still stuck in his arms. The round face of a man appeared above him. The blue letters stitched on his lab coat told Bucky it was Dr. Harrison from Palmdale Regional Medical Center. A nurse stood next to him.

Dr. Harrison leaned over him and asked, "How do you feel?"

"What time is it?"

"A quarter after nine."

"Morning?"

The doctor nodded.

"What day?"

"Monday. They brought you in yesterday afternoon around three. Do you remember what happened?"

Bucky's head throbbed. He recalled Chief Vlasic talking to him about a drug test then leaving 129s and driving out into the desert to the spot of the explosion. He had walked through the debris of the blast and thought about his sister. That was Friday and today was Monday. Everything in between was a jumble of images and scents. He touched the side of his head and felt the bandage.

"You have a bad laceration there," the doctor said. "Someone hit you with something flat, maybe a shovel. Any idea about that?"

Bucky sat up, felt the tug of the IV tubes stuck in his right arm and waited for his head to clear. He stared at a plastic container, the repository for used needles, on the far side of the room. Large red letters announced HAZARDOUS MATERIAL. He tried to get out of bed, but the doctor put a hand on his chest and pushed him gently back. "You need to rest and rehydrate. You've probably lost 15 percent of your body weight, you've got a nasty sunburn, some kind of a heat rash and you got smacked on the head."

Bucky struggled to remember. "I found an earring and part of a chain. In the sand."

"We have it," the nurse told him. "It was in your pocket when they brought you in. And we have your firefighter ID. Did you have a wallet?"

"Yes, and the keys to my Bronco." Bucky also had a scent memory of the body odor of a man, but he didn't mention that.

"We're going to keep you until this evening and let you rehydrate," the doctor said. Can we contact a family member to pick you up?"

"I don't have any family." More memories hovered on the edge of Bucky's consciousness, just beyond reach. "Call Detective Ortiz at the sheriff's station in Lancaster. He'll come for me." Bucky closed his eyes and dropped back into the soft hospital bed. He struggled to recall what had happened. He was certain of only one thing—he had found one of the amethyst earrings he bought for Brandy in Canyon City and that meant she had died in the explosion.

Canyon City was a little pissant town of 16,000 people in the middle of Colorado, home to thirteen federal and state prisons, including the Supermax, America's new Alcatraz. Bucky drove over 1,100 miles to visit his sister. Brandy was on an extended visit to Colorado Women's Correctional Facility, where she was five months into a three and a half year sentence for selling drugs. The last time

Bucky had seen her, she was leaving for Nevada on the back of a Harley. He remembered the smell of the exhaust.

After she called him, Bucky filled out a family visit request, waited nine weeks and finally received approval for a five-hour visit on a Monday in May. He drove straight through and arrived exhausted, late on a Sunday night. On Monday morning, Bucky drove out past the Colorado State Penitentiary surrounded by three rows of 12-foot high fences topped with spiral razor wire, to the women's prison on Grandview Avenue, enclosed by only one fence and no razor wire. When he arrived, the prison was in lockdown and they told him he would have to wait another day to see his sister.

Bucky returned to his motel, slept several hours and then walked the streets of Canyon City in the late afternoon, looking for somewhere to eat. It wasn't much of a city, or even a town. It was a collection of prisons surrounded by cheap motels for visitors, low-priced housing for corrections personnel and a collection of bars, restaurants, convenience and liquor stores. Aside from the nearby Royal Gorge suspension bridge, strung 1,000 feet over the Arkansas River, the only other tourist attraction was the Museum of Colorado Prisons, featuring the first gas chamber.

Bucky caught the distinctive scent of pine trees wafting in from the distant mountains, and then the greasy smell of burgers frying in a nearby restaurant. When he came around a corner, the odor of unwashed bodies assaulted him and he saw a group of Indians squatting on the sidewalk outside a bar. An old squaw perched over a filthy blanket with a few rings, bracelets, earrings and necklaces. Her skin was dark and creased, marked by years in the sun. Two braids of coarse black and gray hair hung down past her shoulders. She looked ancient.

Bucky stopped and tried not to inhale her body odor while he looked at the jewelry. He pointed to a ring. "How much?"

"Silver." When she opened her mouth, Bucky saw that she was missing half her teeth.

How much?" he repeated.

She looked at him as if trying to decide how much he could pay. "$35."

Bucky didn't know Brandy's ring size. He eyed a pair of earrings, each with an amethyst stone the size of a dime. "I'll give you $20 for the earrings." He pulled a bill from his wallet and waved it at the old woman. She nodded, leaned forward, snatched the money from his hand and pointed to the earrings. Bucky bent down and picked them up. "What kind of Indian are you?" he asked.

"Ute," the old squaw said.

Bucky continued down the street and began to wonder whether Brandy could even wear earrings, or any jewelry, while she was in prison. He decided he had blown twenty bucks.

The room smelled of bodies. Inmates and their visitors huddled together, head to head, engaged in muffled conversations. Bucky guessed the visitors smelled worse than the inmates did. His little sister, dressed in green pants and a yellow T-shirt—both marked with Colorado Department of Corrections number DOC216-477—sat across the table in the visitor's room. She twisted her hair around her fingers and looked at him with hollow eyes. In the three years since Bucky had seen her, she had retained some of her underlying beauty, but was pale and thin. Her skin was a sallow color and her face had red patches. He had no idea what to say to her. He opened the palm of his hand and showed her the amethyst earrings. "I bought these for you from an Indian woman."

She looked at him as if he were from another planet. "Your bought me earrings? Are you fucking kidding? What am I supposed to do with earrings? I need money, not some Indian crap."

"I thought you would—"

"They don't allow us to wear jewelry." She looked at the earrings and shook her head. "The girls are jealous about anything you have. Somebody would just try to steal them anyway. There's enough going on in here without getting punched for some fucking Indian earrings. The first girl I shared a cell with got hit on the side of the head with a coffee pot because someone wanted a crucifix she kept in her pocket."

"I'm glad to see you," Bucky said, trying to change the subject. "How are you doing?"

"How do you think I'm doing? I'm in prison and it's fucked up shit in here. I'm trying to stay out of fights or other kinds of trouble and avoid write-ups. I can't survive without some money."

"Slow down, Brandy." When he tried to put a hand on her shoulder, she pulled away. "Start at the beginning. Why are you here?"

She extended her arm and showed him a line of old needle scars leading up the inside of her arm. "I sold some crank to a guy, and he turned out to be a cop."

"That's what you get for hanging out with biker lowlifes." Brandy gave him an angry look and as soon as he said it, Bucky knew he should have kept his mouth shut. "Are you clean now?"

"When I got here, I had to go through detox. It was terrible. I felt awful and I was sick for weeks. They didn't give me anything to help; I went cold turkey. I had the shakes and vomited and crapped all over. A few of the girls helped me and somehow I got through it. After I got better, I sassed a guard. She shoved me into my cell and I lost it. I went after her and scratched her face. The bitch deserved it, but assaulting the personnel is a big fucking no-no and they put me in the lower unit, in a segregation cell. I was by myself for a month." Brandy wouldn't make eye contact. She looked all around the room as she spoke. "I had a small slit of a window on the wall. They buzzed me at 4 a.m. and that's when I went to the shower. They cuffed me to the pipes and I had ten minutes to wash myself with one hand. I screamed a lot during the first two days, so they made me take Elavil every night. They watched me until I swallowed it, then they did a finger sweep in my mouth. It made me feel like a zombie." She paused and twirled her hair around her finger again. "I'm not going back down there. I wanna stay in the day room and watch TV with the other girls, do my time, and get out of here." She finally looked at Bucky.

"What can I do?"

"I told you, I need money. In my account."

"Your account?"

"My prison account. So I can order from the store. Snacks, shampoo, soap, stuff like that."

"How about drugs? I heard you can buy drugs in prison. Are you going to buy drugs?"

She leaned toward him and he got a whiff of an antibacterial smell from the prison soap on her body. "Shhh. Keep your voice down." She looked behind her at the guards standing behind a glass window at the far end of the room.

"Answer me, Brandy. Do you want the money for drugs?"

Her anger flared again. "Christ, Bucky, I didn't say I was gonna buy drugs. You're my brother and you're supposed to help me. That's why I called you.

Do you wanna help me or not? If you do, then deposit some money in my account."

Bucky searched her face for any trace of the little sister he loved and remembered.

"How much have you got?" she persisted.

"About $150. I need enough money to buy gas to get home."

"Whatever." She stared at Bucky. "When you go out, tell them you want to leave some money for me." She looked as hard as any other prisoner in the visitor's room.

"Please don't use it to buy drugs. Promise me," Bucky whispered.

She glanced again at the guard behind the glass and hissed, "Are you gonna do it or not?"

Bucky nodded. "OK." Brandy never had a job—an honest job—and Bucky could only imagine what she might do in prison to get cash. He thought it was better to help her out than to let her try to get it some other way. "I'll leave $100."

She gave him a slight smile and said, "Thanks for coming to see me; you're the only one I have." Bucky wanted to stay and talk to her, but she stood up, gave him a weak hug and walked back toward the guards. She didn't turn to look back.

Bucky had driven seventeen hours to spend less than fifteen minutes with his little sister—except she wasn't his little sister any more, she was inmate number DOC216-477. He still had the earrings in the palm of his hand. On the way out, he left them with her personal belongings and deposited $100 in her prison account.

The amethyst earring swung in front of his eyes from a blackened chain. Back and forth, until Bucky descended into a dreamless sleep on the hospital bed.

NINE

"**H**EY BUCKY! OVER HERE."

Bucky looked up and saw Mike waiting in an unmarked patrol car in the NO PARKING zone in front of the entrance. Bucky felt weak and unsteady as he walked out of the hospital. He was crashing mentally as well as physically and was dying for a pick-me-up. He desperately needed a Perc to energize him and help bring everything back to normal. He decided he would take two—twenty milligrams—the minute he got home.

"You OK, Buck?" Mike said as Bucky wobbled toward the car. He leaned over to open the passenger side door.

"I'm a little shaky. Thanks for picking me up."

"*De nada.* What happened?"

"I'm not sure. I went out to see what was left of the doublewide. Someone hit me on the side of the head. The doctor said it could have been a shovel." Bucky touched the bandage. "They took my wallet and the keys to my Bronco and dumped me. I was wandering around in the desert for two days."

"At least you're alive."

"Mike, I found an earring on a chain out in the sand. I bought those earrings for Brandy. I'm sure she was killed in the explosion."

"Right now you've had a really bad physical experience, and you don't even know exactly what happened to you. Take it easy and recover, then you can deal with this."

"I'm pretty sure Brandy's dead."

"We'll talk about it. Come by the station in the morning. We have to fill out an assault and robbery report."

"I smell Mexican food. "Did you eat tacos for dinner?"

"Burritos."

"In the car?"

Mike nodded. "What? I'm doing you a favor by picking you up, and you're complaining about what my car smells like?"

"Sorry," Bucky said. "Mexican food brings back one of the worst memories of my life. It happened over twenty years ago and I can still remember every detail."

"Is there any odor that doesn't remind you of something?"

Bucky ignored Mike's comment. "Did I ever tell you this? I was six or seven and I was with my dad in his pickup out on Highway 14. A bunch of motorcycles roared past us, and my dad says, 'I hate those guys. They're all one-percenters.' At the time, I had no idea what a one-percenter even was. So then, my dad accelerates and cuts in front of the last straggler, who shakes his fist at us. 'Watch this,' my dad says, 'he's gonna eat asphalt.' Then he flicks the pickup's lights on and off and the guy swerves and nearly crashes. My father laughs and says, 'The sucker thought I was hitting my brakes.' The next thing I know, the biker pulls up next to us, gives us the finger and shouts something."

"Oh yeah, thunder on the road. They must have been 'white-lining,'" Mike said. "A whole club will go out on the highway and ride at seventy or eighty miles an hour down the white line, inches away from the traffic."

Bucky fastened his seatbelt and turned to Mike. "I can still picture this guy flying along, riding next to us in the oncoming lane, staring at my dad and flipping us the bird. I remember he was wearing black leather gloves with the fingers cut off. My dad didn't seem worried by the biker's anger and said, 'OK, mister, I'll teach you another lesson.' He slowed and pulled off the highway into the parking lot of a Mexican restaurant. By the time he was out of the car, the biker had jumped off his bike and was running toward us."

Bucky lowered his window to get some fresh air. "This was the first fistfight I had ever seen and it involved my father. I'm a kid and I think my dad's invincible because he's a firefighter and firefighters are strong and fearless. Right?"

"Right," Mike said.

"So my dad throws the first punch, hits the biker in the face and knocks him down. The problem was, three more Harleys roared into the parking lot and one of the bikes clips my father and knocks him down. I was terrified. The bikers jump off their hogs and pile on top of my dad. One of them keeps

punching him while two others hold him down. My dad starts to bleed and I
think they're killing him. At that point, the first biker gets back in the fight and
kicks my dad in the ribs. You know, with those square-toed boots bikers wear.

"I'm just a little kid and there isn't anything I can do. I'm crying my eyes
out and I run into the Mexican restaurant screaming for help. By the time the
Highway Patrol arrives, the bikers are long gone. I remember seeing my father
lying on the cement, doubled up in pain from two cracked ribs. While all this
is going on, I smell Mexican food coming from the kitchen exhaust fan at the
restaurant. The whole thing was over in less than five minutes, but it stayed
with me. I don't have a lot of memories of my dad. This is the most vivid, and
it's really painful."

"I can see why."

"And I still feel sick whenever I smell Mexican food."

"Hey, what are you going to use for wheels? I could probably get you a
junker from the motor pool for a few days."

"Thanks, Mike. I'm going to use an old pickup from 129s. If you drop me
off there, I can get it."

They drove in silence for a few minutes. Bucky pressed his bandage again
and felt a stab of pain. "Why would someone attack me out there, Mike?"

"Good question. If bikers were using the trailer, they might have come
back to look around. Maybe they had drug money buried out there. Let's talk
about it in the morning when you come by the station. Do you remember
anything else?"

"I thought I saw some guys riding an OHV in the middle of the night."

Without his keys, Bucky had to force his back door open. He entered through
the kitchen, and without turning on the light, took two Percocets from the
bottle by the sink. He downed them with a glass of water and felt the cool liquid
carrying the pills down into his stomach. Bucky waited for the Percocet
to dissolve in his gut, enter his bloodstream and spread its magic throughout
his body.

He walked into his bedroom and saw the blinking red light on his answering machine in the bedroom. No one used that number; everyone called his
cell phone. Bucky knew it was a call from the coroner. He took the amethyst
earring and the remains of the chain out of his pocket and laid it out on his

night table. He rubbed the carbon off the chain with the corner of his T-shirt until the silver underneath sparkled. He cleaned the stone until the purple color reflected the light from his lamp. This was all the DNA he needed. He already knew the message that awaited him.

Bucky pressed the PLAY button and listened to the flat female voice report that they had a match and that the coroner's analysis had verified that one of the individuals killed in the methamphetamine laboratory explosion on the early morning of September 22 was Brandy Michelle Dawson, his sister. Bucky sat down on the bed and played the message twice more. Each time he heard the same bad news. Bucky erased the message and lay back on his bed.

TEN

"THE AMERICAN MOTORCYCLE ASSOCIATION BELIEVES that 99 percent of motorcyclists are decent, honest people.... Motorcyclists are decent, honest people ... decent, honest people." Bucky sat tied to a chair in the middle of the Mojave. Gangs of bikers on Harleys rode past him, chanting the mantra from the American Motorcycle Association. Their bikes sprayed sand and dust. He was suffocating.

Bucky woke up Tuesday morning and felt like he hadn't slept. He seemed to be having more dreams, most of them nightmares, and wondered if the painkillers were affecting his sleep. As soon as he got out of bed, he remembered his dream about motorcycle gangs—the men who were proud to call themselves one-percenters because they were neither decent nor honest. The next thing he remembered was that he had seen a biker in the desert at the blast site.

Outlaw motorcycle gangs had been causing trouble in the Antelope Valley for as long as Bucky could remember. When methamphetamine production came to the high desert in the '90s, the national gangs took over from the local bikers in Lancaster and Palmdale. National gangs like the Grim Reapers and Vagos moved in, and fights, stabbings, shootings and beatings became common at the late-night bars. Local law enforcement mobilized for war. Soon, one-percenters were everywhere, riding in convoys on the local highways and shaking neighborhoods with the thundering sound of straight exhaust pipes. They rode only American cycles. That meant hogs—Harleys—with ape hanger bars and bobbed rear fenders that sprayed a rooster-tail of water during rain-storms. They wore bandannas or helmets shaped like World War II German army issue, black T-shirts and their "cuts"—the sleeveless leather vests with their outlaw club colors and patches. Their club patches were sacred, never to be disrespected, relinquished or washed. The round center logo was the club's emblem. The top rocker displayed the club's name and the bottom rocker the chapter's location. Only "full-patch members" of a gang could wear a complete set of colors. Smaller insignia had special meanings. The number 13 indicated a member dealt in marijuana and methamphetamine. The number 22 indicated he had been in prison. Patches of colored sets of wings represented the performance of obscene sexual acts with women. The bikers who could afford it wore iron crosses around their necks and silver jewelry on their fingers and wrists. Tattoos covered thick hairy arms, necks and chests. Their mustaches grew down around their mouths into goatees or beards. The ones who had hair let it grow wild, or tied it in braids. The skinheads shaved and tattooed their skulls.

As far as Bucky was concerned, every one-percenter in Southern California belonged behind bars.

On his way to see Mike, Bucky stopped for gas on Lancaster Boulevard. The old fire department pickup was a piece of junk, but it still had a light bar on the roof and a working radio system inside and it was transportation until his insurance company reimbursed him for the loss of the Bronco. The pump whirred away, filling the tank and draining money directly from Bucky's bank account. He stood aside and tried to avoid inhaling the gasoline fumes. He recalled the body scent he had picked up in the desert and tried to remember details about the biker who stood in the sand in front of him.

The sheriff's station smelled of stale smoke. Bucky detested smoking—it polluted his nose and made it hard to smell anything else. Secondhand smoke was just as bad. Most cops were smokers; some even smoked cigars. Despite the Percocet he had taken that morning, Bucky still had a throbbing headache. When he walked in to his friend's tiny office, Mike nodded and continued his telephone conversation. Bucky sank down onto the lone chair and waited for Mike to finish.

"DIE POCHO," Mike said. "They rigged up a huge hunting knife on a pendulum. It had two bottles of water for weights, so when you trip the wire, the blade comes swinging down from the ceiling and hits you in the stomach. While you're lying on the floor bleeding to death, you're supposed to look up and see the sign that says, 'DIE POCHO.' Yeah, that's right. Yeah. Hey, I've got someone in my office, I'll have to call you back." Mike hung up. "Hi, Buck. How's the head?"

"Still hurting. What's a Pocho?"

"A Mexican American. We raided a biker stash house yesterday. They're big on booby traps. When we got inside, we found a dead Mexican with a V carved on his forehead and his stomach. That's V for the Vagos motorcycle gang, the Greenies, a really dirty club. The coroner said the cutting was done before he died." Mike put his feet up on his desk and leaned back in his chair until it rested against the wall. "You know what? There's more than the usual amount of meth on the streets right now and I think something big could be going on here in town. For the last couple of years, all we've had are small-time users, but lately things seem to be picking up. There's more meth for sale and more being used and I think it's coming from around here. We thought we were on to something the night of that disaster out at the doublewide." Mike shook his head. "It would be fun to go back to the days of Whac-a-Mole again."

"Whac-a-Mole?" Bucky asked.

"You know, that game at Six Flags. You whack it in one place and it pops up in another. When I joined the Narcotics Squad, that's the way it was. We'd shut down a meth lab and within days, another one replaced it. We were going full out, 24/7. Very exciting times." Mike took his feet off his desk and let his chair settle on the floor. "You know Buck, I worked my way up the drug ladder arresting users, sellers, distributors and the guys doing the cooking. I was inside meth houses with little makeshift labs in the bathroom, bigger operations in garages, and even a few full-size labs in the desert laid out like factories. Looking back, I thought it would never end, but it did. The Mexicans went home where it's easier to operate, and now they just send finished product back into the states for sale. And we put so much heat on the motorcycle gangs that most of them moved to Nevada and Arizona. Ever been in Bullhead City, Arizona? Now *that's* a meth town." Mike picked up his paper coffee cup, realized it was empty and put it back on his desk. "The biker gangs around here are bad news, but now they're into all kinds of other bad stuff like guns and prostitutes, and the ATF is in charge of all that." Mike paused. "Jesus, I'm just going on and on. Have you heard from the coroner? What about Brandy?"

"There was a message when I got home from the hospital yesterday.

The DNA confirmed it was her, but I already knew. Finding the earring out there was all I needed."

"I'm really sorry. What a way to end a life."

"I remember a time when Brandy was in first or second grade. She came into the kitchen one morning and asked me, "Bucky, what's an addict?""

An argument going on between two detectives at the far end of the hall interrupted their conversation.

Bucky rubbed his eyes, which made his head hurt more. "Mike, what do you know about the tweakers killed in the explosion? Were they bikers?"

"We don't know yet, but I'm working on it. We flipped a guy who's up on drug charges and he was supposed to be feeding us information. *Reliable* information. Our G-2 from him was that there was a big meth operation in that trailer—Mexican illegals, surveillance equipment, weapons, a major drug lab out there waiting to be taken down. In fact, as far as we can tell, they were just some small-timers. We call them producer–consumers and I guess your sister was one of them. About a month ago, the owner of a storage facility reported that a girl and a couple of guys with long hair rented a locker and paid in cash. He thought it was suspicious from the get-go. That could have been Brandy. Sometimes they cook meth in those storage facilities."

"I can't believe she was here in Lancaster and never even told me. When she was doing time in Colorado, I tried to stay in touch. She wrote to me once, two years after I went out to see her and said she expected to be released in less than a year. I was worried about what would happen to her when she got out, and told her to come home and stay with me. I never heard from her again and she just disappeared. If I had known she was back, maybe I could have helped her."

"I'm sorry about what happened out there." Mike looked into the empty coffee cup again. "If we had the right information, that whole operation the other night could have been done differently. If we had just done a 'knock and talk,' Brandy might still be alive, but that's my own, unofficial statement."

"It is what it is," Bucky sighed. "She might have opened the door just as you were about to knock. She could have lit the cigarette and taken you with her. Don't second-guess."

"I always thought Brandy was so good looking. I can't believe she ended up a meth freak."

When they were younger, Bucky had often joked that someday Mike could start dating Brandy. It never happened. Before Bucky went to high school, Mike moved to Santa Clarita and found a girlfriend, and he went on to marry her. Mike went into law enforcement, like his father, and Bucky became a firefighter, like his father, except Bucky's father was dead. Through it all, they remained close friends. By the time Bucky became a HazMat specialist, Mike had made it to the rank of detective in the North County Narcotics Task Force. If he had been dating Brandy, he might have had to arrest her.

Mike shrugged his shoulders. "I'll let you know when we find out who else was in the trailer. You off duty for a while?"

"Yeah, I'm taking bereavement leave for a week. I really don't want to do it, but my battalion chief insists on it."

"Well, take it easy for a few days. Give your head a rest."

"I'm starting to remember a few things. I saw a biker out at the trailer before someone hit me. As soon as my head stops hurting, I'm going to find out who it was."

"If it was bikers, especially the Vagos, stay away from them."

"They can have the Bronco, but I want my wallet back."

"You're way out of your league, Bucky. Do you know what OMG stands for?"

"Sure. "Oh My God." Anyone who ever sent a text message knows that. Why?"

"In law enforcement, OMG stands for Outlaw Motorcycle Gang, and it's no joke. There's a Vagos nomad chapter out here and they're a crazy, violent group doing all kinds of bad stuff. Take my advice—they are not people you want to get mixed up with."

"Yeah? Well right now the score is bikers one, Bucky zero. I'm not going to let that stand."

"You know what the Hells Angels are about? Well, the Vagos are just as bad. Stay out of it. The days of fists and knives and bike chains are long gone. They use semi-automatic weapons and grenades and don't play around. Last year back East, they used an RPG against an ATF vehicle."

"I could have died out there in the desert, dammit."

"Well, you didn't. So unless you want a V carved in your forehead, don't get involved."

"I already am. Actually, it's bikers two, Bucky zero. I owe them for what they did to my dad." Bucky felt a sudden surge of anger. "Screw the bikers."

"C'mon Bucky, that was what, twenty years ago? Let it go." Mike checked his watch. "Sorry, we'll have to continue this another time. I've got stuff to do. Cool it and stay away from the bikers or you'll end up with a tag on your toe."

"A tag on my toe? I don't think so." Bucky stood up to leave. "Hey Mike?"

"Yeah?"

"If someone was using, say, Percocet, and stopped. How long before it disappeared from, uh, his urine?"

"You trying to tell me something?"

"It's just a question."

"You want to know the elimination half-life?"

"I guess so."

"Well, for example, meth builds up in your spinal fluid and hangs around for quite a while, but opiates tend not to accumulate in your body, just run through your bloodstream. It depends on the strength of the dosage, the size of this hypothetical person and his metabolism. His piss would probably be clean in three days."

"Thanks, Mike."

"Unless, of course, you're eating a lot of poppy seed rolls."

ELEVEN

"THE OUTPOST: Desert Beauties—Stop—Look—Touch."
When Bucky left the air-conditioned sheriff's station, his head throbbed and he felt the depression seeping back into his body. The thought of going home, watching TV and talking to Zoll was more than he could bear. A visit to the Outpost might help. He knew he could stop and look. The problem was touching.

Outside, the wind was blowing. It was a constant—it blew every day. Some days it blew harder than other days, and occasionally it got serious and unleashed its full fury. Today was one of those days. Bucky drove east on the Mojave Barstow Highway, a straight, flat road flanked on one side by a line of telephone poles that disappeared on the horizon. In the distance, he saw a brown veil of dust and dirt moving in from the northeast. It was unmistakable and he knew there was nothing he could do to avoid it. Pileups involving a dozen or more cars and trucks were common in the reduced visibility of a sandstorm and the only safe place was at the side of the road. Bucky turned on his headlights and pulled over, along with several other vehicles and an eighteen-wheeler. He continued along the shoulder of the highway to put some distance between the pickup and the big rig in case the wind blew the trailer over. Bucky waited and watched as the storm approached across the floor of the valley. After years of below-normal precipitation and summer brush fires, much of the ground cover was gone and the land was quick to give up its top layer to the wind. Before weather advisories to close windows and secure outdoor objects could be broadcast, the sky filled with dust and the hills and distant mountains disappeared as the grit from the desert cut off the light and began to blow across the road. Tumbleweeds, chased by the storm, appeared out of the dust cloud, rolled across the highway and caught on barbwire fences and under the bumpers of cars. Bucky hated these useless weeds that the wind severed from their roots and sent blowing across the landscape, spreading their seeds for another cycle of growth. The gusts rocked the pickup and Bucky listened to the air whistle in around the windows. Visibility on the highway dwindled to a few feet and Bucky sat isolated, cut off from the rest of the world.

Twenty minutes later, after tons of fugitive dust had been blown from one spot in the desert to another, the sky began to clear. People caught outside would be blowing sand out of their sinuses for hours. Homes where windows had been left open—even a crack—would have a fine coating of dust everywhere. Bucky pulled back onto the highway and continued out past the sign that said: WELCOME TO MOJAVE—THE ENTRANCE TO SPACE. He had always regarded it as a cynical joke—a reference to the wide-open Mojave terrain rather than to the heavens above.

In his rearview mirror, he watched a biker appear and follow close behind him as he approached a forlorn cluster of weather-beaten buildings: the Flying Saucer Restaurant, the Space Haven Trailer Park and the Outpost. When Bucky turned into the parking lot, the biker shot past without stopping.

Bucky wasn't about to leave the pickup, marked Los Angeles County Fire Department Station 129, in front of a dilapidated bar and whorehouse. He drove around to the back and parked in the shadow of an old shipping container used for storage. He put a Percocet into his mouth, chewed it into tiny, bitter pieces and washed it down with water from a bottle. He waited for a few moments until he felt the effect of the drug. He knew he had a date with a pee cup next week, but next week was next year. When he opened the pickup door, the smell of Jet-A kerosene fuel drifted out from Edwards.

He knew before he went in to the Outpost that he would be disappointed. The last time he was with one of these women, he wanted to wash her in alcohol and scrub her down to neutralize her odor. Bucky hadn't felt raw sexual desire in weeks, and wondered if it was because of the painkillers. Nonetheless, driven by the emptiness he felt, he desperately needed some simple physical contact. The girls working at the Outpost didn't stay around very long. It was just a way station on their journey up, or down, the ladder of life. He hadn't visited in two months and hoped he might find a new girl with a decent fragrance.

Bucky walked in through the back entrance and paused to let his eyes adjust to the dim light. The odors came first, as he knew they would. He smelled cheap perfume, cigarette smoke and the residue of cleaning solution used on the glassware. Six girls, in cutoffs and brassieres, wearing flip-flops, sat at the bar in the mid-afternoon heat. No one came for a blowjob at 3:00 p.m., and when Bucky entered, they looked at him with bored glances. There were no giggles and no sexy attitudes. The bartender ignored him as well and continued to wash glasses. For all the interest Bucky attracted, he might have come to deliver bottled water.

Overhead light came from an old wagon wheel wired as a candelabra and suspended from the ceiling. Two of the bulbs flickered, struggling to stay alive, while the remainder cast a golden light in the dark interior. On the far wall, a yellow and red neon Dos Equis Beer sign illuminated the wooden stairway leading up to the tiny rooms where ecstasy started at $50 an hour. A barrel filled with peanuts stood at one end of the bar and crushed shells littered the floor. The small, ancient Asian woman who owned the Outpost sat alone at one of the tables. She ate out of a bowl using chopsticks and occasionally stopped to puff on a cigarette burning in an ashtray. When she saw Bucky enter, she stubbed out her cigarette, pulled herself slowly out of her chair and approached him. "Yes mister. You want girl?" She smelled of cigarette smoke and Chinese food.

Bucky hesitated. He wanted to flee. "Maybe. I uh—"

"You look, find nice girl. All nice girls."

The full effect of the Perc hit Bucky's bloodstream and he felt energized, but when he approached the bar, the combined perfumes overwhelmed him.

"Hi, sweetheart," a blonde with long hair said, trying to sound interested. "What happened to your head? Your mamma hit you with a frying pan?" In the dim light, Bucky thought she might be thirty. Outside, in the unforgiving desert sunlight, she might be ten years older. He leaned toward her and then drew back abruptly. She wore a cloying, sweet perfume that was overpowering.

The second girl was much younger, closer to twenty, and decent looking. She had a red glass jewel stuck on her temple next to her right eye. Bucky took a step toward her and then stopped. She reeked of a mixture of sour perfume and harsh mouthwash.

He turned to the third girl and bent to smell her neck, trying to screen out the other scents around him.

"You trying to see my tits?" she said, tugging down her brassiere to give him a view of her nipples. "What d'ya think?" She arched her chest toward him.

She was exceptional. She exuded an almost neutral scent with a touch of pear fragrance. He tugged gently at her arm, drawing her off the barstool toward him. "What are you wearing?" he asked, looking at her face for the first time. Yes, he thought, he could do it with her.

"What am I wearing? What does it look like I'm wearing?" She pulled her bra back up over her breasts. "Did you get hit on the head or something?"

Bucky drew her across the room, away from the maelstrom of scents, toward the front door and fresher air. He placed his nose directly on her skin at the base of her throat and inhaled.

"Hey, you're weirding me out. What're you doing?" She pushed his head away. "This is too fucked. Leave me alone."

"Never mind," Bucky said, letting go of her arm and heading for the back exit. He already knew what she would smell like in the heat of sex, and it wouldn't be good.

"Mister?" the Asian woman said.

Bucky shook his head on the way out. "Sorry to bother you." He pushed open the door and walked out into the daylight.

The air conditioning in the old pickup sent out a weak flow of cool air as Bucky drove home. The San Gabriels, their peaks hidden in gray clouds, were in the midst of a thunderstorm and by early evening, rainwater would be coursing through every desert gully in the area. Bucky glanced in the rearview mirror and saw the same biker on the big Harley appear out of nowhere and again come up behind him. Bucky wondered what it felt like heading into a blast of hot desert air on a bike at seventy-five miles per hour. The guy wore tinted goggles and a black sleeveless leather vest over his bare chest. His muscular arms held on to the ape hanger handlebars at shoulder level. A foot-long braid of black hair trailed out from underneath his bandanna. So much for the helmet law, Bucky thought.

The rider accelerated, disappeared from Bucky's rearview mirror and sped past. Bucky took his foot off the gas to let the motorcycle go, but the rider slowed as well, and stayed just ahead of the pickup. He looked back at Bucky, pointed to the side of the road and motioned to Bucky to pull over. He was a one-percenter; Bucky saw motorcycle gang colors on the back of his vest. He wore a patch shaped like an inverted neon green triangle that said VAGOS. In the center, a red devil sat astride a single-winged motorcycle wheel. His vest was missing the rocker above the patch with the club name as well as the one below it with the club location. The man in front of him was still coming up through the ranks; he was a prospect, not yet a full member of the gang.

When Bucky failed to pull over, the biker moved out into the left lane and drifted back until he was abreast of the pickup. He seemed unconcerned about oncoming traffic as he turned and again pointed at the side of the road with his finger. The highway was straight and flat. Bucky looked ahead and saw a truck in the distance. He slowed to forty miles per hour and the biker slowed to match his speed. The rider seemed to be looking at him, although Bucky couldn't see his eyes through the goggles. Bucky thought again of his father's beating and humiliation years ago in the parking lot of the Mexican restaurant. His heartbeat increased. The damned one-percenters! A jolt of adrenaline coursed through Bucky's body and he felt a surge of anger. Did the biker recognize Bucky? Was this one of the bastards who hit him on the head and dumped him in the desert?

The man on the Harley was still riding next to him and pointed yet again toward the side of the road. Screw you, Bucky thought. Whatever the biker had in mind, it couldn't be good and Bucky didn't need a V carved on his forehead. He pressed hard on the accelerator and the old pickup struggled to gain speed. The engine howled as the speedometer needle edged up toward eighty and began to quiver. Bucky thought the truck might be on the verge of a heart attack and eased up slightly on the gas pedal. The Harley drifted back into the right lane to avoid the oncoming truck and then pulled up close behind the pickup.

Bucky watched the rider in the mirror and thought of his father again as he turned the pickup's lights on and off, causing the taillights to flash. The biker applied his brakes abruptly and his Harley fishtailed and swerved out into the left lane in front of the oncoming truck. Overcorrecting, the Harley veered back across the right lane behind Bucky and off into the desert, crashing onto the sand. Have a nice day, asshole, Bucky thought.

He continued on, turned south on the 14 and headed home. He checked his rearview mirror several times. Cars and trucks followed him, but no motorcycles. Bucky's heart rate slowed. He was certain he would see the biker again and decided next time he needed to be better prepared.

The minute he walked into the house, the depression descended upon him. It was like a physical weight, pushing down on his shoulders. The silence in the house was deafening. Bucky turned on the heat lamp for Zoll and watched as the lizard climbed to the top of a rock and remained motionless, soaking up the warmth. The reptile's eyes were open, unblinking. Bucky felt it staring at him. What was it thinking?

Bucky grabbed a pear out of the refrigerator and fled to the garage to pump iron, but his usual therapy didn't help. He couldn't concentrate on his workout and he quit halfway through his routine. He walked out onto the driveway and watched an early sunset as the glowing sphere disappeared behind high cumulus clouds over the Tehachapi Mountains. He stared at the spot on the cement where Brandy's boyfriend Kenny had parked his hog years ago, revving the engine, waiting to depart for Nevada.

The late September days were getting shorter. Worse than the silence in his house, Bucky hated the early darkness. He went into the bathroom and took the Percocet bottle out of the medicine cabinet. Even with the loss of three pills taken along with his wallet and keys, he still had more than enough to last until his order from BuyDrugs arrived. Bucky was thankful he had ordered more P online. He wasn't about to go doctor shopping, chasing around Lancaster for a new prescription from some sleazy doctor. He planned to stop taking the painkiller soon anyway, but he still needed the comfort of knowing it was available if he wanted it. He opened the plastic bottle, dropped a pill into his hand, popped it into his mouth and slammed it dry—it was a skill he was learning in case he wanted to take a Perc when he didn't have water handy. Once he was sure he had swallowed it, he drank from the tap to hasten the drug's dissolution. Swallowing a Perc was becoming a comforting ritual, a regular part of his life, something he looked forward to doing three or four times a day. Bucky scratched his chest and pulled off his T-shirt to look at his upper body. The doctor at the hospital had given him a spray for his irritated skin and for a day, the itching had diminished.

Now it was coming back to life and Bucky was certain it wasn't from the heat.

He walked out onto the deck, sat down in the dark and waited for the pill to take effect. The cool wind, which sometimes reached fifty or sixty miles per hour, blew against his bare chest. In the summer, high pressure over the ocean drove the air northeast through the surrounding mountain passes toward the Mojave. In the winter months, the wind reversed direction when cooler weather in Nevada created the Santa Ana winds that descended southwest toward Los Angeles. One way or another, the wind was present every day and whichever direction it blew, it brought Bucky a fragrance or an odor of something from somewhere. The smell of ozone from the distant lightning had moved on earlier in the evening and now he detected the same faint, sweet chemical smell that lately had come drifting across the desert at night. It drove him crazy because it was vaguely familiar but he couldn't identify it. Like so many scents he picked up, no one else ever noticed or remarked about it. Whatever it was, the wind carried it to him from the desert.

He relaxed on the deck as the Perc flooded his senses. He gave up trying to identify the chemical scent and thought about the Vagos prospect who had followed him from the Outpost. It was definitely time for some protection. Bucky went inside to his bedroom, opened his closet, reached to the top shelf and took down the box that contained his Beretta 85FS Cheetah. The box was covered with dust and he couldn't remember the last time he had touched it. He had purchased it several years ago, after a series of burglaries in Quartz Hill. When he took the Cheetah out into the desert for target practice, he discovered he was a lousy shot. He had planned to practice regularly, but soon lost interest and left the gun to collect dust in the closet.

Bucky sat down on the bed and opened the box. The pistol lay in its gray Styrofoam niche. The black matte finish of the gun swallowed light and gave it an ominous look. Bucky picked it up and held it. In his initial enthusiasm, he had replaced the plastic handles with dark mahogany grips that fit his hand perfectly. He had forgotten the solid feeling of power the .38 imparted. The Percocet in his bloodstream told him the Cheetah would be his new family member and loving companion that would defend and protect him. No asshole one-percenter was going to try to carve a V in his forehead. Bucky, the Percocet and the Cheetah would make sure of that. He released the empty magazine and it fell to the floor. He pulled back the slide, racked an imaginary bullet in the chamber, pointed the gun at his bedroom window and squeezed the trigger. The snap of the firing pin made a solid, reassuring sound. "Kapow," Bucky said, pulling the Beretta up in mock recoil. "A biker goes down. Kapow, another biker messing with my sister hits the blacktop." The Cheetah had a 9-round magazine and Bucky squeezed off seven more imaginary shots at an outlaw motorcycle gang. Kapow—a one-percenter slumps over his handlebars and crashes. Kapow—mayhem. Kapow—Dead Greenies and metal on the pavement. Kapow, kapow, kapow—tattoos covered with blood. KAPOW —a biker massacre."

After years on the shelf, the gun needed cleaning and lubrication. Bucky went back to his closet and took down the cleaning kit. He opened the small bottle of bore solvent and didn't even have to inhale to smell it. It was a chloroalkane, and its thick, sweet odor filled his nose. Bucky looked at the warning on the back of the bottle: Harmful or fatal if swallowed. Trichloroethane. Avoid prolonged inhalation of vapors.

Bucky slapped his forehead and said, "Of course, you idiot."

TWELVE

"YOU SMELL WHAT? WHERE?" MIKE searched through the mess on his
desk for his notebook. "Trichloroethane?"

"I'm sure," Bucky said. "To be exact, it's 1,1,1-TCE, methyl chloroform.
It drifts in sometimes at night when the wind comes from the east. It's faint
but I've picked it up three or four times. I knew it smelled familiar, but I
couldn't place it until last night. Someone's dumping solvent from a meth lab
out there, Mike."

"They use a dozen different chemicals in extraction and purification.
It's all bad stuff—volatile, flammable and toxic. Acetone, methanol, ethanol,
ether, benzene, trichloroethane, you name it. How do you know it's
trichloroethane?"

"Yesterday I went to clean my Beretta. As soon as I opened the bottle of
bore cleaner, the odor hit me. It's definitely TCE."

"You have a Beretta?"

Bucky ignored the question and went on. "These goddamn one-percenters
are dumping their lab residue in the desert."

"How much do they have to dump for you to smell it?"

"It depends on where they are and how strong the wind is blowing."

"Well, they're not dumping it at the end of your street. It has to be somewhere off-road, in the middle of nowhere. They're not gonna unload it anywhere
where someone will see them."

"This isn't very scientific, Mike, but I couldn't smell a quart, or even
a gallon at any distance. It would have to be a significant amount. Maybe
someone's emptying something like a 55-gallon drum."

Mike stood up, his eyes gleaming. "Fifty-five gallons? Of solvent?

A little tweaker lab would use a coke bottle full."

"I didn't say *exactly* fifty-five gallons, Mike. Maybe it's thirty-five gallons. I don't know how much, but enough for me to smell, and a lot more than one gallon."

"Anything close to that would mean a huge lab. Do you know what kind of yield that would be? You're talking about meth worth millions of dollars on the street. It fits with the increased drug activity."

"Maybe they have a bunch of small labs and they collect the solvent from each one."

"Not likely. Is there any way you could track the scent to the dump site?"

"I don't know. There's what, eight million acres of desert out there? Like I said, it depends on where they're dumping it, how strong the wind is and which direction it's blowing. We'd have to get lucky. Once it's absorbed into the sand and evaporates, the smell will just about disappear."

"This could be huge—a major drug bust. We could put together a team and do aerial surveillance. It could be the biggest thing in my career. I could get another stripe."

"I can't smell anything from a plane."

"I'm talking about a drone, not a plane."

"A drone? Like in Afghanistan?"

"That's right, but smaller. One with a 6-foot wingspan and an optics package. We've been working with Homeland Security. Last year the Sheriff's Department staged a series of crime scenes while a SkyScan drone did surveillance. Ever heard of them?"

"No."

"They make small military drones over in the Plant 42 complex. Now that the Space Shuttle program is over, all kinds of new high-tech defense companies are moving in out there." Mike regarded Bucky for a minute. "What're you doing with a Beretta?"

"I've had it for years. I'm gonna carry it for protection."

Mike shook his head. "Jesus, Buck, you are one stubborn son of a bitch. I'm telling you the bikers are vicious and violent." Mike dug through a pile of papers on his desk. "Here, listen to this. The ATF just brought charges against a Mongols chapter in Vegas. They included murder, rape, assault, bombings and execution-style killings. You want to get involved with stuff like that?"

"I may already be involved. Yesterday, a Vagos prospect followed me out on the Barstow Highway. He kept coming up next to me and tried to get me to pull over. I have no idea what he wanted and I wasn't about to stop to find out. Maybe it was one of the guys who jumped me. Maybe they want another set of keys to my Bronco." Bucky almost said, "Maybe they want more of my Percocet," but refrained. "I don't know what's going on, but they took my wallet and know where I live, so from now on, my Beretta is gonna keep me company."

"You have a license to carry a concealed weapon?"

Bucky shook his head. "No. Right now I don't even have a driver's license."

"Fired your gun recently?"

Bucky shook his head again.

"Can you hit the broad side of a barn?"

"Depends on how close I am and how big the barn is." Bucky aimed his finger at Mike.

"You wanna bring it by and practice at the range?"

"That would be good."

"I'll get on this solvent thing," Mike said. "Maybe your crazy sense of smell can help us make a drug bust. A *big* drug bust."

Bucky smiled. At least trichloroethane was one of the 10,000 chemicals he recognized, instead of one of the 70,000 unknown to his nose.

"My son has hallucinations," his father was quick to tell friends when Bucky was growing up. "He has smell hallucinations, if there is such a thing. What's the word? *Old-fac-tory.* He has *oldfactory* hallucinations. He thinks he can smell things across town."

Bucky was in fact born with an unusual number of receptor cells and had an extraordinary sense of smell. He went through childhood smelling dinner cooking on each stove in the neighborhood, trash rotting on every street and jet engine exhaust drifting across the desert from Edwards Air Force Base. The barrage of fragrances, scents, odors and stenches was at first disorienting—he was continually bombarded with stimuli—and Bucky had trouble concentrating. In elementary school, one doctor diagnosed him as having attention deficit disorder.

Bucky remembered the first time he understood he was different.

He was almost eight, and his dog, Pepper, had been out in the yard barking all afternoon.

"If that goddamn dog doesn't shut up," his father screamed, "I'm gonna strangle her. Bucky, bring Pepper inside and keep her quiet."

"Dad, she's barking at coyotes." Pepper was always out in the yard, at the fence, yelping at something.

"Coyotes? Where? How do you know?"

"You can't see them, Dad, they're out in the hills. Can't you smell them?"

His father gave Bucky a strange look and replied, "No, stop the bullshit. I can't smell them, and neither can you. Now keep Pepper quiet."

But Bucky could smell the coyotes, as well as other animals nearby. He could also smell the chlorine in the pool at the Youth Center across town and the odor wafting from the public restrooms. At the supermarket, he could detect women's fragrances and men's sweat throughout the store. As he grew older, he began to test the limits of his unusual ability. He was careful at first, often asking his friends, "Do you smell that?" or, "Phew, what's that stink?" At home, when he sensed a particularly strong scent, he watched carefully to see if anyone else in his family showed any awareness. His parents and Brandy were forever oblivious and Bucky soon learned to be silent about the aromas and odors that surrounded him. Pepper was his only ally. Pepper always had her head to the ground, the nostrils on her long snout quivering, tracing scents, and inhaling information.

Bucky wished Pepper could speak so they could compare the various odor prints and he could learn what she had picked up that he had missed. A year later, Pepper was killed by a car and his mother didn't want another dog in the house. Bucky cried for Pepper and was left to explore the olfactory world alone. Throughout his life, he felt a special kinship with canines and was able to approach even the meanest stray dog on the street. Years later, when he learned that a human has about 6 million receptor sites for smell while dogs have between 200 and 300 million, Bucky wondered if he were part canine.

By the time he was a teenager, Bucky's brain had learned to filter out the unnecessary sensory input from the thousands of inhalations he took each day. While he was always aware of the melody of smells swirling around him, he was no longer distracted. His cognitive ability developed to the point that, when he needed specific information, he drew air into his nostrils and his nose told him what he needed to know long before anything registered in his eyes or ears. Once his brain learned to control and use the input from his nose, Bucky's concentration improved, his grades rose and his teachers began to rate his intelligence as above average.

Bucky used his sense of smell as others used their vision. His memories of people, places and things were in the form of scents and odors. His nose acted as a collection point for important information, channeling odorants— chemical molecules—to his olfactory cortex, the place in his brain where scent memories are created. His brain was quick to forge a link between a new scent and the person, thing, or event associated with it. He began to build his own mental reference library of every aroma, good or bad, that passed into his nose. His mother's odor print was that of stale cigarette smoke, liquor breath, and the funk surrounding a body that had spent several days in bed without washing. Bucky remembered his father as the dry smell of dust in the hot garage the day he stood watching him pack his fire gear in duffle bags for deployment to Kuwait. After his death, Bucky sometimes went out to the garage to summon the memory of his father. He didn't own a camera and wished he had a picture of his sister, but he had the scent of Ivory soap on her body as a child and the institutional smell of the prison soap when he visited her in Colorado.

As Bucky's mental reference library of odorants expanded, a particular fragrance could suddenly bring up a powerful emotional response. His first experience at making love remained clearly embedded in his mind as a kaleidoscope of sweaty perfumes. Bucky picked his girlfriends by how they smelled— looks were not as important as fragrance. When he met Patricia, the woman who became his wife, her fresh, healthy bouquet, which reminded him of pears, attracted him immediately. On their second date, he pressed his nose against her neck and said, "You're the woman I want to marry." It wasn't a happy union. They fought about everything—money, their respective friends, and the hardships of Bucky's work schedule. Most contentious, however, was Bucky's desire to start a family and Patricia's refusal to have children, which she said was non-negotiable. When she decided to leave him after three years, her final smackdown was, "You let your nose make all your decisions." He never found anyone else whose body produced Patricia's fragrance. He still loved the memory of her particular scent and as time passed, he realized that was the only thing about Patricia he had really loved.

When he entered the fire service, his special ability helped him to excel at what firefighters call "situational awareness." Bucky was always the first to smell smoke and could often tell what was burning before anyone else even saw flames. When he moved into HazMat, Bucky often knew immediately what substance they were dealing with, but learned to keep quiet and to rely on the special equipment instead of his nose. HazMat command frowned on opinion—only the readings from the meters and detectors were reliable.

Battalion Chief Vlasic took an immediate dislike to Bucky's reliance on his sense of smell. "I don't care how many pounds you can bench press, how fast you can climb a ladder, or what you think you can smell," Vlasic once told Bucky. "Every situation is dangerous, and you've got to go slow, use the equipment and find out exactly what you're dealing with. That's the way we do it. The *only* way."

"How about using my nose?' Bucky had asked.

"Your nose?" Vlasic sneered. "The average person can recognize a few thousand odors. You have to deal with 70,000 different chemicals and a lot of them are toxic. There's shit you don't want to breathe; it'll kill you. Ever heard the word 'coptometer'? That's a cop who runs into a HazMat situation without a breathing apparatus. If you see him fall down, it's probably because he's inhaled something lethal and he's dead. If you don't have a coptometer around, you better be using your breathing apparatus. If you're suited up and on air and you whip off your mask to take a deep breath, you could get a snout full of Anthrax or Ricin. Is that what you want? Or it could be a low-seeker, and you could get down on your stomach, get a whiff of gas and never get up. Learn to use the meters—that's what they're for."

Bucky listened and did as he was instructed. He became proficient with the measurement devices, the detectors and the sampling tools. He learned to calibrate the PIDs and CGIs—photo ionization detectors and combustible gas indicators—for chemical and vapor analysis. He practiced with the biological detectors for airborne pathogens, and he hoped never to have to use the devices they sent into buildings on robots to detect radiation and chemical terrorism. Bucky trained using the Level B chemical splash protection suit. When he practiced in the Level A vinyl/butyl chemical gear, wearing the double layers of gloves and integrated boots, with every possible opening zipped, taped shut or sealed with Velcro, Bucky could smell his body as never before. Sometimes, he could identify ingredients from the meals he had recently eaten leaking from his pores. Occasionally, he could smell diesel exhaust residue on his skin.

"You men are the 9-1-1 for the 9-1-1, and you're dealing with the unknown," Vlasic told the HazMat class at graduation. "You don't want someone else to have to come rescue you. Park uphill, stay upwind, use your binoculars, wear your protective gear and be goddamn careful."

As Bucky left Mike's office, he knew he had smelled trouble. Trichloroethane was drifting across the desert—not tetrachloroethane, not trifluoroethane, not tricholorofluoromethane, nor any of the other related aromatics. It was trichloroethane and it was from a meth lab. The bikers who humiliated his father, destroyed his sister's life and left him in the Mojave to die were dumping their toxic crap out in the sand. He would wear protective gear. He would pack his Beretta. He would be goddamn careful. Bucky swore he would even the score.

THIRTEEN

"How would you like to spend your life in a glass tank?" the owner of the Critter Center pet shop asked Bucky. "Cut off from everything?"

"If I let it loose, would it survive?" Bucky asked.

"Look, I don't sell you anything if I tell you to turn your lizard loose, but yes, the truth is, it could probably survive in the Mojave. Monitors eat anything—insects, mice, birds, even dead animals. There's plenty to eat out there."

"Thanks for telling me."

The owner slid a plastic container across the counter. "In the meantime, you want to try some live crickets instead of the worms?"

"Sure," Bucky said, and slapped down a five-dollar bill.

It was Thursday, 11:15 a.m., a week since his sister was killed and the third day of his bereavement leave. Bucky cruised down Sierra Highway and wondered how he would survive with nothing to do until he went back to work the following Tuesday. He turned on the communications radio in the pickup and like every firefighter, listened to the broadcasts and intermittent bursts of static from dispatch without actually paying attention.

Engine 109 on scene at garage fire. 10399 Dexter Street. Request paramedic.

Station 88. Squad and engine, respond to injury collision on PCH at Las Flores Canyon.

HazMat Squad 129 respond to report of dead animals.

Bucky turned up the volume.

... meet BLM range conservation officer, east on El Mirage Road, look for dirt road marked Moody Springs. GPS coordinates latitude 34 55 18, longitude 117 65 88.

Dead animals? Bucky had nothing better to do and decided to kill some time by driving out to see what kind of dead animals had been discovered. He entered the coordinates into his smartphone. El Mirage Road ran due east from Plant 42. Approximately fifteen miles out, it intersected Moody Springs.

He missed the turn-off and had to turn around. Moody Springs wasn't a dirt road; it was a trail winding through the desert brush, marked by a faded sign riddled with bullet holes. He checked his GPS and confirmed he was headed toward the coordinates called in to dispatch by the conservation officer. A dust devil formed and whirled along, following the pickup for a few minutes before it died out. Waves of heat shimmered up from the sand. Tracks from all-terrain vehicles crisscrossed the area and it looked like a popular riding spot even though it was miles from the El Mirage Off Highway Vehicle Recreation Area. Bucky drank half a bottle of water and continued until he saw the red profile of the HazMat Squad in the distance. He rolled down the window far enough to take a deep breath and picked up the faint smell of rotting flesh. Whatever was dead hadn't been killed recently.

As he approached, Bucky saw men from B Shift standing in the shadow of the enormous vehicle. They weren't suited up and sweat stains showed on the backs and underarms of their blue T-shirts. A sheriff's car and white pickup from the Bureau of Land Management baked in the sun nearby. A man in a brown uniform, wearing aviator glasses and a baseball cap kneeled on the sand, bent over one of three small manhole covers.

Bucky parked and the moment he opened the door, the hot desert air brought him the faint, familiar smell of trichloroethane, as well as the dense feral odor of decayed flesh. Bucky got a closer look at the manhole covers and realized the tan and dark brown objects were the shells of desert tortoises, each over a foot in diameter. Two of the three were upside down, their undersides ripped open.

The BLM man wore a ROGERS nameplate with "Bureau of Land Management" embossed underneath. He was scribbling on a clipboard. "This is an endangered species," he said, as Bucky approached. "You're not even allowed to touch a desert tortoise. If one dies, it's a problem. If two die, it's a crisis. Three dead tortoises? A national disaster. The Secretary of the Interior will hear about it."

Fire Captain Browne and a sheriff's deputy stood sweating in the sun, listening to Rogers and looking at the dead tortoises.

"How did you find this spot?" the deputy asked Rogers.

"We monitor sheep and cattle grazing," Rogers said. "Pure coincidence."

Browne looked up and saw the bandage on the side of Bucky's head. "What happened to you?" he said.

"Hey Brownie," Bucky said. "I ran into the side of a shovel."

"Hear anything about your sister?"

Bucky again saw the thin figure standing outside the door to the trailer. She twisted her hair around her finger. She pulled out a cigarette and lit it. Bucky wondered if he would ever forget those images. "She was killed in the blast," he said.

"Oh man, I'm sorry to hear that. You on leave?"

"Yeah, but I was in the neighborhood. What's going on here?"

"You heard the man," Browne said. "We have a national disaster on our hands." He pointed at one of the dead tortoises.

"I would guess they've been dead two or three days," Rogers went on. He tapped the shell of an overturned tortoise with his pen. "It's mating season and we've got two females and a male. Natural causes wouldn't explain the death of three of these creatures at one time. They live to be a hundred."

The sheriff's deputy bent down to look at one of the overturned carcasses. "That really stinks," he said, and backed away. "Looks like some predator had a pretty good meal."

"Probably coyotes," Rogers said. "These tortoises weigh around fifteen pounds. They turn them over and rip out the soft underside. Then the birds finish it. Hawks and ravens." He pointed to the tracks in the sand. "We may have a crime scene here. Look at this. Off-road vehicle tracks. This is a DTNA —a Desert Tortoise Natural Area. It's illegal to ride an OHV here."

"A crime scene?" the deputy said. "Were they shot?"

"Maybe an OHV killed the tortoise," Browne said. He turned the single upright tortoise over with a shovel and looked at the underside.

The BLM man flipped the dead tortoise back on its stomach. "I know it's dead, but it just goes against my nature to see one on its back."

"We respond to dead animals," Browne said. "But big animals like horses and cows. This isn't really an incident for Hazmat."

"As long as you're here," Rogers said. "Could your men bag them up while I take some pictures and call this in? Hold your nose and try to keep the flesh intact. There's a special procedure for dead tortoises. I have to take them back to the office, fill out a detailed report, pack them in ice and ship them off to the Fish and Game lab in Oregon."

Bucky bent down to look at one of the overturned tortoises, or what was left of it. The guts were partially torn away and the head and two of the legs ripped off, leaving open flesh, now black in color and filled with tiny crawling insects. The remaining legs, ordinarily round like tiny elephant legs, were limp and shrunken. "What do they do for water out here?" Bucky asked.

"*Gopherus agassizii*," Rogers said. "They can live in 140-degree heat and get their water directly from plants. They have huge bladders and recycle their piss. If you touch one and scare it, it'll start hissing and then let go. If you've ever smelled desert tortoise piss, you won't forget it."

"*Gopherus?*" Browne said. "Are they related to gophers?"

"No," Rogers said. "That's just the scientific—"

"Tortoise piss?" Bucky exclaimed. "Uric acid and nitrogen?" The reek came back with total clarity. His mind filled with disjointed images. He struggled to put the pieces together and remembered his night in the desert when he touched the dark form of a tortoise. He recalled the halogen headlights. Bucky looked around. He had wandered for two days. Could this be the spot where the creature pissed on him?

"Tortoise piss?" Rogers said.

"One of them let loose on me one night when I was lost in the desert," Bucky said. He looked for something familiar, but the sand and brush looked like all the other sand and brush in the Mojave. He saw a five-foot wide spot on the sand that was a darker color. Bucky went to it, kneeled down, placed his nose against the ground and took a deep breath. He scooped out a hole with his hands, stuck his face into the depression and took another breath. Bucky stood up and looked around again. Was it possible? He picked up a handful of sand and held it out to Rogers. "Here. I think they dumped it right here. You can still smell it."

"Dumped what?" Rogers said.

"Solvent. TCE." Bucky let the sand trickle out of his cupped hand. "I think this is the spot where I spent the night. I saw an OHV. They must have come out to dump another load and I was there to see it." Bucky stood in the heat, sweating, remembering the halogen lights. If they had emptied a container of TCE, why didn't he recall the odor? He understood—the wind had been at his back, blowing in the wrong direction.

"Trichloroethane?" Rogers said. "Someone dumped trichloroethane? Bad stuff. It was used as an industrial and aerospace degreaser for years, but now it's banned. It's toxic and builds up in the body. It causes central nervous system disorders, birth defects, cancer, you name it. Twenty-five years ago it was dumped everywhere, especially at air bases. They're still cleaning it out of the sand at Edwards. It got into the groundwater, and then the sage and grass and cacti picked it up. It worked its way up the food chain. A bunch of tortoises were poisoned out there in the '90s."

"What kind of plants do they eat?" Bucky asked Rogers.

"Any kind of succulent or grass," Rogers said. "This stuff." He pointed to a patch of Mexican bladdersage, pods filled with seeds, growing within the darkened spot on the sand. He bent down to examine it. "If someone dumped TCE here," Rogers said, "it could have been absorbed by these bushes. This plant was chewed on recently. The tortoises could have been poisoned." Rogers sniffed the spot where Bucky had scooped away the sand. "There is a faint chemical odor. Is that what TCE smells like?"

"That's it," Bucky said. "They also use it in meth labs."

Bucky went to talk to the sheriff's deputy who had retreated to the air conditioning of his car. Bucky opened the door, felt the rush of cool air, leaned in and said, "I think you should get your lab guys out here to collect some samples. This is a solvent dump from a meth lab."

"A meth lab?" the deputy said. He looked out through the open door. "Where? If I call the criminologist out for a chemical dump with no glassware or other evidence, not only will they not come, but I'll end up directing traffic for the rest of my life."

"This is important," Bucky said. "Call Detective Mike Ortiz in the Narcotics Squad. He's looking for this spot."

Rogers joined them. "You calling your lab technicians?" he said. "When they get here, ask them to take extra soil samples. Fish and Game has to do its own analysis." Rogers shook his head in disbelief. "Tell your sergeant we have a new kind of crime. Meth freaks have killed an endangered species."

The deputy frowned, but got on his radio.

Bucky walked back to the dark spot, kneeled down again and looked closely. He scraped up a tiny pile of surface sand, held it in the palm of one hand and pushed it around with his finger. "There's something else here," he said. "Some kind of white residue." He held it to his nose, but could only smell the trichloroethane. Wait until Mike hears about this, he thought.

Bucky sat in the sheriff's car talking with the deputy. The HazMat team had finished bagging the dead tortoises, piled them in the back of the BLM pickup and returned to 129. Rogers had departed to complete his paperwork and Bucky and the deputy waited for the sheriff's lab team.

"I still don't understand why our lab people need to be involved in this," the deputy said to Bucky. "It's an endangered species matter. Not our jurisdiction."

"I promise you, it's a narcotics matter," Bucky said, shifting around in the passenger seat and adjusting the air-conditioning vent. The cool air had a slightly sour smell as it blew directly on his face. Through the windshield, he watched a distant dust cloud, which soon became a white forensics van coming across the desert. Bucky and the deputy waited in the cool car until the van pulled up. Two forensics technicians emerged wearing white jumpsuits with the sheriff's six-sided star and the words CLANDESTINE LABORATORY RESPONSE TEAM underneath. One of the men went around to the back of the van, opened the double doors and pulled out a large equipment case. The second man approached the sheriff's car. The deputy and Bucky got out to meet him.

"Where's the crime scene?" he asked, and scanned the area. "What're we after?"

Before the deputy could respond, Bucky pointed to the stained area on the sand. "That's the crime scene. Someone dumped solvent out here and poisoned three tortoises. It's TCE and it came from a meth lab."

"You are?" the man asked.

"Bucky Dawson, I'm a HazMat specialist with County Fire."

The forensics expert didn't volunteer his name. "How do you know it's TCE?"

"I can smell it."

"You can smell it?" He laughed and said, "Well thanks for setting us straight. I guess our work is done."

Bucky ignored his comment. "Just check in with Detective Ortiz. This may have to do with a major meth lab operation."

"For any kind of prosecution, you need evidence—glassware, some finished product, stuff relating to a meth lab. Is this it? A spot on the sand?"

"That's it," Bucky said.

"Fish and Game wants some soil samples too," the deputy said.

The forensics man shrugged his shoulders. "OK, I hope you guys know what you're talking about." He joined his partner, who had spread a plastic sheet on the ground and placed the equipment case on top of it. Bucky watched them begin their work as they took a precise GPS location, snapped several photographs of the discolored sand, measured the spill area and prepared to take soil samples.

"If it is solvent from a meth lab," the second technician said, "it's gonna have something else mixed in with it. Pseudoephedrine, Red P, hydriotic acid, something."

"There is something else," Bucky said. "There's some kind of white residue."

"Let's take a look," the first technician said. He bent down and examined the surface of the sand with a magnifying glass. "Yeah, you're right. It looks like the scum left when they separate out the ephedrine from the binder." He used a small brush to sweep up several surface samples and placed each in a separate container.

The second technician removed what looked like a three-inch diameter pipe from sealed plastic wrapping marked DECONTAMINATED. He pounded the pipe several inches into the sand with a rubber hammer, twisted it around and then pulled it up. He checked to see that the sand was packed into the pipe, placed a cap over both ends and placed it back in the plastic wrapping. He repeated the process several times in different locations within the stained area on the sand. "Direct-push soil sampling," he said to Bucky. "Not exactly rocket science."

"And how did the tortoises get poisoned?" the first technician asked. "Did they ingest something?"

"Brush. The Mexican bladder-whatever-it-is. It absorbed the TCE and they ate it."

"Where is it?" the first man asked. "I need some samples."

Bucky led the technician to the bladdersage. "What happens next?" he asked.

"We send everything to our lab in Downey. They use X-ray fluorescence and infrared scanning to identify the chemicals. We'll send samples to Fish and Game. They run everything through an Inductive Coupling Plasma Mass Spectrometer. Only the Feds can afford equipment like that. It's a lot more sensitive."

"Never heard of any of that stuff," Bucky said. "I just use my nose,"

"Your nose?" The lab man smiled and gave him a strange look, then turned to help his partner pack away their equipment.

Bucky watched them drive off, followed by the deputy, who trailed the forensics van on the dirt road at a distance, trying to avoid the dust. He stood around for a few minutes, looked at the sand and brush and thought about his sister. Heat waves shimmered in the air. Joshua trees dotted the landscape. The San Gabriel and Tehachapi mountains were a faint blue-gray presence in a hazy sky. The wind blew in Bucky's face. It rumbled in his ears. It filled his nose with a parched, dull smell of emptiness. The wind lived in the desert; the humans were visitors.

As he drove back toward Lancaster, Bucky collected saliva in his mouth and swallowed a Percocet.

FOURTEEN

"**D**O NOT MIX IT UP with these bikers. You're way out of your league. They're vicious and violent."

On the way home, Bucky thought of what Mike had said to him. His anger flared again. I can handle the bikers, Bucky thought. Mike was treating him like a child.

Bucky was almost home when the Harley roared past him travelling in the opposite direction. He watched the biker in his rearview mirror and saw the large Vagos center patch without the rockers on the back of his vest. A foot-long braid of black hair trailed out from a German military type helmet. It was the same one-percenter who followed him from the Outpost on the Mojave-Barstow Highway. Bucky wondered why the biker was in his neighborhood. It was time to start carrying the Beretta. It wouldn't do him any good in a drawer in the kitchen.

When he pulled onto his driveway, Bucky saw that his mailbox was open. He parked alongside it, rolled down the window and shined his flashlight inside. He had heard of pipe bombs left in mailboxes and even remembered a story about someone bitten by a coiled rattlesnake. Bucky didn't see any rattlers or pipe bombs; just a small pile of mail. He pulled out a bunch of junk advertisements, his telephone bill, a letter from the California State Firefighters' Association, a sealed white envelope with no address or stamp and a small package with a Toronto return address. Bucky was most interested in this parcel from Canada that contained his Percocet order. He went into the house and directly to the bathroom, where he dumped the mail by the sink. He hesitated for a moment, then took another Perc from the bottle in his shirt pocket and drank from the faucet. If he downed one more before going to sleep, that would be five, more than he had ever taken in one day.

His fingers shook with excitement as Bucky opened the small priority-mail package and took out two plastic bottles. Each label had the same information: *Percocet 30 10 mg.* Bucky opened both bottles, spilled sixty pills out on the counter and gazed at them. It was more than he had ever had at one time and yet he wondered if he had enough. He counted the weeks since his back had begun to hurt. That episode began in June and lasted a month. He had continued to take the Percs for almost eight more weeks. Was that long enough to become addicted? Initially the painkiller had muted thoughts about his mother and father and had helped him feel as though he could still conquer the world. Now it was becoming harder to get that special sensation, even though he was swallowing more pills each day than a month ago. It was as if he were taking painkillers for his mind instead of his body and he didn't like the feeling when the pills wore off. Bucky had two choices—quit altogether, or increase the dosage and feel better.

He went into the kitchen and checked on Zoll. The lizard was on top of the rocks, holding on with sharp claws. Its long, forked tongue flicked in and out, and Bucky thought she might be hungry. He took the container of crickets out of the refrigerator and grabbed a pear at the same time. The crickets were sluggish from the cool temperature, but still alive. Bucky held one of the insects by its hind leg and dangled it in front of Zoll. In a blur of motion, the reptile pulled the cricket into its mouth with its tongue. Bucky thought the lizard was getting fat. She had nothing to do, nowhere to go and spent her existence resting motionless on top or behind the rocks in her tank. While Bucky reached for another cricket, Zoll retreated behind the rocks.

Bucky sat down at the kitchen table and bit into the pear. It was overripe and the special fragrance that he liked was dominated by the buildup of malic acid. Bucky set the fruit aside, booted up his computer and googled "Percocet Addiction." It was on the page with "Oxycontin Addiction," and he was surprised to learn that Percocet was simply Oxycontin mixed with Tylenol. Bucky knew all about the problems with Oxy, but had no idea that Percocet was the same drug. Now he understood the doctor's comment about Percocet being Oxycontin's ugly little sister. The website emphasized that Percocet addiction is a craving for morphine, which Bucky found frightening.

He read through the questions listed on the website and answered them mentally:

- *Do you feel like you need to have the drug regularly, every day?*

No, Bucky thought. I have gone months in the past without taking it.

- *Do you need the drug to function normally?*

I function normally every day. Not a problem.

- *Do you have mood swings during the day? Do you find yourself getting angry for no reason?*

I'm even-tempered and don't get angry. Except maybe lately, but I'm under a lot of stress. It's an emotional thing that will pass.

- *Do you want to stop, but just can't?*

No, I can stop anytime I want.

- *Because you can't stop, do you do things you normally would not do to get drugs?*

Bucky considered his Internet purchase and decided that didn't count. The answer to this question was also no. He wasn't doing the kind of crazy things addicts do to get drugs.

- *Do you make sure you have a steady supply of the drug on hand?*

Yes, but so what? I have back pain. If I get hurt on the job, I have to have a painkiller. I can't miss work.

Bucky concluded he was not an addict. Addicts were the lowlifes he had seen leaning against the walls of buildings or sprawled on the sidewalks in downtown Lancaster, oblivious to what was going on around them. He was a firefighter, a trained HazMat specialist, a regular working guy, not an addict. Bucky decided he was OK and besides, he was going to quit soon. It was Thursday afternoon. He planned to quit Friday evening, to be clean as a whistle for his drug test on Monday. Friday was a day away, no problem. Bucky chose not to read further on the website. He logged off and went back in the bathroom to retrieve the rest of his mail.

He picked up the blank envelope and pressed it to his nose. It was odorless. He held it up to the light and saw that it contained handwriting. When he ripped it open, he found his name misspelled on a message printed in crude letters:

> *Buckey – I have important information for you about your sister. Tomorrow afternoon at 5:00 sharp. Mach 2 Bar. East on 90th street to the dead end. Come alone.*

Information about his sister? It was no secret that he had a sister—or *had* a sister—but what information could anyone have about Brandy that was important? Was this really about Brandy, he wondered, or did someone have another agenda? The message must have been left by the biker who followed him back from The Outpost; the same one who roared past him earlier in the day on his way home. What did a Vagos want with him? Maybe it was Vagos bikers who assaulted him at the site of the explosion. Bucky thought about his stolen wallet. They had his driver's license and knew his address. Was this about the meth labs? Did the bikers somehow know he had discovered they were dumping solvent? No, that discovery came *after* he was attacked. Bucky's head began to spin. There were too many possibilities; too many unanswered questions. What if it really was about his sister? After all, she had been involved with bikers for years before she went to prison.

Bucky thought for a moment longer and decided the only way he could find out what was going on was to keep the date. He would not go alone, however. His close friend, Cheetah the black Beretta, wearing her exotic trichloroethane gun cleaner perfume, would accompany him. He went into the kitchen and pulled the Beretta out of the drawer. He held it in his hand and felt its weight. Bucky was glad he had taken the Percocet and thankful he had ordered more.

FIFTEEN

"How can something this big be going on under our noses and we have absolutely no intel on it?" Mike paced around his tiny office. "We got the lab results back this morning. You were right, it was trichloroethane. Score one for your nose. The lab tech out at the dumpsite thought you were bullshitting him when you told him that's what it was. Here's the kicker, Buck. The white residue? Lithium. Lithium, for Christ sake. Lithium's used in a meth manufacturing process called the Birch process. Our lab says it yields a very high-quality product. It's an expensive process because you have to use pure lithium metal." Mike drained his coffee cup. "It's all starting to fit together. Lithium ribbon is expensive, so somebody with some bucks has to be bankrolling the operation. Lithium reduction is a high-volume process, so it's consistent with a big solvent dump. Our lab estimates that thirty or forty gallons of TCE were dumped, all of it suffused with lithium residue. Somebody's running a big meth lab out here in the desert."

In all the years Bucky had known Mike, he had never seen him so animated. "And you know what?" Mike continued. "Sentencing guidelines are based on production capacity, so if we apprehend them, we can put them away for a thousand years." Mike sat down but was so wound-up, he stood up again and started to pace around.

"Hey, take it easy," Bucky said.

"This is huge. The good news is, we're going after them. We've got controlled substance violations and endangered species crimes. Fish and Wildlife is chipping in and we have funds to set up a small taskforce. BLM assigned a special agent to help us. I didn't even know the BLM had special agents. The first thing we're gonna do is throw up a drone and see it we can't find out who's doing the dumping. We'll work a grid, starting with the place where the turtles were poisoned. Have you remembered anything else?"

"Nothing that relates to this investigation."

"Is there some other investigation?"

"Don't mention this to anyone, OK?"

"Sure Buck."

"After the tortoise let loose on me, I had these weird visions, and they involved my mother."

"What? Your mother? What's she got to do with anything?"

"According to what I've read, the first memory a child has is the smell of his amniotic fluid, when he's still inside the womb."

"I still don't get it. What's that got to do with tortoise piss?"

"Urea. Uric acid. It's in urine and it's in amniotic fluid."

"Christ, Buck, what's the matter with you? You're starting to act weird. If you ask me, you've got too many strange memories."

"C'mon Mike, I'm under a lot of stress." Bucky held his head in his hands for a minute. "I guess I'm just tired. I'm having trouble sleeping and when I do, I keep dreaming about bikers. The one-percenter I told you about who followed me on the highway Tuesday? I saw him coming out of my neighborhood yesterday. He left this in my mailbox." Bucky unfolded the paper with the message and handed it to Mike.

Mike read it and said, "What's this about your sister?"

"I don't know. Do you think they're trying to get to me out there for some other reason? Does anyone know that I've been smelling solvent or that I figured out how the tortoises died?"

"A couple of people on the narcotics team. That's all. Mach 2? That crummy biker bar out near Edwards? You're not planning on going, are you?"

"Yeah, I thought I would."

"You're setting yourself up. Ten miles out of town? Alone at a biker bar? You're out of your fucking mind."

"Well, I'm bringing a friend."

"If you're planning what I think you are, I don't even want to know about it. How about if I send a deputy with you?"

"Sure, Mike. That would be great. I walk into a bar full of one-percenters with a sheriff's deputy? Thanks, but I'm not ready to commit suicide. I'll handle it myself."

"You may be committing suicide. Ever heard of death by cop?"

"So?"

"This is called death by biker. It's a lot worse."

When Bucky left Mike's office, he smelled ozone in the air and saw cumulus clouds building into thunderheads over the San Gabriels. As he watched, faint bolts of lightning—white electricity—descended from the sky. It was the time of the year when moisture from the Gulf of Mexico was sucked up into the Antelope Valley through the gaps in the ridgelines. The wet air, trapped by the surrounding mountains, formed bands of dark clouds and let loose heavy rainstorms. By early evening, torrents of water would scour the hills and drain down into the Antelope Valley. Flash floods cascading through the dry gulches and creek beds on the desert floor would nourish the sparse vegetation for a few hours. After the rain passed, Bucky knew a pungent smell would hang in the air. The creosotebush, a pervasive Mojave shrub, released the odor when rainwater touched the waxy coating on its leaves. Some people liked the smell because they associated it with rain. Others thought it smelled like camphor. To Bucky's sensitive nose, it was the pungent, bitter smell of a phenolic compound.

Before leaving home late Friday afternoon, Bucky downed two Percocets and placed several in a small plastic baggie. Now, he didn't leave the house without his pills; they accompanied him everywhere. Tonight he needed the P to dull his anxiety about the meeting and gave him a surge of confidence.

He drove into the deserted parking lot in front of Mach 2 at 5:05 p.m. Two decades earlier, the place had been a hangout for clean-cut aerospace engineers and test pilots. Now it was a joint, deserted during the day and frequented late at night by the Greenies, the Vagos biker gang. The bar stood alone at the corner of two intersecting hard-packed dirt roads, miles outside of Lancaster. Once covered with pink stucco, Mach 2's exterior was now a stained and faded brown color, with large chunks of plaster missing. The fuselage and tail of a small Beechcraft had been mounted on the roof, made to appear as though the plane had crashed nose first into the building.

When Bucky walked in, the bartender looked up in surprise, shocked to see a customer while it was still daylight. He was a fat man, wearing a dirty Jack Daniel's cap on top of greasy hair that cascaded down to his shoulders. He had a bushy mustache, dark, deep-set bloodshot eyes, and his T-shirt, embossed with "Support Our Troops," could not cover the enormous belly hanging over his belt.

"Howdy," the bartender growled. "What happened to your head?"

"Hey," Bucky said. He was tired of explaining the bandage on his head. He smelled charred meat and saw a half-eaten hamburger on the bar. In the dim light, he saw interior walls covered with dark wood paneling. A few round metal tables filled the center of the room, resting on an uneven gray cement floor. Queues lay across an old pool table, illuminated from above by a fluorescent bulb mounted in a plastic shade shaped like a NASCAR racer. In the corner, a jukebox, unplugged and dark, waited for the late night carousing to begin. An assortment of beat-up stools stood empty in front of the bar and strands of tiny Christmas tree lights hung from the back wall. Half the bulbs were out, but Bucky could see an old sign for Muroc Airfield, the predecessor to the giant aerospace facility that was now Edwards Air Force Base. When he looked up, he saw plastic aircraft models hanging from strings and old NASA stickers and aerospace mission patches stuck to the ceiling.

Bucky needed a plan. He sat down at one of the tables and the barrel of the Beretta, tucked into the back of his pants, pressed into the crease in his butt. The Cheetah was plan B. He was still working on plan A.

"You want something?" the barman asked.

"A beer."

"What kind?"

"Got Coors?"

"No."

"Whatever you have."

Bucky sat facing a wall of torn and faded jet fighter posters: the F-101 Voodoo; the F-102 Delta Dagger; the F-104 Starfighter; the F-105D in the air over Vietnam; and the F-106 Delta Dart high over Edwards. The pictures called forth a memory from his childhood when he visited the small outdoor air museum at the west gate of Edwards with his father. A collection of old jet aircraft baked in the desert sun and he stood looking at memorial plaques embedded in the cement while his father read them aloud. Bucky had never forgotten one inscription: *Captain Richard Davies – found God at Edwards – 1957*. Did Davies really find God? Bucky didn't believe in God—all the rotten things that had happened to him and his family proved to him there was no God. Bucky looked around and thought if Captain Davies's ghost ever came back to visit Mach 2, he would be very disappointed.

The bartender opened a Budweiser and waddled around the counter to Bucky's table. Considering how grubby the man looked, Bucky was surprised that he didn't smell worse than he did. The bartender put the bottle down, turned a chair around backwards, straddled it and lowered his fat body onto the seat. "Wanna hear a joke about the Jew and the Chinaman?" he said, exhaling a blast of tobacco breath.

"I don't think so." Bucky heard the first drops of rain on the roof as he took a swig of his beer.

The bartender gave him an angry look and pulled himself up off the chair. "You know, you look like a cop," he said. "In fact, you sound like a cop. You a drug clown?"

"No, I'm not a cop." Bucky stared at the bartender until he retreated to the bar to finish his hamburger in silence.

Bucky checked his watch. It was 5:15 p.m. He would give the biker another fifteen minutes and almost hoped he wouldn't show. He nursed his beer, picked at the damp label on the bottle, watched the second hand move around the face of his watch and listened to the increasing rainstorm outside. In a few minutes every Arizona crossing—the places where dry creeks and arroyos crossed the roads—would be flooded. By the time the storm ended, rainwater would inundate the desert and the lakebed out at Edwards would be submerged. The wind would blow the water back and forth over the hard clay until it filtered down and sealed the cracks, leaving a 44-square-mile landing pad as smooth as glass for the space shuttle.

A small rivulet of water began to leak from the ceiling, falling to the cement and forming a puddle in front of the bar. The bartender belched, farted and headed to the toilet.

Bucky waited and enjoyed the buzz from the Percocet. He was still day-dreaming when he heard the deep growl of a Harley arrive outside and go silent. The front door to the bar banged open and the man who walked in was drenched.

Water dripped off his German-style helmet and leather vest. His T-shirt and jeans were soaked through. Bucky saw black boots, a black belt and a silver chain. A vague recollection stirred in his memory and the instant he caught the body odor, Bucky knew. This was the biker he had seen standing in front of him at the site of the explosion; the one who had picked him up like a sack of potatoes and dropped him in the back of the pickup after he had been hit in the head.

The biker came to the table and sat down without saying anything. When Bucky saw his long braided ponytail, things began to make more sense. This was also the guy who had been following him around Lancaster. The biker was wild and tough looking, definitely a one-percenter. Up close, Bucky saw a cluster of scars on the left side of his face, probably the result of going face first through a pane of glass. He folded his thick arms over his chest and stared at Bucky. When he shifted his head, only one eye moved; the other stared straight ahead. Bucky wondered if it had taken a piece of glass.

"Hey, dude," the biker finally said.

"Hey," Bucky said.

The biker stared at Bucky with one good eye.

"You got a name?" Bucky asked.

"Jack."

"Nice to see you again, Jack." Bucky touched the bandage on his head. "Thanks for this and for dumping me in the desert."

"Ya gotta do what ya gotta do," the biker said. "We was out there to see if anythin' was left of our fuckin' trailer. Tough luck for ya—we thought ya was a cop. If I'd a known at the time ya was Brandy's brother, ya might've gotten a pass."

Bucky tried to remain impassive when he heard the biker utter his sister's name. "I almost died in that desert."

Jack shrugged his shoulders. "We're even. Ya could a killed me with that asshole stunt ya pulled on the Barstow Highway."

Bucky shrugged his shoulders. "We're not even. Where's my wallet and my Bronco?"

"Yer Bronco's probably in Mexico. I dunno about yer wallet." The biker smiled at Bucky, showing irregular teeth. "Ya gotta keep a sense a humor."

"I don't have a sense of humor," Bucky said.

The bartender returned from the toilet. "Howdy," he said. "You want something to drink?"

The rain thundered down outside.

"Usual."

Bucky saw a man sitting across from him who probably came from a screwed-up family, was a poor student who left school early, and who struggled through life, getting kicked in the teeth. He was just like Brandy, someone who desperately wanted to be part of something, even if it was an outlaw motorcycle gang. "You a Vagos prospect?" Bucky asked.

"Yeah, I'm gonna be a full-patch member soon. I just gotta get my rockers. A year after that, I can get the patch tattooed on my chest, in color."

"So what do you have to tell me about my sister?"

"Yer sister. Yeah. Nice lookin' chick—at first."

"What about her?"

"I met her after she got outta prison. That had to be … uh … three years ago. She was hangin' with the Vagos."

"Three years ago? Here in Lancaster?"

"That's right. One time we rode by yer house."

"My house?" Bucky imagined himself watching television and hearing a motorcycle outside on the street.

"So we get friendly and I nail her a few times and all of a sudden she wants to move in with me. She says she's clean since she got outta prison and she's goin' to them NA meetings. What a joke. She was fucked up even without drugs." The biker drained his beer and signaled to the bartender to bring him another. "So she stays with me for a while until one day I come home and she's gone. No explanation, no nothin'. I start askin' around and one of the brothers tells me she's moved up the food chain."

"Moved up the food chain? What the hell does that mean?"

The bartender brought a beer to the table. The biker drained it, put the bottle down on the table and continued. "So she's outta sight for almost two years, no one sees her and then all of a sudden, she's back and she's on drugs big time and doesn't look so great. She tells me she wants to live with me again and I tell her, 'No fucking way, honey.' So she starts hangin' with the Vagos again, gets passed around to every biker in town and keeps comin' back for more."

That would be Brandy, Bucky thought. Taking sexual abuse, maybe even beatings from one-percenter thugs, and mistaking it for a sense of family and belonging.

"She was deep inta' meth and couldn't even think about anythin' else. She was stealin' shit and turnin' tricks and I saw she was just another slut tweaker-chick who would do anythin' for a rail of crank."

The bartender brought another bottle of beer to the table. The biker took a long drink, wiped his mouth with the back of his hand and looked up with his one good eye at the water dripping from the ceiling. He was a lefty, and Bucky saw scars on the back of his hand and wrist. More likely, he went through a glass door than a window.

The biker drained his beer and leveled his one-eyed stare again at Bucky. "Last Wednesday your sister musta hooked up with the two assholes who thought they was meth chemists, and she takes them out to the Vagos' trailer. She had no fuckin' business being there; it belonged to the club and we kept important stuff there. So what happens? They decide to cook up some crank and then it gets blowed up."

Bucky waited for more.

The biker fell silent.

"Is that it?" Bucky said. "You dragged me out here to tell me my sister was a meth freak? I already knew that. That's why she was in prison."

"No, that's not all." He leaned close to Bucky. "She had a kid. A little girl."

"A daughter?" Bucky was dumbfounded. He was speechless. Of all the things Jack the biker might have said, this was the most incredible, the most unexpected. Bucky felt as though the biker had punched him in the stomach.

The sound of the rain pounding on the roof of the bar grew louder. The puddle on the floor expanded and began to run toward the center of the room.

"When she tried to come back to live with me, she tells me she has a little girl."

"A daughter?" Bucky repeated.

"Yeah, the kid's name is Sherry. No. Sharon. No, I dunno, a weird name."

"Schare? Is her name Schare?" Bucky asked.

"Yeah, maybe."

"That was my sister's nickname."

"She said if anythin' ever happens to her, ya should know about the kid.

I'm supposed to tell ya the kid has a necklace made out of some earring. Yer sister said ya'd know what I mean." The biker signaled for another beer.

"Where's the child? How old is she?"

"I never saw her. Ya know, I bet yer sister must a been a terrible mother, with all the shit she was doin'."

"I can't believe it," Bucky said.

"This is important information, right? How much would it be worth to ya? Ya know, for me to help ya find the little girl? I could locate her."

"What? You want me to pay you? This is about money?"

Over the noise of the storm, Bucky thought he heard a motorcycle approaching.

"A helpless little kid needs someone to take care of her." The biker leaned toward Bucky. "Don't ya think?"

A cauldron of emotions boiled up in Bucky. He was astounded—was Jack telling the truth? Could Brandy really have a baby daughter? He was anxious—if there was a baby, what had happened to her, who was taking care of her, where was she, who was the father? He was angry—the slime ball sitting across the table wanted money before he would give Bucky more information. At least one thing was clear—Bucky knew why the one-percenter had been following him.

Bucky heard a motorcycle outside.

Jack heard it as well, frowned, stood up and went to one of the windows. He pulled the shade aside and said, "What the fuck?"

The front door of Mach 2 opened and a lone biker walked in. He spotted Bucky and Jack and came directly over to them.

"Hey, Kicker," Jack said. "What's happenin'? What're ya doin' here at this hour?"

Kicker was wearing jeans and just his cuts. He was soaking wet and rainwater ran down the rug of black hair growing on his chest and extended belly. "Prospect!" he growled. "I'll ask the questions and you do the answerin'. Otherwise I'll ride yer ass all the way to Vegas." He took a drag on his cigarette and blew the smoke in Jack's face.

Bucky began to cough.

"I got some business with this dude," Jack said in a subdued voice.

"Yeah?" Kicker said. "Well, we're havin' Church here. The Dwarf called it. Was you invited?"

"Ah, maybe he couldn't get hold of me."

"Yer cell phone work?"

"Yeah."

"Did he call you?"

"No."

"Then you wasn't invited."

Bucky now heard an insistent rumble of motorcycles, a lot of them, over the sound of the rainstorm. They rolled into the parking lot and the bar began to vibrate to the resonance of several 1,200 cc Harley Big Twin engines.

"Time for you to clear out," Kicker told Jack. "And take this dude with you."

Bucky still had questions. Before he could say anything else, the front door of Mach 2 burst open. The first biker who came in was a giant, at least a foot taller than the ones who followed him. Bucky tried to get a good look at his face. He was strange looking, almost deformed. A dozen Vagos, all soaking wet, piled into the bar. The giant saw Jack, walked toward him and said, "You mother-fucker. You know what happens to snitches? They get shot."

"Aw, shit!" Jack exclaimed, and ran for the exit at the back of the bar.

"Get that fucker," the giant shouted.

"Hey," Bucky yelled. "Wait a minute. What about her daughter? Where is she?" He bolted after the biker.

When Bucky ran out the rear door of Mach 2, he entered another world. Between flashes of lightning and thunder, a dim evening light shone over the desert as heavy gray clouds dumped sheets of rain from the sky. Water pummeled his face. He was soaking wet in seconds. He heard a roar that sounded like an approaching freight train. Bucky looked at Armagosa Creek, which passed behind the bar, and saw a flash flood coming from the direction of the San Gabriels. The creek, dry fifty weeks a year, was about to overflow from a torrent of water and the roiling flood of mud, branches, rocks and debris that came along with it. The desert surface, heat sealed from months of intense sunlight, could not absorb this deluge.

Through the rain, Bucky looked for Jack and saw him trying to cross the swollen creek. He charged after him through the downpour, screaming, "Wait a minute, where is she? Where's the little girl?" If the one-percenter heard Bucky, he didn't stop to answer.

Bucky looked behind him and saw three bikers emerge from the back door of Mach 2. The storm took on a different sound when the giant fired a shot. Bucky heard a crack from the pistol and flash from the muzzle. When Bucky heard a second shot, he ran for his life.

Maybe it was the fear, or the adrenaline, or the effect of the Percs, but Bucky's perceptions slowed to a crawl. He examined each thought in slow motion. He wanted to catch the fleeing one-percenter and find out more about Brandy's daughter—that was critical. He didn't want the Vagos to carve a V on his forehead, or put a bullet through it—that was important. He didn't want to get swept away by the approaching wall of water—that was a passing notion. Bucky reached for his Beretta—that was an afterthought and it was too late. The Cheetah was gone; it was no longer tucked into the back of his pants.

Bucky ran after the fleeing biker just as Armagosa Creek gushed up over its sides. The water, transformed into a fast-moving wall several feet high, spread out over the road, the Mach 2 parking lot and swept across the sand toward the bar. The flood hit Bucky with a powerful jolt and knocked him into the maelstrom of the creek. Bucky's thoughts were no longer moving in slow motion. He was in a full, all-out panic as he felt himself tumbling around in a murderous torrent. Up was down. Debris slammed into him. The bandage on his head ripped away. Water and mud blinded his eyes, filled his nose, flooded his mouth and finally gushed down into his throat. His sense of smell was gone. He was choking, trying not to swallow the brown, muddy sludge churning around him. He attempted to lift his head out of the water and suck in some air. He tried to stop himself from being swept away. Something hard slammed into his forehead. Before everything went black, Bucky wondered whether the giant biker with the gun was the last person he would see before he died.

SIXTEEN

"HEY, SPORT."

Bucky knew he was alive because of the familiar odor of disinfectant in the Palmdale Regional Medical Center. The doctor's voice sounded a lot like Mike. Bucky opened his eyes and saw it was Mike. Doctor Harrison stood next to him.

"He lives," Mike said.

Bucky touched his head.

"This time your forehead was split open," Doctor Harrison said.

"Big night at the biker bar?" Mike said. "You're lucky Search and Rescue got called out. They pulled you, a horse and two dead goats out of the riverbed about a half mile from Mach 2."

The throbbing in his head and the pain behind his eyes had returned. Bucky felt a gauze bandage wrapped around his skull. "Jesus," Bucky said, "I feel like I was run over by a truck."

"What the doctor is telling you," Mike said, "is that you've got stitches from your hairline to your eyebrow. The question is, did you get some sense knocked into you this time? I can't believe you actually went out there."

"The biker ..." Bucky said.

"Which biker?" Mike said.

"The one I went out to meet."

"What about him?"

"He told me she had a daughter."

"Who had a daughter?"

"Brandy. My sister had a little girl."

"Brandy had a daughter?"

"That's what the biker wanted to tell me. He wanted money."

"Well, I hope he told you everything you need to know, because he's gone."

"He said his name was Jack. Can you locate him?"

"No, he's gone for good. He took a bullet in the stomach and drowned. That was One Eye Jack. Years ago he went through a plate glass window and lost an eye."

"What day is it?" Bucky asked.

"Saturday morning," Doctor Harrison said. "You've had another bad blow to the head. It'll be a miracle if you don't have a concussion. Do you have anyone to watch you at home?"

Bucky shook his head. The minute he moved, the pain behind his forehead increased.

"Then you're staying here over the weekend," the doctor said. "You can go home tomorrow evening."

A nurse handed Bucky a cup of water and two white pills.

"What's this?" Bucky thought of his drug test on Monday.

"Just ibuprofen," the doctor said. "To minimize brain swelling"

"As soon as you get straightened out," Mike said, "we need a statement from you. We're working with the ATF on this and we're going to nail the biker who tried to kill you and shot our boy."

"Your boy?"

"Jack was our informer. He was trying to avoid a federal drug charge. The problem was, his information was never accurate. Turns out he was exaggerating everything to make himself more important. The misinformation on the doublewide came from him and that was the last straw. He told us there were a bunch of armed Mexican illegals making meth out there."

"Before the shooting started last night," Bucky said, "they were shouting about killing a snitch."

"It was just a matter of time before the Vagos found out who was talking."

"Do you think he was telling the truth about Brandy's daughter? Would he lie about something like that?"

"To get money out of you? Yes."

Bucky became agitated. "I have to find out, Mike. If my sister did have a kid, it's my niece, a living relative. She would need me."

"Did you lose something last night, Wyatt?" Mike said.

"Wyatt?" the doctor said. "Is that your real name?"

"Wyatt Burp," Mike said, "the slowest and dumbest gun in the West" Mike leaned over, pointed his index finger at Bucky, cocked his thumb and fired. "Bang. We found your Beretta. It was in the mud about ten feet from the back door of Mach 2. Consider it confiscated." Mike stepped back from the bed and shook his head. "Buck, what were you thinking? That was the Vagos gang. You're lucky you didn't get shot."

Bucky ignored Mike's question. "What if the kid was born an addict?" Bucky said. "What if the one-percenters have her?"

After Mike departed and the doctor and nurse left Bucky alone, he sank back into the pillows on the hospital bed. Bikers three, Bucky zero, he thought. The score was going in the wrong direction. Bucky was trying to think of a plan for revenge when he fell asleep.

SEVENTEEN

TWO AND A HALF DAYS without a Perc.

It was Monday morning. Bucky felt terrible and threw up his breakfast. It was eighty degrees outside but he had the chills and his body was starting to ache. The only good news was that the continual itching had disappeared. His head throbbed and waves of nausea shook him as he stood looking in his bathroom mirror at his pale face and the gauze bandage wrapped around his head. Doctor Harrison had told him when he left the hospital Sunday night that nausea and vomiting were a sure sign of a concussion. The doctor also warned that he might have double vision and should not drive. Bucky had no choice; he had a date with a pee cup at 10:00 a.m. He fed Zoll, put his packet of Ps in his pocket and checked his watch. It was 9:40 a.m. If everything went on schedule, he would give his sample and by 10:15 a.m., he could take a couple of Percs. Maybe he would even take three, just to catch up and restart his body. He felt like he had the flu.

Bucky arrived at 129s and intended to go straight up to Chief Vlasic's office without stopping to talk to anyone. Unfortunately, the men from A Shift were outside doing their morning physical training in the back of the station, and they saw him drive in.

"Hey, towelhead," one of the firefighters yelled at Bucky when he got out of the pickup.

"Some guys will do anything not to come to work," another yelled.

"Nice turban, Bucky-roo," was the final insult.

"Watch it, guys," Bucky said, and started to walk toward them. "I'm a suicide bomber. I'm wired with a ton of explosives."

"Then head directly up to Chief Vlasic's office. Don't come over here," the first firefighter said.

Bucky ascended the stairs and according to his watch, his knuckles hit the chief's door at 9:59 a.m.

Chief Vlasic, in a spotless uniform, opened the door. "C'mon in, Dawson." He looked at the bandage on Bucky's head. "What's going on now? Is this the same injury?"

"No sir," Bucky said. "I fell into the Armagosa Creek during the flash flood on Saturday night. I was hit in the forehead by something, probably a piece of wood." Bucky was sweating and felt another wave of nausea building in his stomach.

"Just remember," the chief said, "any time you take off after your bereavement leave is on your nickel." He turned to a pale-looking man wearing wire-rim glasses and holding a small white paper sack. "This is Richard from Security Test Services. He'll collect the specimen."

Bucky reached for the bag.

"No," Richard said, "I have to observe you giving the sample. That's the only way we can be certain of the chain of custody."

Bucky followed Richard out of the chief's office and down the hall. "Do you have to hold my dick too?" he asked.

"No, just watch." Richard blinked behind his wire-rim glasses and looked dead serious.

Bucky walked into the men's room just as the nausea hit full force. He lurched over to the sink, gagged several times and threw up a small amount of green fluid from his empty stomach. He turned on the water, let it clean the sink and then splashed it on his face, soaking the bandage on his head in the process. "Concussion symptoms," he said to Richard.

"Looks like opiate withdrawal to me," Richard said.

Bucky glared at Richard and then took the white sack, withdrew the plastic bottle, broke the seal and unscrewed the top. He turned away and unzipped his pants. When he finished, he screwed the top back on the container. It felt warm in his hand when he handed it to Richard. "Thanks for coming," Bucky said. "Hope you enjoyed the party." As soon as Richard left the men's room, Bucky took out his pill packet and emptied three Percs onto his palm. He put one pill back, reconsidered, and added it again to the two he was holding. He tossed them into his mouth and drank a mouthful of water from the spigot.

When Bucky walked out of the second-floor toilet, he just a few feet away from Bobby Alvarez, captain of the A Shift, who was standing on top of the HazMat Box. The vehicle was so high that they were almost at eye level. Alvarez was inspecting the rotating satellite dish mounted on the top of the cab. When he heard the men's room door close, he turned and said, "Hey, Bucky, happy ending?"

By the time Bucky reached the pickup, the three 10-milligram Percocets from *BuyDrugs.com* were already making him feel better. He made a mental note to order more and then began to think about his niece. He tried to imagine what she looked like. He remembered his little sister celebrating her fourth birthday with friends. Even then, people said Brandy would grow up to be a beautiful woman. Would the child turn out to be as striking as Brandy? Was it already obvious she would be attractive? Was she somewhere in Lancaster, and who was taking care of her? Bucky felt a wave of anxiety wash over him. Jack was right. His niece needed him. She needed a home and someone to love her. Bucky had to find out if any of the bikers knew where she was. He made a decision—he was going back to Mach 2.

EIGHTEEN

"I JUST CAME TO FIND out about a little girl ...." Bucky tossed down two Ps, and continued. "I'm looking for a baby girl ...." He waited for the wonderful sensation to seep into his body. "I'm wondering if anyone has seen ...."

He stood in front of his bathroom mirror and tried to think of what to say to the bikers at Mach 2. Nothing sounded right. He removed the gauze wrapped around his head so that it didn't look like he was wearing a turban. He still had a large bandage covering the stitches in his forehead, and the shaved left side of his head showed an ugly purple bruise above his cheekbone. He wore a blue fire department T-shirt and jeans and hoped the members of the Vagos motorcycle gang would see that he wasn't carrying a weapon tucked into his ass, or anywhere else. Bucky was an inch over six feet, had been in his share of brawls and had taken his lumps. Nonetheless, with stitches in his forehead and the bruise on his temple just starting to heal, he didn't need an explosion of mayhem resulting in more injuries. He hoped his firefighter status would earn him at least neutral treatment from the violent group of bikers.

When he arrived at Mach 2, it was almost midnight on Monday, three days since the flash flood. Bucky couldn't believe the debris deposited across the parking lot by the water. His headlights revealed rocks the size of bowling balls, tree limbs, pieces of rotted wood and assorted metal and plastic objects. What remained of a smashed horse trailer lay strewn around the far side of Armagosa Creek, which now had only a trickle of water passing through it. A three-quarter moon hanging low in the sky reflected a golden light from a black sky punctuated by stars. A single spotlight mounted on the roof of the bar illuminated two dozen Harleys parked in the lot and a lone biker standing watch over them.

A faint glow came from the open door at the entrance and music from the jukebox, played at maximum volume, echoed across the desert.

When he entered the bar, Bucky caught the reek of some of the worst body odor he had ever experienced. It reminded him of the stench he had smelled in an empty bear's den in the Angeles National Forest after the winter hibernation. It was almost as dark in the bar as it was outside. A thick haze of cigarette and marijuana smoke hung in the air and filled Bucky's nostrils, but couldn't trump the body odor. The Christmas lights over the bar, along with the faded red, white, and blue colors of the jukebox, did little to illuminate the room. His eyes were drawn to the pool table where two women were playing a game of eight-ball under the fluorescent bulb with the NASCAR shade. They wore only G-strings and high heels. Both had long, shapely legs, oversized breast implants and hard-looking faces. They walked slowly around the table, tapping their cues on the floor and studying the lay of the balls. Before taking a shot, each woman bent over, pressed her breasts onto the dirty green felt and raised her ass to the eye level of the bikers standing around the table. The one-percenters ogled the women, poured beer on their naked bodies, shouted obscenities, applauded, and took turns slapping them on their behinds. No one cared who was winning.

"Hey, this here's a private party." A beefy arm covered with tattoos of skulls and daggers came up in front of Bucky and stopped him just inside the entrance. "I'm talkin' to you. Where d'you think you're goin'?" A biker, wearing a green bandanna so far down over his forehead that it almost covered his eyes, blocked Bucky from taking another step inside. The man's bare chest showed beneath a black leather vest.

Bucky tried to ignore him and push past.

"Who the fuck do you think you are?" the biker snarled. "You can't come in here."

Bucky raised his hands, tried to smile and hoped the P would get him through the next few minutes. "I just came to get some information."

"Information? What are you, a narc?"

"No, I'm a firefighter with a head injury." Bucky pointed to the insignia on his T-shirt, which was starting to soak through with nervous sweat.

The biker stepped toward Bucky. He flexed the fingers on both hands and made fists.

115

Bucky saw the letters "VFFV" tattooed on the biker's fingers. He took a step back. "I came to ask about a little girl."

"A little girl?"

They were joined by another biker, who had full-sleeve tattoos on both arms. "A little girl?" the second biker echoed. "We don't mess with little girls. We like big girls with big asses and big tits. And they gotta be at least fourteen." He laughed in Bucky's face. "You some kinda sex deviant?"

"No, I—"

"Hey brothers," the second biker shouted over the noise in the bar. "We got someone here who's lookin' for a little girl. We got any little girls?"

Several other one-percenters started to mad-dog Bucky, hoping he would throw a punch.

"Cool it, cool it," Bucky said. "I'm not here to start a fight. I think my sister used to roll with you. Her name was Brandy. I'm looking for her daughter."

"Roll with us?" a biker said. He came face to face with Bucky. Bucky smelled marijuana on his breath. "The brothers here are full-patches. No woman rolls with a full-patch unless she's his ol' lady. Was your sister somebody's ol' lady?"

"I don't—"

"Or was she just a mamma? You know what a mamma is, fireboy?"

Bucky shook his head.

Another one-percenter joined the discussion. He wore dark glasses in the gloom of the bar. "A mamma is a biker chick that is the property of the whole club," he said. "A mamma is a cunt and any full-patch can do whatever he wants to her, whenever he wants, however he wants. Is that your sister?" The biker looked at Bucky over his dark glasses.

"Maybe fireboy came to slam some meth with us," someone at the bar said.

"Let's buy this dude a drink," said another voice from the crowd. "Anyone related to one of our mammas deserves a drink. Don't he, brothers?"

Bucky did not hear any hospitality in the invitation. He looked around at the local members of the Green Nation—the meanest, ugliest looking group he had ever seen. Some of them were old and fat, but some of them were not. They were all big. Most had nasty looking facial hair—mustaches drooping to the chin, braided goatees, and unkempt beards. Some wore black knit caps pulled down just above their eyes. Others wore bandannas, ear studs and metal jewelry. Bucky was surrounded and did not see a friendly face. What he saw was anger and hostility in the eyes of a bunch of outlaws decked out in the green Vagos colors, itching for a brawl to add to the night's entertainment. Bucky realized he had made a mistake, knew he was in for trouble and wondered if he would get out of Mach 2 in one piece.

The giant who fired the gun the night of the rainstorm appeared and pushed through the crowd of bikers to confront Bucky. Up close, Bucky saw a cruel mouth turned down in a permanent sneer, a nose that had been broken more than once, and hard dark eyes. A prominent jawbone and forehead gave him a deformed look. "What the fuck do ya want?" he snarled.

The bikers crowded around Bucky and jostled him toward the bar. He came face to face with the fat bartender with the greasy shoulder length hair and the Jack Daniel's cap. The man was either too drunk or too high to recognize Bucky. "What'll you have?" he slurred.

"I'll have a Bud," Bucky said in a low voice.

"Fuckface is havin' a beer," the big man announced and bent over the bar top to inhale two lines of powder through a dollar bill. His hands were the size of baseball gloves and even in the faint light, Bucky could see that they were bruised and filthy, with dirt under long fingernails. He straightened up, wiped his nose, looked at Bucky's bandage and said, "What happened to you?"

"I fell in the river."

He nodded. "Yer the fucker who was here the other night with the snitch. Ain't you?"

"The former snitch," someone added.

"You know, snitches are a dyin' breed," the big man said, and made a sound that Bucky thought was supposed to be laughter. He pulled a pistol out of his belt, placed it on the bar and spun it around. He stopped it so that the barrel pointed at Bucky and put his oversize finger on the trigger.

Bucky was silent, waiting for something terrible to happen. He smelled his own fear.

A Vagos standing near Bucky reached inside his vest. Bucky expected to see a knife or another gun, but the biker pulled out a small baggie with powder inside. He emptied some on the bar, pushed it into a crude line with his fingers and handed the bag to the man next to him.

Bucky heard an obscenity from the direction of the pool table, followed by the sound of an open hand smacking flesh. One of the girls let out a yelp and Bucky looked to see what had happened. In that moment, the big man standing next to him picked up Bucky's beer bottle. "Hey, pussy, yer not drinkin' yer beer," he said, and brought the bottle down hard on Bucky's left hand, which was resting on the bar. The biker's aim was slightly off and the bottle only crushed the knuckles on Bucky's fourth and fifth fingers.

The agony was so great that Bucky couldn't move. He stood with his hand still on the bar while a blinding flash of pain erupted in his fingers, shot up his arm and lodged in his brain. Bucky clenched his teeth and swallowed a scream just before a fist caught him in the chest, sending him onto the cement floor. The first swipe of a boot missed his head but the second caught him in the ribs. Bucky instinctively went into the fetal position to protect himself, covering his head with his hands before he caught a hard kick on the butt and another on his thigh. Two bikers, on either side, lifted him up by his arms and someone punched Bucky in the stomach, knocking the air out of him. While Bucky gasped, trying to fill his lungs, the bikers dragged him across the floor to the door and threw him out into the parking lot. Bucky landed on several sharp rocks left by the flood, but he was already in so much pain he barely noticed it.

"Tell yer cunt sister we said hello."

Bucky lay on the ground for a moment, gasping for air and unable to move, his entire body on fire with pain. When his head cleared, he managed to crawl over the flood debris to the pickup, which seemed to be miles away. He lay on the ground next to the door and tried to suppress the pain. He struggled to pull himself upright, clinging to the door handle for support. He stuck his good hand into his jeans pocket and vaguely realized with gratitude that they had crushed the fingers on his left hand. After he pulled out the keys and unlocked the door, it took a lifetime to climb into the driver's seat and even longer to get the key in the ignition. He drove out of the parking lot without closing the door, barely holding the steering wheel with his right hand as the pickup bounced over rocks and pieces of wood in its path. Bucky rolled down the dirt road until the light from Mach 2 disappeared. He stopped, leaned back in the seat and tried to control the pain in his body. He took two Percs from his baggie and swallowed them. This time, he thought, there was a good reason for taking them.

Bucky was thankful that a fire department first aid kit was still lodged behind the passenger seat of the pickup. He pulled it out and removed an old roll of Kerlix wrap. He looked at his fingers in the overhead light of the pickup and saw bruised skin, starting to swell and turn purple. A throbbing sensation, which matched his heartbeat, took over his left hand. He tried to straighten out the damaged fingers and gasped in pain. Bucky taped them to his index finger with the flex-wrap, tearing it with his teeth. He sat back in the seat and tried to sort out the various pain signals coursing through his body. His chest and stomach hurt from the bikers' fists. He felt a burning sensation in his ribs, thigh and butt, where they had planted their boots. That pain merged into the throbbing of the stitches in his forehead and the ache on the side of his head. These were the least of his injuries. His fingers were a disaster—the pain was excruciating. Bucky was afraid the bones were crushed and wondered if he could get to the Palmdale Community ER before he passed out.

On the way to the hospital, Bucky realized he wouldn't be able to go back to work until his hand healed and wondered how long that would take. At the least, he was looking at weeks of unpaid medical leave, not something he could afford. He wondered how bad his injury was and whether his fingers could even be repaired. He had heard paramedics tell of accidents that left the victim's fingers forever stiff and unbending. What a disaster. He had suffered through a terrible night and had found out nothing about Brandy's daughter.

The damn one-percenters! Years ago, they had beaten his father. They had treated his sister like a dog. They had left him for dead in the desert, stolen his Bronco, beaten the shit out of him and crushed his fingers. He felt humiliated. Now the score was bikers four or five, or ten or twenty, or whatever, while he, Bucky, still hadn't struck a single blow for the good guys. He felt his anger rise up, and used it as an antidote to the pain coursing through his body. It was not over yet. Bucky resolved to pay the Vagos back. Every single one. He had an idea.

Bucky held the steering wheel with his right hand and cradled his left in his lap. At 1:00 a.m., he didn't expect to see his new friend Doctor Huntington in the ER.

A teenager with a knife wound to his stomach and a gang member holding a towel over a flesh wound on his arm took precedence over Bucky's injured hand. After they took X-rays, he waited almost two hours, sitting in a cubicle behind white drapes in the ER, listening to the groans from people injured that night on the violent streets of Lancaster.

"You're lucky; all you have is a crush injury," the ER doctor said, waving an X-ray. "It would take more than a beer bottle to break the bones in your fingers, but you've got pretty bad bruises, and your tendons and nerves have some trauma. It's going to hurt for quite a while. I don't see any cracked ribs or anything broken anywhere else, so I guess you had some good luck."

"Do I need a painkiller?" Bucky got his hopes up. Something positive might come from the evening after all. It never hurt to collect some extra Percs. "Do I need a painkiller? Maybe some Percocet?" Bucky asked the doctor.

"I don't like painkillers; they can be addictive. I'll give you Diclofenac. It's an anti-inflammatory. It'll help with the swelling and stiffness in your hand."

"When can I go back to work?"

"What do you do?"

"I'm a HazMat firefighter."

The doctor shook his head. "It could be four to six weeks before you can use your fingers. I'll immobilize them with a metal splint. After you take a shower, rewrap them with dry tape and continue using the splint. Keep the hand quiet and elevated for a couple of days and ice your fingers for fifteen minutes several times a day. Do you have an orthopedist? Go and see him. You'll need some physical therapy to keep your fingers working."

When Bucky got home, it was 2:45 a.m. He tossed his X-rays on the kitchen table, took two more Percs and fell asleep in his clothes.

NINETEEN

"BORIS DUBKOVA?" BUCKY SAID. "What country is he from?"

"I think it's a Russian name," Mike said. "But he was born in Chicago and he went to MIT." Mike played with his laptop. "Here's the profile of SkyScan. They build drones for the Defense Department. He looks pretty young, but he's the CEO." Mike pushed his computer across the desk and it grazed the metal splint holding Bucky's two smashed fingers.

"Ow." Bucky almost jumped out of his chair. "Jesus, Mike, be careful." He held his injured hand against his chest.

"Are the bones broken?"

"No, the ER doctor said it was a crush injury. The problem is, I'll be off duty for weeks, and it's not a work-related injury, so no paycheck. It's a disaster."

Mike shook his head. "You know those movies where zombies with bruises and stiches and bandages go after college kids? That could be you, Buck. That's what you look like. The living dead, or the dead living. You're a mess."

"Thanks Mike, I needed to hear that. I get the crap beat out of me, spend three hours at the ER, barely sleep, and then I have to listen to my best friend tell me what a mess I am."

"If your friends won't level with you, who will?"

"I've been meaning to ask you, what does 'VFFV' stand for?" Bucky said.

"Where'd you see that? On a biker's knuckles?"

Bucky nodded.

"It stands for Vagos Forever-Forever Vagos. It's a standard tattoo; each club inserts the letter of its name. It goes along with the one-percent tat, the daggers, the spiders, and 'TCB' for taking care of business, which means the biker won't back down."

Bucky shook his head. "These guys are really animals."

"No shit. If you have a tattoo of the club patch on your arm or chest and you want out, it has to be taken off. It's usually done with a blowtorch." Mike closed his laptop. "You want to join us? We're meeting at noon today, out at the spot where the tortoises were poisoned. We have a special agent from the BLM, someone from Fish and Wildlife, and two people from SkyScan. The guy Dubkova will be there to kick it off." Mike slammed his fist into his palm. "We're gonna get these suckers, I just know it."

"Every guy in that bar was snorting meth," Bucky said. "They were passing it around."

"Then they're manufacturing it. It's easy to be generous with your drugs when you have a constant supply and you're not paying for it."

"I'll meet you out there. I have to go home and ice my fingers first."

Bucky left Mike's office holding his left hand up against his chest and walking slowly, feeling the pain throughout his body from the bikers' kicks and blows.

On the way out to the desert, Bucky took two Percocets. Somehow, he had now worked himself up to five pills a day, and yet felt like he was getting less of a bump each time he took them. The supply he had purchased online was already dwindling, and if he wanted to keep taking P, money was going to be a problem. Without a paycheck, his money would disappear fast if he started buying painkillers without health insurance reimbursement. He tried to understand the signal in his body that demanded more Percocet when the prior dose wore off. It was not so much a specific thought as an urge, a demand for more, a longing that kept asserting itself until he satisfied it.

When he arrived at the spot where the tortoises died, the only vehicle Bucky didn't recognize was the black Hummer with tinted windows and raised suspension. Mike and five other men sat around a folding table, shielded from the hot sun by a rectangular canvas umbrella.

The BLM agent had brought a set of the 3-foot long topographic DAGs—Desert Access Guides—and had spread the one for Lancaster and the surrounding area out on the table. "It's divided into 1,800 squares," he said as Bucky joined the group. "Each one represents 1,500 square meters. This pink area in the center is Edwards Air Force Base." A gust of desert wind lifted the map and he put his hands down to keep it in place.

"Can I draw on it?" Mike asked.

"Sure, that's what it's for," the agent said.

Mike traced a line with a yellow marking pen that ran along the southern edge of Edwards. "No one's gonna have a meth lab on the base," he said. "We can leave that area out." He drew a yellow rectangle and then laid his pen against the mileage scale at the bottom of the map. "We have a potential area here of maybe one hundred square miles. We want to look at any unusual building or trailer that might house a meth lab. It'll probably be off by itself, away from any neighbors. We're also looking for anyone who might be doing something that looks suspicious. We want to check out anyone riding on an OHV outside the recreation areas, especially if it looks like it's transporting liquids. Finally, check on anyone wearing leather and jeans, black T-shirts or club colors."

Bucky stood looking over Mike's shoulder.

Mike turned and said, "This is Bucky Dawson, a HazMat firefighter. Buck, this is Boris Dubkova, president of SkyScan; Andy Levkov, one of his engineers; Special Agent Lopez from the BLM and Officer Duarte from Fish and Wildlife. I think you know Deputy Richards."

Bucky nodded his head and said, "Don't let me interrupt."

Dubkova looked at Bucky and said, "Were you in a car accident?"

"No, I ran into some hazardous material."

Dubkova turned to Mike and said, "Our drones are used for a lot of things, but this is the first time we've looked for a meth lab."

"They've been dumping solvent," Lopez said.

"Poisoning tortoises is a federal crime," Duarte added. "Maybe worse than cooking meth."

"Dumping solvent?" Dubkova raised his eyebrows. "How do you know that?"

"Bucky has some special talents," Mike said. "He's the one who got wind of it." Mike smiled and looked at the other men around the table to see if anyone caught his joke.

"Nice, Mike," Bucky said.

"Solvent," Dubkova said. "How much solvent? What kind?"

"We know it's TCE, but we aren't sure how much," Mike said. "We're guessing around forty gallons."

"That's this time," Bucky said. "I think there's been more than one dump."

"It just so happens, some tortoises got poisoned," Duarte said. "That's how we found this spot."

"How do you know there's been more than one dump?" Dubkova asked.

"I can smell it blowing across the desert," Bucky said. "It has happened several times."

Dubkova gave Bucky a skeptical look.

Mike traced another rectangle on the map on the west side of Edwards. "This is a secondary area of interest and most of it's in San Bernardino County. We have a lot of space to cover, but the drone can handle it." Mike looked at Dubkova. "Right?"

"Right," Dubkova said. "This is small potatoes."

"We'll start here where the tortoises died and work outward," Mike said. "I want to cover the L.A. County area first. I don't know how far anyone would drive through the desert just to dump solvent. If someone's cooking meth, my bet is it's going on nearby, but who knows? If we move on to the second area, I'll have to coordinate with the Sheriff's Department in San Berdoo."

Bucky studied Dubkova, the first person he had ever met who was smart enough to go to MIT. Was there something in Dubkova's physical appearance that would indicate how smart he was? Bucky didn't see a big forehead or an oversized skull and thought Dubkova looked a lot like the Pillsbury Doughboy. He was in his late thirties, wore thick glasses and had milk-white skin. He looked as though he never went outside. Bucky watched Dubkova's pudgy white fingers dance across the keys of his laptop. How could anyone live in the Antelope Valley without getting a tan? Bucky guessed Dubkova had been the kind of nerdy kid who spent his entire childhood inside. While other boys were playing football, riding their bikes and engaging in friendly fistfights, Dubkova was probably inside screwing around with video games and computers.

Dubkova turned on his laptop and when it booted up, the screen flashed pictures of jet fighters and aerial drones.

"So how does this aerial surveillance work?" Mike asked.

"It's really simple," Dubkova said. He opened an Excel file on his screen and began scrolling through columns of numbers. "SkyScan has its own proprietary GPS navigation software, enhanced by geographical information systems and digital elevation modeling. We refer to it as GIS and DEM." He pointed to numbers on the edge of the map in front of them on the table.

"Latitude and longitude are standard coordinates, and everyone starts with degrees, minutes and seconds. The problem is, from our point of view, maps like this one are pretty crude."

Mike glanced at Bucky and gave the tiniest shrug of his shoulder.

"So," Dubkova continued, "We integrate our own geodetic grid mapping data with the land-based coordinates on the BLM map."

"I don't think I'm following you," Mike said.

Levkov, the SkyScan engineer interrupted. "If we were using United States Coast and Geodetic Survey—USC&GS—maps, which are based on the North American datum, that's the '84 datum, not the '27 datum, then we could determine accurate coordinates for every rock and tree in California. But if we're looking at a BLM DAG, we have to convert to precise ground coordinates by using the UTM—Universal Transverse Mercator—grid projections developed by the military."

"Oh," Mike said, "That explains everything."

"I thought we were just gonna send out a drone and see whether we could find any unusual activity," Duarte said. "You know, try to identify a meth lab."

"We are," Dubkova said. "That's exactly what we're going to do here."

"So why do we care about the Universal Transversal, or whatever it is?" Duarte said.

"Because SkyScan drones are used all over the world for surveillance and reconnaissance," Dubkova said. He sounded exasperated. "When the military or one of the intelligence agencies uses one of our drones to spot something they're looking for, they have to know exactly where it is, and I mean *exactly*. We have to be super precise about any locations we identify because someone might want to send a rocket down a chimney or into a doorway without taking out any civilians. I guarantee you, if we find one of your meth guys out there and we're calibrated properly, we'll be able to tell you where he is, within a couple of inches." Dubkova smiled, then added, "That is, *if* we find anyone."

"This little surveillance gig came at the right time though," Levkov said. "We're beta-testing some advanced software."

"Levkov and I are going to do a quick setup and test flight right now to check our mission interface," Dubkova said.

"So when do we actually start?" Mike asked.

"First thing tomorrow," Dubkova said. "We'll show you a map grid and explain how we're going to search each area." He wiped the sweat from his forehead. "I'll tell you one thing: I'm not sitting out here in this heat all day. We can pilot the drone and monitor the pictures remotely from your office."

"We've got funding for four days." Mike said. "How much of the area can we cover in a day?"

"We could cover all of it," Levkov said. "The drone we're using can fly for four hours at up to fifty miles per hour as high as 1,000 feet on a single battery. We've got a forward and side-looking color video camera with zoom, pan and tilt control. That should do everything we need to do. It depends on what we find, and whether you want to take a closer look at something or run surveillance on a specific location."

"What about at night?" Mike asked.

"We have infrared capability." Dubkova said. "The surveillance goes slower, but we're prepared to work at night."

Mike made some notes on his pad. "What do you call this thing?"

"We refer to our drones as 'eyes in the sky,'" Dubkova said. The military likes macho names for their equipment so they call this one the Cyclops." Dubkova looked at the blank faces of the men sitting around him. "C'mon guys, you know, the Cyclops. The monster with one eye, like a camera lens?"

"Yeah," Bucky said. "We know." He had only known Dubkova thirty minutes but was already starting to dislike him.

"OK," Mike said. "Here's the drill. Duarte and Lopez will spend the next couple of days out near El Mirage patrolling on an OHV. I'll watch the pictures with Mr. Dubkova at the station. If we come up with anything, I can have a sheriff's helicopter in the air on a moment's notice and we'll be on it like flies on shit."

Dubkova turned to Levkov and said, "Let's get her up."

Duarte looked around. "Where is it? This ... uh ... Cyclops?"

"Over here," Levkov said. He went to the black Hummer and reached for a 5-foot long case on the roof. "You've heard of UAV's, right?

"Unmanned—" Mike said.

"Unmanned aerial vehicle," Dubkova said. "Except, that term is no longer used. We're now talking RPAs—remotely piloted aircraft. The men flying drones in Afghanistan are all sitting in Arizona."

"Cyclops is one of our smallest RPAs," Levkov said. "Thanks to Velcro, we can assemble this model in less than five minutes." He pulled the case down, placed it on the ground and opened it. He took out a single wing, the body of the drone, a small electric motor with a propeller, and a black box containing electronics and lenses. "This, gentlemen, is the Cyclops."

"Does it have wheels?" Bucky asked. "How does it take off and land?"

"We hand launch this version," Levkov said. "When we bring it back, we send it up into a stall, it dives, hits the ground and comes apart. The electronics and optics are in this little black box, which is almost indestructible. Everything's attachable and detachable. We just put it back together for another flight with a fresh battery."

"We're a full-service intelligence provider," Dubkova said. "U.S. troops on the ground use our HALAD—hand launched drone—version. They carry it in their backpacks. Our biggest model, the UASys—unmanned aircraft system—is a medium-altitude, long-endurance drone. It's more complex, flies higher, lasts much longer and does everything but cook breakfast."

"We're also developing a new HuKi, that's a Hunter Killer," Levkov said. "It's incredibly strong and lightweight, made out of carbon fiber–reinforced composite materials. You know, carbon nanoparticles."

Mike turned to Bucky and whispered, "I'm getting a BFH—big fucking headache—from all this."

Bucky wasn't listening. He was thinking about how much he needed more Percocet.

TWENTY

"HALAD, RPA, UAV, GIS, DEM."

Bucky drove back toward Lancaster and imagined Dubkova the doughboy, sitting around a table at the Pentagon with the military brass. They were discussing drones and secret intelligence missions, but were speaking in abbreviations and acronyms. Not a single word of English crossed their lips. Was there a special class for that at MIT?

When he hit the Antelope Freeway, Bucky didn't exit in Lancaster, but kept going on to Santa Clarita. He hadn't visited Gram, his paternal grandmother, in almost a year. Several times he had thought of going to see her, then found an excuse. It didn't really matter, because she didn't recognize him or anyone else. Gram wasn't suffering from anything fancy, just plain old dementia. The knowledge that Brandy had a daughter started Bucky thinking about family, and now he felt guilty about not visiting the poor old woman, even if she wouldn't remember his visit five minutes after he left.

Santa Clarita was a boomburg, a rapidly growing suburban city feeding off the growth of Los Angeles. Rated one of the safest cities in the United States, most of its residents focused on its other label: brushfire capital of North America. Before Bucky moved into HazMat, he spent several summers battling the fast moving wildland fires that originated in the hills around the city. Santa Clarita was much more upscale than Lancaster, but Gram's home for over a decade, the Comfort Care facility, was one of the bleakest places Bucky had ever seen. It stood at the end of a cul-de-sac, a long, white single-story structure with a high fence around it. The trees and bushes, initially meant to provide landscaping, were stunted and shriveled, adding to the desolation. The first time Bucky visited, he promised himself he would find some way to kill himself before he ended up in a dementia facility like Comfort Care. What frightened him most was the thought that he might not even grasp his mental deterioration and never know the difference. Comfort Care told families that the center was designed more for the safety of the patients than for their standard of living. The exterior doors were secured, no cooking was allowed in the rooms and the single-story floor plan was simple—a straight hallway—with rooms off to either side, so that no one could get lost.

After years of alcohol abuse, Gram had begun to show apathy, memory loss and confusion. She was only fifty-two when she deteriorated to the point where she was unable to function by herself and the family knew they had to move her to a dementia care center. Over the years, her condition worsened and her final move took her to Comfort Care.

When Bucky entered the facility, the scent inside was bitter. He smelled medicine, antibacterial solutions and incontinence. He also smelled hopelessness and death. At the reception desk, a young nurse introduced herself as Lexie and accompanied him to Gram's room. As they walked down a wide hall covered with ugly green linoleum and handrails mounted on both walls, she looked at him and asked, "Were you in some sort of accident?" Her eyes locked on his for a moment, and then she looked away.

"Not exactly," Bucky said. He had never seen anyone with pale green eyes. They were beautiful. Lexie was young and attractive, but amid the smells in the building, he couldn't get a sense of her particular aroma.

"Not exactly?" she persisted.

"I … uh … had some trouble with some bikers."

"Ouch," she said, and looked at Gram's file. "I see it's been over a year since you were here to see Mrs. Dawson."

Bucky shrugged his shoulders. "Does it matter? She doesn't recognize anyone."

"That's true," Lexie said. "But most of the patients here are abandoned. Some family members don't even know if they're alive or dead; sometimes they don't want to know. When someone shows up and discovers that a relative died weeks or even months ago, then the regret sets in. People ultimately feel guilty about not making that last visit."

Poor old Gram, Bucky thought, stuck here, waiting to die. She was only seventy-one and her life had already been over for some time. Payment for her care came every month directly from the Veterans Administration, part of her dead husband's benefits. Bucky wondered who would stop the checks, or if they would continue to come after Gram was gone.

The nurse led him to Gram's small room. A yellow happy face was stuck to the door. As soon as Lexie opened it and he stepped inside, the odor of Gram's incontinence enveloped him. "Oh," Bucky said. "You don't know how bad that smells."

"I *do* know," Lexie said, and closed the door behind him.

The thin woman on the bed was almost unrecognizable. Much of her hair was gone and what remained was white and gossamer, hanging in long strands. Her wrinkled skin hung loose on her body and had an unhealthy sallow color. She was so much smaller than Bucky remembered, smaller than the last time he had seen her. He wondered if she would continue to shrink a little each day until she just disappeared. Maybe one day a nurse would come to the room and find no trace of Mrs. Dawson.

She turned toward Bucky, but looked at him without focus or recognition in her eyes.

"Gram, it's me, Bucky." The odor was unbearable. "Do you remember me?" Gram ran her tongue over her dry lips.

"Can you hear me, Gram? Do you understand what I'm saying?" Bucky looked closely, but nothing in her slack face indicated comprehension. "Gram, I came to tell you something. Something important."

Gram shifted around on the bed and smoothed the blanket with her frail, wrinkled hand. She looked at Bucky again with a blank expression.

He knew she wouldn't understand anything he was about to say and thought of just leaving. It would be so easy. He could walk out, be rid of the smell and forget about the frail old woman sitting on the bed in front of him. Bucky started for the door, then stopped. No, he decided, as long as she was alive, she was still his grandmother. Now that he had come, he couldn't just walk out on her. "Gram," Bucky said. "Brandy had a baby. I thought you should know. You have a great granddaughter. I'm going to find her and take care of her. What do you think of that? Do you remember Brandy?" Gram stared at him.

Gram had only a few personal items, but Bucky felt claustrophobic in the small room. A picture of her long-gone husband, Bucky's grandfather, sat on the top of a wood dresser next to a black Bible with a worn cover. Two walls had cheap framed prints—one showed a golden sun rising over mountains; another showed a sailboat on a deep blue sea. A small tan area rug in front the bed covered part of the green floor. The nightstand and bed frame were metal, both painted a pale cream yellow. The unmade bed had two large doll pillows. One was either a panda or a raccoon, Bucky couldn't tell which, but the doll had black patches around its eyes. The other was a large green turtle. Its eyes were missing and he thought of the dead tortoises upended and ripped open by predators out near Edwards. The recollection of the scent of the rotting flesh did nothing to dispel the odor in Gram's room.

Bucky looked out through the single window at the drooping trees and a sense of panic rose in him. The odor of death was seeping deep into his brain. He couldn't bear to be penned in with this silent apparition who had once been his grandmother. He felt queasy, almost physically sick, and the Percocet he took earlier wasn't helping. He wondered why he had come. It was a stupid idea and he had to get out of the room before the walls closed in and crushed him. "I love you, Gram," Bucky said, but couldn't bear to get close enough to kiss her cheek. To himself, Bucky whispered, "I'm going to find your great granddaughter." He took a last look at his grandmother and fled, slamming the door behind him. Outside, in the hall, he leaned against the wall, breathing heavily, trying to flush the disgusting odors from his nostrils.

Lexie, the nurse, met him halfway down the hall to the exit. "Your grandmother is frail," she said. "She hasn't got long." She handed him Gram's medical file. "D'you want to check your contact information and make sure it's up to date? In case we have to reach you when she passes?"

The first page contained Bucky's name, address, telephone number. The file was heavy, thick with notes and observations scribbled by doctors and nurses over the years. He thumbed through the file and looked at the bottom page, which contained the first entry when Gram arrived at Comfort Care: Diagnosis – suspected onset of Korsakoff's dementia, neurological disorder. "What's Korsakoff's dementia?" he asked.

"It's dementia brought on by chronic alcohol abuse. It's caused by a loss of vitamin B-1 in the brain."

Bucky was shaken. Here was yet another member of his family affected by addiction. He hadn't thought about the cause of Gram's mental deterioration. He had no idea it was alcohol related. He handed the file back to the nurse, looked at her eyes again and tried to estimate her age. She might not even be thirty, too young and hopeful to be working in a place like this, where no one had a future, only a past. "What kind of a name is Lexie?" he asked.

"It's short for Alexandra, which means 'defender of mankind.'"

"Quite a name to have to live up to. I doubt if I'd be brave enough to do this job," Bucky confessed.

Lexie looked at him. "What do you do?"

"I'm a firefighter."

"You have to be fearless to do that job. I know how hard that is—my dad was a firefighter in Oklahoma City. Firefighters get hurt all the time." Lexie reached out and touched his arm. "It's good you came to see your grandmother. You'll be happy you did."

Her hand on his arm was cool and electric. "Thank you," he said.

"My dad used to say 'stay safe.'"

"Every firefighter says that."

"Well, you take care. I hope you recover from your injuries. Maybe I'll see you again sometime." She gave him a radiant smile and walked back toward the reception desk.

Bucky stood for a moment on the green linoleum in the middle of the hall and watched Lexie. He couldn't remember the last time a woman had smiled at him like that. He couldn't remember when a woman had smiled at him, period.

Once outside the facility, Bucky searched his childhood memories but remembered little about Gram. He must have been too young to know that she was an alcoholic. Now he could add her to the list of addicts in his family—his mother, dead of liver failure, his sister, killed in a meth lab explosion, his grandmother, soon to die of alcohol-induced dementia. Bucky was determined to find Brandy's child and save her from going down the same path.

When he opened the door to the pickup, he saw that he had left his cell phone on the seat. A text message from Chief Vlasic showed on the screen: *Dawson – I am away tomorrow. Please be in my office at 9:00 a.m. Thursday.* He read it again and wondered how much longer he would be a county firefighter.

TWENTY-ONE

"**B**INGO," MIKE SAID. A SMILE crossed his face and he leaned closer to look at the screen on Dubkova's laptop. "Where are they?"

"You want the exact UTM coordinates?" Dubkova asked.

"No, dammit," Mike said. "Just show me on the map."

Dubkova pulled the DAG closer and pointed. "Here. They're south of the Edwards fence and north of Buckhorn Canyon Road."

"Makes sense," Mike said. "That's about ten miles north of the spot where the tortoises were poisoned. Can we get a closer look?"

Dubkova tapped his keyboard and the screen enlarged to show two OHVs moving across the sand. They were four-seaters with camo paint. Each had a cargo rack on top, loaded and covered with brown canvas. The front overhang of the racks obscured the drivers.

"I've never seen OHVs like that," Bucky said. "They almost look like military vehicles."

"I'd like to know what's under the canvas," Mike said.

"We don't have X-ray capability yet," Dubkova said, "but we can zoom in." He enlarged the picture again and stared at the screen. "Square shapes under there. Maybe large boxes? Do you want me to bring the drone down to get a horizontal view to see who's driving?"

"No," Mike said. "I don't want to tip them off until we get our chopper out there." Mike punched a frequency into his radio. "This is Detective Ortiz. Sergeant Anderson, do you copy?"

The radio crackled. "Is it a go, Mike?"

"It is, Dave," Mike said. "Get your bird up. We have two OHVs on the south side of Edwards, carrying cargo covered by canvas. We need an intercept."

"What does your primary suspect look like?" Anderson asked.

"Don't know," Mike said. "And we can't see who's driving. I don't want to take the drone down any lower or they'll spot it."

"We're on our way. Give me a lat-long," Anderson said.

"Hold on," Mike said, "I'll put someone on." Mike handed the radio to Dubkova.

Dubkova hit a button on his keyboard, and a set of numbers appeared. "They're moving," he said, "but as of five seconds ago, the current location was latitude 34 83 18 41 14 98 28 655 and longitude 117 89 42 87 10 93 75. The two vehicles are headed south-southwest at about fifteen miles per hour. We're tracking them in real time."

"Copy that," Anderson said, and laughed. "I don't think our aerocomputer ever got coordinate input that precise. We're lifting off now; be there in nine minutes."

Dubkova handed the radio back to Mike and pointed to the OHVs on the computer screen. "Those are Kawasaki Mules," Dubkova said. "Very reliable, with good torque. They can really move if you take off the speed governor, but I don't like the suspension and they have lateral drift. My preference is the Polaris Extreme. Better handling, better differentials front and back."

Bucky looked at Dubkova and wondered if there was anything the nerdy doughboy didn't know.

Mike put down the radio and picked up his cell phone. "I'm gonna call Duarte and Lopez and see how far away they are." He asked Dubkova, "Can you send this video to their cell phone?"

"Sure," Dubkova said. "I just need the telephone number."

"Hold on," Mike said. "I'm not getting an answer."

"So are these the bad guys?" Dubkova asked. "The ones dumping the chemicals?"

"We're about to find out," Mike said. "Highly suspicious, I'd say."

Bucky watched Mike fidget as if he'd had ten cups of coffee. His eyes gleamed with anticipation.

"Those aren't picnic baskets under the canvas," Mike said. He called Duarte again, but still couldn't connect.

Dubkova seemed to have a smirk on his face. Something about him really annoyed Bucky. He wanted to plant his fist in the doughboy's face. Bucky rubbed his forehead. The stitches were starting to itch and that was good; it meant healing. His smashed fingers were starting to throb and that was bad; it meant he needed another painkiller. "I'll be right back," he said, and walked outside to the pickup. He unlocked it and sat on the passenger side with his feet hanging out. He opened the glove compartment, took out the envelope and removed two Percs. Bucky looked at the pale yellow pills in his hand before he popped them into his mouth. He leaned back against the seat for a moment and closed his eyes. He had so much on his mind. He was worried about losing his job tomorrow, certain that Vlasic had called him in to say he had flunked the drug test. Bucky couldn't begin to imagine what would happen if the fire department cut him loose; it was his whole life. And, he couldn't stop thinking about Brandy's daughter. Where was she? Who was taking care of her? What if she was living in a filthy motel room with another addict or a biker's girlfriend? He had to find her before something terrible happened. Bucky was also beginning to worry about taking the Percs. Maybe he *was* addicted. Each day he planned to stop, but instead found himself increasing his dosage. *Could* he stop? Just this morning, he had vowed to limit his intake to six pills a day. Six pills—almost twice what he was taking ten days ago! How had it come to this? He had taken two at breakfast and now, five hours later, two more. He was on his way to an eight-pill day. He decided to ignore the pain in his fingers, cut back to four a day and then work his way down to nothing. He put his hand to his forehead and touched his stitches with his fingertips.

The only positive thought he had was the plan he had devised to even the score with the bikers.

When Bucky walked back into the conference room, he heard Sergeant Anderson report from the helicopter, "We're a minute away."

Mike was still trying to reach Duarte. "C'mon, c'mon," Mike said. "Drive up on a damn sand dune and connect with the cell tower."

Dubkova was making computations on his computer and talking to Levkov on his phone at the same time. He kept pushing his glasses up the bridge of his nose with his forefinger. "How much battery time do we have, Andy?" he asked.

Bucky looked at Dubkova's glasses. Were they prescription? They were thick, but looked clear. Dubkova didn't seem accustomed to them. Why would anyone who didn't need glasses wear them?

The noise from the helicopter echoed through the radio. Above the roar, they heard Anderson say, "We have them in sight. Two OHVs traveling west. Brown canvas covering something on the roof racks."

"Alright!" Mike exclaimed.

Dubkova stopped his calculations and took the drone up above the copter to watch it close in on the two OHVs.

Mike watched the screen and told Anderson, "Get in front of them. Let them see you. Use your speaker and tell them we have to see what they're carrying under the canvas." He tried again to get Duarte on his cell. "Dammit, where are you?" he said.

Dubkova zoomed the lens in on the top of the Kawasakis. "What's under the canvas?" he said. "Maybe weapons of mass destruction?" He smiled at Mike and Bucky. "This reminds me of a film I saw about the Cuban Missile Crisis. After the Russians backed down and started taking their rockets out of Cuba, they had them under wraps on the deck of a ship. The Air Force did a flyover and ordered them to pull back the canvas so they could count the missiles. It was really tense."

Bucky wondered when the Cuban Missile Crisis happened. It had to be long before he was born.

"Duarte?" Mike said, finally getting through on the cell phone. "We've got something. I'm gonna put you on the speaker." Mike laid the cell phone down on the table. "Can you hear me?"

"Clear as a bell," Duarte said.

"We've spotted two OHVs north of Buckhorn Canyon Road. We're tracking them and the chopper is in the air. Where are you?"

"We're on the far side of El Mirage, too far to intercept."

"OK, we'll stream the video to your phone." Mike looked at Dubkova.

Dubkova held up his hand and said, "Hang on, I'm sending it right now."

Bucky and Mike leaned in around Dubkova's laptop to watch the screen. The drone focused on the sheriff's helicopter as it made a wide circle around the OHVs and started to descend. The men in the vehicles must have seen it, because the OHVs slowed and the dust clouds behind them died down.

"Moment of truth," Mike said.

"I'm following the copter down," Dubkova said. "Let's get a look at these guys."

"You getting the picture, Duarte?" Mike asked.

"Not yet," Duarte reported.

"He should have it … now," Dubkova said.

The drone descended and Bucky saw two men wearing blue jumpsuits in the front seats of the first OHV.

"Sheriff's Department, stop your vehicles, stop your vehicles." The sound from the helicopter's loudspeaker boomed into the conference room through the radio connection.

The OHVs slowed to a stop.

"Hey—" Anderson radioed from the chopper.

"Mike, Mike," Duarte's voice came through the phone speaker at the same time. "Cancel the intercept. Do you copy? Cancel … the … intercept. Those are Head Starters from Edwards."

"Mike, I think we have the wrong target," Anderson radioed a second later.

"What?" Mike said. "What's a Head Starter?"

Bucky watched four men step out onto the desert floor next to their OHVs while the sheriff's helicopter settled onto the floor of the desert, creating a brief sandstorm.

When the dust cleared, Dubkova focused the drone's camera on the men. Three were wearing blue caps that said U.S. Air Force.

"They're from Edwards," Duarte said over the speaker. "They're transporting baby turtles back to their habitat."

"You've got to be kidding." Mike slammed his fist against the wall of the conference room. "We're tracking Air Force OHVs?" Mike radioed to the helicopter, "Dave, these are not our suspects. Do you copy? Return to base." Mike sank down in his chair and deflated like a punctured balloon.

"That's what I was trying to tell you," Anderson radioed back. "We could see they were from Edwards."

Bucky picked up the cell phone and asked Duarte, "The Air Force? What are they doing?"

"Edwards has a Head Start program to help tortoises," Duarte said. "They collect pregnant females, keep them for a year with their babies, then take them back out in the fall and release them. That's what they're doing."

"I can't believe this," Mike muttered.

Bucky, Mike and Dubkova watched the video feed as one of the airmen looked up and spotted the drone circling overhead. He took out a pair of binoculars and zeroed in on it, then took off his hat and waved. The men in the sheriff's office observed the airman through the lens of the drone as he watched it through his field glasses. A second airman climbed on the back of the OHV and peeled the canvas back to reveal two large wire cages holding desert tortoises. He pointed to the tortoises, then out toward the desert. The two men from the other OHV stood by their vehicle, leaving their tortoises covered. One shaded his eyes and looked up at the drone while the other lit a cigarette.

Dubkova called Levkov. "False alarm, Andy. We've intercepted a crew from Edwards. Let's bring the Cyclops back and replace the battery while they decide what to do next." Dubkova pushed his chair away from the table. "I have to pee."

Mike sat slumped in his chair, disappointment written all over his face. "I was sure we had something," he said.

Dubkova left the room and his computer reverted to screen-saver mode. Bucky watched a picture of a drone appear on the screen. After several seconds it faded into a fighter aircraft, then the space shuttle landing at Edwards, followed by a picture of a baby, not more than a few months old, wrapped in a pink blanket. Whoever was holding her was cut out of the picture—two disembodied arms held the child up to the camera. Poor kid, Bucky thought. What a bummer to have Dubkova as a father. As he tried to imagine what kind of woman would be married to the asshole from MIT, Bucky's eyes were drawn to an earring hanging from a silver chain around the baby's neck. He barely had time to collect his wits before the image was replaced by a picture of another fighter jet.

"Mike, Mike, look" Bucky said. He pressed his face closer to Dubkova's computer screen. "Did you see that?"

"See what?" Mike said.

"On Dubkova's computer."

"What are you talking about?"

"The baby. It's Brandy's daughter."

"You're not making any sense, Bucky."

"Yes I am. She had Brandy's other earring on a chain around her neck, just like the one I found out at the blast site. The biker—Jack—was telling the truth. Dubkova has Brandy's daughter. Look." Bucky stared at the screen saver. New pictures of jet aircraft cycled through, but the image of the baby didn't return.

"Dubkova has Brandy's daughter?" Mike exploded. "Jesus, Bucky, let's not get off on something crazy while this operation is going on. I've got enough problems, OK? Just sit tight and don't say anything to Dubkova. Let's finish this job. Whatever you think is going on, we'll get into it later, not now."

Bucky stood up and started to pace around the room. "I knew I didn't like this guy."

"Do not start anything, understand?" Mike said.

Bucky didn't answer.

"Yes?" Mike said.

"OK," Bucky said.

Before Bucky could sit down, Dubkova returned to the conference room. On his heels came Mike's boss, Sergeant Macy, who was in charge of the three-man narcotics team in Lancaster. Macy was a smoker and Bucky could smell it on his clothes the minute he walked in the room. "You ready for this, Mike?" Macy said. He wasn't smiling.

"I know," Mike said, "We just intercepted four flyboys from Edwards by mistake."

Macy ignored Mike's response. "We just got a call from the Fish and Game lab in Eugene, Oregon. They've done their own analysis on the soil samples."

Bucky's fingers were throbbing in spite of the Percocet. It was time to do another icing.

"They've confirmed trichloroethane and lithium," Macy said.

"Great," Bucky said. "I knew it."

"Why do I think that's just the good news?" Mike said. "What's the bad news?"

"Well, you haven't lost your detective's edge," Macy said. "The bad news is that Fish and Game says the lithium is a component of something called Aerospec 200." Macy read from the pad he was holding. "A low-temperature, complex synthetic grease, made by a British company called Rocol."

"It's not elemental lithium?" Mike said.

"What's elemental lithium?" Bucky asked.

"It's lithium in the metallic form. That's what we're looking for," Mike said. "That's what they use in meth production."

"Well, apparently that's not what you found," Dubkova said. "Aerospec 200 is an aerospace lubricant, an ester grease."

Macy looked at him. "That's exactly what I was told. How would you know something like that?"

"I know," Dubkova said, "because I have a degree in aerospace engineering from MIT."

MIT should be tattooed on your forehead, Bucky thought.

"What's an ester grease?" Mike asked.

Dubkova ignored Mike's question. "That means the dump is aerospace related, not a meth lab, right? What you've got is traces of trichloroethane used as a degreaser to clean a lithium-based lubricant off aircraft parts."

"I thought trichloroethane was banned," Bucky said.

"It was used for years in the aerospace industry," Dubkova said. "Still the best degreaser around."

"Is Fish and Wildlife certain about this?" Mike asked Macy.

"Yes," Macy said. "And we just got confirmation from our own lab."

"Sounds like you guys went off half-cocked," Dubkova said.

Bucky wanted to plant his fist in Dubkova's face.

"The surveillance is done as of right now," Macy said.

"After all this," Mike said, "we're not even chasing a meth lab?" This time he brought his hand down so hard on the table that Dubkova's laptop moved. "After all this," he repeated.

"FYI," Macy said, "Fish and Wildlife was ordered to drop the tortoise case."

"Drop it?" Mike said.

"I thought this was an endangered species case," Bucky said. "The ranger said three dead tortoises was a big deal. I don't get it. If TCE is banned, and somebody is dumping it, why are they dropping the investigation?"

"I only know what I heard," Macy said. "Orders came from higher up to drop the case."

"From higher up?" Mike said. "Higher up? Higher up where?"

Macy shrugged. "That's all I know, I'll see what I can find out." He turned to Dubkova. "You're the drone guy, right?"

Dubkova nodded. "SkyScan."

"Sorry, but the search is over and I'm disbanding the taskforce," Macy said. "We have the right to terminate at any time and that's what's happening.

You get paid for the rest of the day, that's it."

"I know what the letter says," Dubkova said, and glared at Macy. "Your payment was chickenfeed anyway. Hell, this didn't make much sense to begin with. Our mission is to chase terrorists, not tortoises." He closed down the camera feed from the Cyclops and called Levkov. "Andy, it's over. The job's terminated. Bring the Cyclops back. I'll meet you at the plant." Dubkova logged off and his laptop reverted to the screen saver.

Bucky leaned in to watch the computer screen and just before it closed down, he again saw the picture of the baby with the chain and amethyst earring around her neck. Bucky wondered about the picture. Would a baby a few months old be wearing a necklace? Could it be some sort of message from Brandy?

Mike sat in his chair with his back to everyone, staring at the wall. "Lithium grease?" he said. "Fucking *lithium grease?*"

TWENTY-TWO

"**D**AWSON, YOU SCREWED UP." As Bucky climbed the stairs to Chief Vlasic's office at precisely 9:00 a.m., he imagined this was the first thing the chief would say to him. The Percocet he had taken two hours earlier gave him little confidence. Bucky's mood was crashing, he felt very depressed. Deep down, he knew his job was on the line. Actually, it was on the line last week when he took the drug test. Now he was probably over the line and his career as a firefighter was finished. Bucky paused outside the door to Vlasic's office and wondered again how things had become so screwed up. He couldn't decide whether the Percs were the cause of his problems, or just one result of a life he had somehow let get out of control.

Bucky knocked and opened the door. Chief Vlasic sat at his desk, wearing his uniform jacket. He thought that was a bad sign, an indication that something formal was about to happen. The chief's aftershave lotion filled the office with a menthol aroma.

"Sit," the chief said.

"Good morning, sir," Bucky said.

"How are all your injuries?"

"Getting better, thanks." Bucky held up his hand with the splinted fingers.

The chief took the top off a Styrofoam cup filled with coffee and sipped from it. He looked up at the ceiling and Bucky thought the chief was trying to make up his mind about how to terminate him from the fire department. It would probably be more formal than "Dawson, you fucked up." The sharp smell of the coffee overwhelmed the menthol aftershave aroma. Bucky's stomach was churning and he wished he had eaten a bigger breakfast.

The chief opened a file lying on his desk and glanced at it. "Dawson ... uh ..."

Here it comes, Bucky thought.

"Do you know how this drug testing works?"

"No sir, not exactly."

"There's something called the Substance Abuse and Mental Health Services Administration, and they have mandatory guidelines for drug testing. It's simple. You pass or you fail. There's nothing in between. If your first test is above the drug cutoff level, they run another test to confirm the results." Chief Vlasic drummed his fingers on his desk. "You failed both."

Bucky shook his head, almost imperceptibly.

Vlasic read from the file in front of him. "For opiate metabolites, including Percocet, the cutoff level is 2,000 nanograms per milliliter." Vlasic dropped the file on his desk and pushed his chair back. "You registered 2,400. What's going on, Dawson? I knew your dad. He was a good man and a good firefighter. You've got a clean record. You work hard and until now, you've never fucked up." Vlasic got up, walked around his desk and sat on the corner. "Look, I'm a HazMat specialist, not an expert on drug addiction. I haven't seen anything wrong with you or your work, but you've just failed a drug test and I hate to see you go down the drain. You wanna talk about this?"

"Chief, the last few days have been a nightmare."

"I'm sure losing your sister was tough."

"I wasn't that close to her, but her death hit me harder than I expected. Now I've found out she had a daughter, and I'm trying to locate her." Bucky couldn't believe he was telling Chief Vlasic all of this, but he went on. "Physically, I'm a mess and I'm in a lot of pain. I've been attacked by bikers twice and I was washed into the creek during the flash flood. I've got two injured fingers, two separate head injuries, bruised ribs and black and blue spots on my butt and thigh the size of baseballs." Bucky paused and decided he had said enough, probably too much. He definitely didn't need to tell Vlasic he had been taking Percs regularly for almost two months before all of this happened.

The chief wrote some notes on his pad. "So you're taking painkillers because of multiple injuries, right?"

"You could say so."

"No," Vlasic said, "you could say so. In fact, you just did. I think we made a mistake here. You've got injuries and you're on painkillers. So of course you failed a drug test. Right?"

"Uh, yes, that's right."

"Look, Dawson, I'm not as big a shit as everyone thinks. If one of my men has a problem, I'll try to help him out. As long as he tries to help himself. Get my drift?"

"I think so."

"What I mean is this." Vlasic went back around behind his desk and smoothed his jacket before he sat down. "You're on unpaid leave until you heal up. At that point, you won't have any reason to take more painkillers. Then, you will pass a drug test. Right?"

"Right," Bucky said.

"I know everyone thinks I'm a control freak." Vlasic waited for a response.

Bucky said nothing.

"Well, I suppose it's true, but having control means having an orderly life, and having an orderly life means you don't go off the track and do stupid things. Do you know what I mean? You stay on track and do what you're supposed to do. That's what life is about. Not being a fuck-up. It's about personal discipline. Do you understand that?"

Bucky nodded. "I think so."

"You've got time to think about it. Come back when your injuries have healed and you can go back to work. Then you can take another drug test and pass. That's it." The chief waved Bucky out.

"Thank you, sir," Bucky said, and started for the door.

"Dawson," Vlasic said, as Bucky was halfway through the doorway. "Is that miserable old pickup still running?"

"Yes sir."

Vlasic gave his version of a smile. "Well, take care of it. It's fire department property."

Bucky walked out of the chief's office, closed the door, pumped his good fist in the air and exclaimed, "Yes." He was still a Los Angeles County firefighter. He was on unpaid leave, but at least he had his job. Bucky felt like he could fly down the stairs. The depression was gone. He felt euphoric.

TWENTY-THREE

"NEXT STEP, BIKER REVENGE," Bucky uttered aloud as he descended from Chief Vlasic's office.

At the bottom of the stairs, he saw AJ's motorcycle parked behind the pickups and SUVs belonging to the other men. AJ was on Bucky's shift, and wasn't supposed to be on duty today. Bucky went into the apparatus bay to find him. AJ was the perfect choice for what Bucky had in mind. He had grown up on the mean streets of Los Angeles, in the part of the city the LAPD referred to as the Ramparts Division. You had to be tough to survive there, and AJ was tough. He was a big man with a broad chest, thick arms and big biceps. He had a thick black mustache that hung over the sides of his mouth. He shaved his head but left a tiny strip of hair in the center, like a Mohawk, but cut close to the skin. He could be very intimidating, liked to mix it up and never backed away from a physical confrontation. AJ was someone who actually liked physical combat. Bucky had often thought that if AJ hadn't become a firefighter, he would have been a one-percenter.

Bucky found him on the far side of the bay, wiping down one of the engines. "Hey, AJ."

"What's up, brother?"

"I've got something going on tonight. Are you on duty?"

"No. I'm on holdover for another two hours. Richards had an accident at home."

"Want to have some fun later?"

"Sure." AJ's eyes narrowed and he grinned. "What do you have planned?"

"I'm going on a mission and I need backup."

"Cool. I'm always game for a little excitement. What have you got planned?

A punch-up?" He held up his oversize hand and made a fist.

"I'm going to even the score with some one-percenters."

"That's not a punch-up, that's a war. How are you gonna pull that off with injured fingers and stitches in your head? Am I gonna have to be your representative?"

"Actually, it's more like a HazMat exercise, but I need your help."

"A HazMat exercise?"

"That's right. Can you bring five or six buddies from your club? On your bikes?"

"I could probably arrange that. You gonna tell me what we're up to?"

"I'll tell you about it tonight. You'll have some fun, I promise."

"What time?"

"Midnight. I'll meet you out on 90th Street, about a quarter of a mile this side of Mach 2. You know where that old house is? The one that burned down?"

"You're on. I'll see how many guys I can get." AJ returned to cleaning the engine.

Bucky went back out to the pickup and wrote up a list of the things he needed. The most important items were a Kappler 300 Level B protective suit, designed for chemical splash resistance, and a breathing apparatus with a full tank of air. Smaller things included a headlamp, his night vision glasses, the outer HazMat gloves to wear over the ones that were part of the Kappler, and adhesive and duct tape. Wearing any gloves was going to be a problem with two fingers splinted and taped together. Bucky also needed Vaseline. He would have to remove the tape and splint, grease his injured fingers and try to slide them into the protective gloves. If he could accomplish that, he could slip on the second set of outer gloves and tape his fingers together from the outside to immobilize them.

Bucky drove the pickup around the side of the station and picked up an SCBA harness and a full bottle of air. The Kapplers were in the supply cache, which was never locked. The suits were disposable, and recordkeeping was so-so. Bucky "borrowed" one.

At home, Bucky struggled with one good hand to wrestle the old 55-gallon fiberglass tank onto the bed of the pickup. Salvaged from his neighbor who had used it to transport water for his horses, it was perfect for decontamination.

Once he had it secured on the back of the pickup, he filled it from his garden hose. There would be no way to rig up a plastic pool at night to collect the decon water and he decided to just let it run off into the desert sand at Mach 2.

Last and most important, Bucky had to choose his weapon of mass destruction and had a list of acids from which to choose. Bucky considered hydrofluoric acid first, but rejected it as too risky. The advantage was that it was stored and transported in plastic containers, but only because it dissolved glass and most metals. One of the first things HazMat responders learn is that HF is the single most dangerous contact poison. It causes deep burns and tissue destruction, and a tiny amount absorbed into the blood through the skin can interfere with nerve function and cause cardiac arrest. HF was definitely out.

Bucky scanned the HazMat list of destructive acids and considered three—muriatic acid, sulphuric acid and nitric acid. He decided the 86 percent solution nitric acid, referred to as fuming nitric acid, would do the job nicely. He especially liked the fact that HNO_3 is extremely corrosive and is used to etch and dissolve metals. He checked the MSDS—material safety data sheet—posted online and read the description of nitric acid's properties:

> *Colorless, highly corrosive, poisonous liquid that gives off choking red or yellow fumes in moist air. Toxic, corrosive and flammable vapors. Very hazardous in case of skin contact, eye contact or ingestion. Skin contact may produce burns. Inhalation of mist may produce severe irritation of respiratory tract, characterized by coughing, choking, or shortness of breath. Prolonged exposure may result in skin burns and ulcerations. Severe overexposure can result in death. Keep locked up. Do not ingest. Do not breathe gas/fumes/vapor/spray. Wear suitable respiratory equipment.*

Bucky knew he could purchase HNO_3 at High Desert Chemical Supply where he had often gone to pick up chemicals for HazMat training exercises. He checked the pricing and was shocked to discover that a one-liter bottle of high purity HNO_3 cost $55. Assuming a half liter for each of twenty bikes, he was looking at a bill of $550. His savings were minimal, the Percocet purchases were costing a fortune and now he was on unpaid leave. Bucky thought about it and decided screw it, this had to be done. He would charge it to his credit card and pay it off later.

TWENTY-FOUR

"DAMN IF I DON'T SMELL Red Hots," Bucky said. A full moon illuminated the skeleton of the half-burned home. It was several hundred yards to Mach 2, but the music blaring from the jukebox and the boisterous shouts of the Vagos members in the bar echoed through the empty desert. As soon as he stopped the pickup and opened the door, he had smelled AJ's candy.

AJ emerged from the darkness. "You want backup, you get me and you get the Red Hots."

Bucky tried to make out the indistinct shapes of the men and bikes blending into the gloom behind AJ. "How many guys are with you?"

"Five," AJ said. "Is that enough?"

"That's great."

"Wanna tell me what we're up to before we start doing it?"

"First, you're coming with me in the truck." Bucky shined a flashlight on the gear in the back of the pickup. "You have to help me on with a Kappler suit. I have some business in the parking lot and there may be a Vagos prospect watching the bikes. You have to either scare him off or take him out. I do not care which; just do not let him run into the bar and alert everyone. After that, wait until I am finished, wash me down and help me get out of the suit. We will drive back here and you will get your people. Then you can ride around the bar and make a lot of noise. Let the Vagos hear your bikes and then take off."

"Are they supposed to come out and chase us?"

"If they do, they'll be on foot."

The shades in the bar were drawn, but light and noise streamed out through the open door. In the dirt parking lot in front of the bar, the single spotlight mounted on the roof illuminated an assembly of motorcycles.

Bucky and AJ walked around to the back of the pickup. They were upwind and the fumes and vapors would drift away from the bar, out across the desert. AJ held the flashlight while Bucky took off his boots, unfolded the Kappler, slipped his feet into the booties and pulled the suit up above his waist. The protective suit was made of a tan material called Zytron and lined on the inside to absorb sweat.

"These things always remind me of the one-piece kiddie pajamas with the little feet attached," AJ said. "What d'ya call them?"

"Doctor Dentons? What do you know about Doctor Dentons?"

"My sister's little boy wears them. They have a trap door you can unbutton if nature calls."

"Right now," Bucky said, "nature's calling for you to hold the flashlight over my hands." He gently unwound the tape, removed the splint and slathered Vaseline over his injured fingers. He gritted his teeth, put his arm into the sleeve of the Kappler and grimaced as he pushed his two crushed digits into the fingers of the tight glove. "Damn, that hurts." He put his other hand into the sleeve and glove, pulled the hood up over his head and sealed the Velcro seam of the suit up under his throat. He pulled on the outer gloves and said to AJ, "OK, now tape my two fingers together, and take it easy. Not too tight and try not to bend them."

AJ placed the flashlight down on the bed of the pickup. "Hold your hand over the light," he said. He pulled off a length of adhesive tape and taped Bucky's fourth and fifth fingers together outside the two sets of protective gloves. AJ went on to tape both outer gloves at the wrist of the suit with duct tape to prevent any liquids or vapors from seeping inside. AJ then held the flashlight again while Bucky put his feet, already inside the booties attached to the suit, back into his own boots and pulled the outer sleeve on the leg of the Kappler down over the boots to provide yet another layer of protection against any fluids getting inside.

Bucky guessed it was around fifty degrees. During the day, the humidity might be 6 percent in the hot desert, but in the night air, it would be closer to 20 percent. As soon as he opened the containers, the nitric acid would absorb and react with the moisture in the air and would quickly start fuming, giving off toxic vapors. His facemask and breathing apparatus would seal him off from this danger. He slung his air pack onto his back and let the facemask hang loose in front of him.

"Let's do it," Bucky said. His body radiated the excitement and energy created by the Percs he had taken before leaving the house. Tonight was an important night, a moment of payback, which had been a long time coming. Bucky was jacked and ready to go. He focused his night vision glasses and scanned the motorcycles in the parking lot. The weak light on the roof sent a narrow beam across a few of the bikes parked near the doorway. Bucky checked the dark areas around the edge of the lot and said, "There he is—one guy—out there guarding the bikes. He's sitting down on the far side. Let's go, AJ. I'm right behind you. Remember, when you turn on your light, shine it directly in his eyes so he can't see anything."

Encased in his Level B chemical protective suit with a 40-pound breathing apparatus hanging off his back, Bucky picked up the box with ten bottles of nitric acid and followed AJ down the middle of the dirt road toward the Mach 2 biker bar.

"On your knees! On your knees, you mother." AJ came charging out of the darkness at the edge of the parking lot and shined his halogen light directly in the eyes of the startled biker. "On your knees, I said. Hands behind your head. Now!"

The biker stood his ground for a few seconds, then fell to his knees and put his hands behind his head.

AJ was in his face immediately. "You carrying a weapon?

The confused man pulled a knife out of his boot.

AJ grabbed it out of his hand and heaved it out onto the desert sand. "How about a gun?"

He shook his head.

"Cell phone? Have you got a cell phone?"

The biker reached into his leathers and withdrew his cell phone.

AJ took it and tossed it in the same direction as the knife.

Bucky stepped out of the darkness and put down the box with the nitric acid. He approached the one-percenter, who put a hand up to shield the beam from his eyes, trying to see Bucky.

"Hands behind your head, I said," AJ bellowed in his face. "I'm not gonna tell you again."

"You're not a full-patch member?" Bucky asked the frightened biker. "Just a prospect, right? I don't see a patch."

"What's goin' on?"

"I asked you, are you just a prospect?"

"That's right. Just a prospect."

"This is your lucky day," Bucky said. "I'm giving you the chance of a lifetime. Do you know why I'm wearing this protective suit?"

The biker shook his head.

"Because the stuff I'm gonna pour on these bikes is so toxic it will kill you. You can head off down the road and disappear right now, or I can pour some of this acid on you and watch your flesh dissolve. You won't enjoy it. It's your choice."

It didn't take the biker long to make up his mind. "Ah, fuck, I'm outta here."

"That's the right decision," Bucky said. "And if you show up again in Lancaster, you'll be history, because you'll have to explain to your Vagos buddies what happened. Now take off!"

After the prospect disappeared, AJ said to Bucky, "What kind of acid you got?"

"Fuming nitric," Bucky said. "Move back to the truck, AJ, while I do my work."

"Be careful with that stuff—its nasty."

Bucky turned on his air, pulled on his facemask, moved it around until it was comfortable over the stitches in his forehead and then drew a breath. He secured the hood of his protective suit, slipped on the headlamp and turned to survey the bikes parked around him. In the limited light cast by the spot on the roof and the beam from his headlamp, he counted eighteen hogs. Some were in excellent condition, with chrome parts and pinstriped gas tanks and fenders, while other bikes were old and dirty, with nicks and dents. Bucky wasn't an expert on Harleys, but he recognized Fat Boys, Nightsters, Road Kings, a Dyna Low Rider and an old Night Train. Most of the bikes were chopped—fenders cut back and unnecessary decorative parts and saddlebags removed. Several had ape hangers or other modified handlebars.

When Bucky stopped by the Lancaster Harley dealer to take a close look at the bikes and figure out where he could inflict the most damage, a salesman told him that a used Harley cost $5,000 to $10,000.

"A new bike, all tricked out, could cost $15,000 to $40,000," the salesman said. "A lot of bikers spend thousands on upgrades and modifications."

"Where do they get that kind of money?"

The salesman just shrugged his shoulders and said, "It's the first thing they spend their money on, to live the biker's life. Every dude who rides a bike wants the excitement, the freedom and the escape." He lowered his voice. "With the one-percenters, it goes further. Their identity's all wrapped up in their bikes. They ride down the highway wearing just a patched vest, showing hair and skin and all their macho tattoos and some bitch is pressing her tits against their back. Half the time they're drunk or high, or both. They're going crazy fast and doing all kinds of shit and they want people to stare at them and think, 'Wow, look at those guys. They're wild, and tough, and mean.' And you know what? They are. If you want to commit suicide, go out and disrespect a gang member's bike. Try kicking it over."

Tonight in the parking lot at Mach 2, Bucky was going to do more than kick over the bikes. He intended the worst kind of disrespect. In his clumsy Level B suit, looking through the facemask of his breathing apparatus and compensating for the fact that two of his fingers on his left hand were taped together, he picked up the first container of nitric acid and went to work. As soon as he removed the stopper, the beam of his headlamp illuminated the deadly yellow fog that began to drift from the mouth of the bottle. Bucky walked to the closest bike.

Drizzling the acid over leather seats and onto the metallic paint and pin striping on the gas tanks and fenders was easy. Destroying lights and instrument gauges was also simple. The HNO_3 immediately began to eat away whatever it touched. Bucky tried to drip it onto the control cables and brake lines, but that took too long. The brake calipers and disks provided easy access to inflict major damage.

As he worked, Bucky thought of his father, held down by two bikers while a third punched and kicked him.

Tires and rubber drive belts dissolved immediately under the attack of the acid. The shift mechanisms took longer. When he poured it on the bikes with elegant chrome wire wheels, it immediately began to etch and corrode the shiny metal. Using bottle after bottle, Bucky ruined the spokes, rims and axles of the bikes.

The fancy chrome-covered exhaust pipes and shock absorbers were also inviting targets. Bucky thought of the fishtail pipes on the bike that Brandy rode years ago to Burning Man in Nevada. Was it possible that the biker, Kenny, was here tonight?

Bucky did his best to drip the acid into the intake manifold between the pistons. If that worked, the HNO3 would eat through the air filter and drip into the carburetor. Finally, he poured acid into each ignition switch. Bucky worked methodically and managed to use about a half-liter of nitric acid on each bike.

When he was finished, he had one bottle left. He thought about his sister and all the things the Vagos might have done to her in Lancaster and poured the entire contents of the bottle on what was left of the finest bike in the parking lot. He thought about his niece growing up around one-percenters as the fumes boiled up and drifted into the air.

Bucky was soaking wet inside the sealed suit and could smell the sweat running off his face and collecting in the bottom of his breathing mask. He felt his T-shirt plastered to his chest and was anxious to get out of the protective suit. If he were working a real incident in a Level B suit, a safety officer would be monitoring him for dehydration and heat exhaustion. In the hot sun, he might only work for ten or fifteen minutes before being pulled back to rehydrate and rest while someone else took his place. Tonight, he had spent almost an hour inside the impermeable suit and he was exhausted. He placed the empty bottles back in the cardboard box and started back toward the truck.

"Sorry about your bikes, guys," Bucky whispered into his facemask. "And by the way, fuck you—each and every one of you."

AJ sprayed water from the tank over Bucky, still enclosed in the Kappler suit, and then removed the tape and outer gloves. Bucky slipped off his mask and breathing apparatus and dropped it on the ground. He pulled off his hood and yanked apart the Velcro seal on the body of the Kappler. He felt the cool night air wash over his damp body, inhaled and thought he could still smell a trace of the nitric acid fumes. Bucky gently worked his fingers out of the inner gloves and peeled the suit down around his ankles. "Damn, that air feels good," he said to AJ. "I was soaking in there." Bucky removed his boots and slipped out of the inner booties. "I don't think a drop of acid even touched the suit, but that stuff was fuming the minute I opened the bottles." He rolled up the protective suit and stuffed it into a plastic bag. "Any sign of the prospect from the parking lot?"

"Long gone," AJ said. "Here, drink some water." He handed Bucky a bottle.

"If he's smart, he'll leave town," Bucky said, draining half the bottle in one gulp. "The Vagos will want to know why he didn't die trying to protect their bikes."

AJ took a box of Red Hots out of his leathers. "You want some?" Before Bucky could say no, AJ emptied them all into his own mouth.

"Love that smell," Bucky said, holding his nose as he slid behind the wheel of the pickup. They drove back down the dirt road to the spot where AJ's buddies were waiting on their bikes. "Go to it," Bucky said. "Act like an outlaw gang, have some fun and let the Greenies hear you."

After AJ and his friends rolled down the dirt road to Mach 2, Bucky leaned back on the seat of the pickup. "Mission accomplished," he said.

TWENTY-FIVE

"ALL HELL BROKE LOOSE LAST night."

"What happened?" Bucky sipped his coffee and tried not to make eye contact with Mike.

"Somebody destroyed most of the Vagos' hogs in the parking lot at Mach 2." Mike moved his face into Bucky's line of sight. "That's like castration. Maybe even worse."

Bucky raised his eyebrows. "How awful."

"Word on this street is that it was the Hells Angels. They used some kind of corrosive acid."

"Mmm," Bucky murmured.

"I've never heard of bikers using acid; it's not their style. At least not that kind of acid. Know anything about it?"

"Why would I know anything about it? Do I look like a Hells Angel, Mike?"

"You look like hell. That's a start."

"It couldn't have happened to a nicer bunch of guys. Sorry if their dicks got chopped off. Wish I could have been there to watch."

"There'll be reprisals and then reprisals for the reprisals. Too bad we can't just let them kill each other off."

Bucky reached into his pocket. "Look, Mike. This is the chain and earring I found out at the blast site. The baby I saw in the picture on Dubkova's screensaver was wearing one exactly like it. It's some kind of message from my sister. I have to find that little girl."

Mike shook his head. "It doesn't make any sense. Are you sure you really saw that on his screensaver? All I saw were jets and rockets. Besides, I don't see any connection. Maybe you're just under a lot of stress and—"

"Dammit Mike, I'm telling you I saw it. I'm not imagining anything." Bucky was surprised at his own flare of temper. "I have to find out. If there's any possibility that my sister really had a child, I have to find her. I'm asking you what you suggest."

"I don't know. Go see him and get it out of your system. Take the necklace and show it to him. See what he says."

"That's why I came by. Can you find out where he lives?"

Bucky turned left onto Airport Road and felt the glow of the two Ps spreading through his body. For the first time in days, he felt happy. He tried to imagine the scene at Mach 2 when the Vagos heard AJ and his friends on their motorcycles, came out to the parking lot and found their own bikes destroyed. The poor Hells Angels. The Vagos might be on their way right now to dish out retribution. Bucky wondered how they would travel without their bikes. Maybe they would have to charter a bus—an outlaw bus. Bucky chuckled; he had more than evened the score. He was tempted to drive out to Mach 2 and check out the ruined bikes, but he had something more important to do.

He continued down Airport Road past the faded billboard for the Mojave Air and Space Port. A mile farther, he came to the cement K-rails blocking the entrance and a much smaller sign indicating that the airport was closed. Ten years earlier, the Feds had designated the tiny airfield a spaceport and for a time, hope was high in the Antelope Valley that it would attract commercial air traffic. Today it was deserted.

The empty spaceport was located inside a six-square-mile, high-security area surrounded by barbwire fences and signs warning: RESTRICTED AREA – UNLAWFUL TO ENTER. Fortified gates with guard posts manned by armed federal officers controlled the main access roads leading to the secretive aerospace defense plants and no one entered without identification and authorization. At the west end was the Lockheed Skunk Works, known in Lancaster as Plant 51, which developed black program aircraft and satellites. At the east end, NASA's Production Air Test Facility occupied several enormous, tan hangars. Dubkova's company, SkyScan, was located behind the abandoned spaceport in one of the buildings that were part of Plant 42. Small clusters of structures with radar, microwave, and satellite dishes dotted the area and military aircraft landed and took off from the shared runway. Nearby residents told stories of transport aircraft loaded with unknown cargoes taking off in the middle of the night and large flatbed trucks carrying covered loads coming out of Plant 42 headed for Edwards.

Bucky turned off the pavement in front of the cement barricade and drove across the sand to a fire access road that led around to the back of the airport. Might as well try to look official, Bucky thought, and turned on the light bar on the roof of the pickup. A gate with barbwire and a set of locks blocked his entry, but members of HazMat Task Force 129 knew the combinations, which were changed on a regular basis. It looked as though the gate hadn't been used in years and when Bucky swung it open, the metal hinges groaned. As he closed the gate behind him, he heard the deep rumble of a large jet and looked up to see a gray KC135 refueling tanker flying low overhead. As it roared past, two fighter aircraft of a type Bucky couldn't identify followed it. The tanker banked and prepared to land on the shared runway. Its lights flashed even in the bright sunlight.

Before Bucky could get back into the pickup, a black extra-long SUV skidded to a stop and blocked his departure. Three men in dark blue jump suits, wearing badges, lightweight tactical boots and aviator glasses confronted him. "Federal Police," one of them announced. Another trained a machine pistol with a laser scope on Bucky's chest.

"This is a restricted area, sir," the first man said.

Bucky held up his injured hand and said, "I'm reaching for my badge. I'm a firefighter." Bucky withdrew the silver badge and showed it to the federal officers.

"Do you have an ID, sir?"

Bucky nodded.

"Can I see it please?"

Bucky handed him his fire department card. "I'm from 129s. Checking a hydraulic leak on the 747."

"That's a job for the fire department?"

"It's make-work." Bucky held up his injured hand again. "I'm on partial disability."

"Hold on a minute." The first man got back into the SUV, holding the ID. Bucky caught sight of a computer, similar to the one most police cars carried, mounted on the center console. The man closed the door and Bucky stood in the hot sun for a moment with the other officer, who lowered the pistol with the scope.

The KC135 roared overhead again with its landing gear down.

The first man got out of the SUV and returned Bucky's card. "OK, Mr. Dawson, sorry to trouble you. The fire department shows this vehicle is out of service. If it's in use, make sure it's on the active list."

"Thanks," Bucky said.

"Have a good day," the man with the machine pistol said.

The black SUV drove off and disappeared behind a group of nearby buildings, leaving a cloud of dust in its wake.

Bucky headed past the vacant spaceport terminal, the empty hangars and the old fire station. Parked on a cement apron at the end of an access runway, he saw the Polar Air Cargo 747 with registration number N653854 on the tail, corresponding to the information Mike had given him at the station.

"Dubkova lives in a 747?" Bucky had said.

"I guess so," Mike had responded.

Bucky's only experience with jet travel was a few flights to Northern California and a trip to Denver, all in small 737s. The distinctive 747 loomed ever larger as he drove down the runway toward it. He parked in the shadow cast by the huge aircraft and when he stepped out of the pickup, he smelled diesel exhaust, heard the noise of a generator and saw that the aircraft was hooked up to a large power unit near the tail.

Standing directly under the nose of the aircraft, Bucky got a sense of its overwhelming size. At six foot one, Bucky was only a few inches taller than the tires on the front landing gear. Each wing stretched out one hundred feet or more. Four huge engines, each the size of a school bus, hung under the wings, plugged with round wooden covers at both ends. Bucky looked down along the underside of the aircraft and thought the tail might be in the next county. For the first time, he noticed the small surveillance cameras and motion detectors mounted at different places under the wings and body of the 747. They were close together and Bucky guessed there were no blind spots in the coverage. A scaffold of pipes and wooden planks supported a stairway leading up to a door in the fuselage. He walked to a small intercom and camera at the bottom of the stairs, looked straight into the lens and pressed the button.

"Who is that?" A disembodied voice echoed from the speaker.

"It's Bucky Dawson, the HazMat firefighter." Who do you think it is, he thought. Dubkova was playing games. If his cameras could pinpoint someone from 5,000 feet in the sky, they could certainly send a clear image of someone whose nose was six inches away from the lens. Bucky stepped out into the sun, shaded his eyes and looked up at the front of the jet towering above him. He caught sight of Dubkova move back through the open hatch and saw a reflection of light on metal. It looked as if Dubkova were holding a chrome pistol against the side of his leg. He reappeared seconds later, leaned over the edge of the scaffold and stared down at Bucky. "Dawson? What are you doing here?"

"I want to talk to you."

Dubkova looked down as if considering whether to invite Bucky up. Finally, he said, "OK, but just for a minute. I'm busy."

Bucky ascended the steep stairs, struggling with the various pains in his body as he climbed up through the forest of pipes and wood planks. Dubkova met him outside the jet, blocking his entry. Bucky didn't see any sign of a pistol and wondered if he had imagined it. The look of the nerdy aerospace engineer was gone. Today Dubkova wore a dark blue T-shirt, dark green cargo pants and square-toed black boots. The thick eyeglasses were missing. Dubkova had shed the look of the Pillsbury Doughboy. He was still pudgy and his skin was still snow white, but Bucky could see muscle under the fat. Today Dubkova looked more like the Michelin Man.

"How'd you find out where I live?" Dubkova's gaze wasn't friendly. "Oh, I know. It was your amigo Ortiz, the narcotics detective, right?" He stepped aside. "You're here, so you might as well come in." He suddenly smiled. "Yeah, it's good you're here. We can perform an experiment."

When Bucky walked into the aircraft, he was astonished by what he saw and for the first time, realized the true meaning of a "wide-body aircraft."

"One of the first 747s," Dubkova said. "Actually, a 747-100 built in '69. It has over 170 miles of wiring and 900 lights, gauges and switches in the cockpit." Dubkova glowed with pride at his recitation of the details. "It cost about $24 million."

"That's what you paid for it?" Bucky said, awestruck.

"No, of course not." Dubkova gave him a "How stupid are you?" look. "That was the original cost. It was a cargo carrier. The airframe is stressed, the engines are too noisy—they guzzle jet fuel—and there are newer models. No one would pay anything close to that today."

"You actually live here?" Bucky asked.

"Live and work. It's quiet and I do my best thinking here. Besides, it's a short trip over to our facility at Plant 42."

Bucky found himself standing in what was once an air cargo compartment. Computers, hard drives, screens and other electronic equipment filled the space. Much of the equipment Bucky had never seen before, but he did recognize an enormous device used to print engineering drawings, similar to one at the county fire department headquarters. Wires, cables and electrical cords were everywhere, snaking down from each piece of equipment and disappearing into countless outlets and conduits on a raised aluminum floor.

Structural reinforcement beams crisscrossed the curved inside walls of the aircraft, and hooks and other devices used to secure air cargo were welded in place. Bright fluorescent lights ran down the center of the unfinished ceiling and the sunlight sent slanted columns of a different light through the few windows not covered. Bucky saw aircraft parts on drawings and printouts that Dubkova had taped to whiteboards. Monitors showing multiple views from the outdoor surveillance cameras were placed in strategic places around the space so that one or another of the screens could be seen from any position. The only non-industrial items were a large pine table and matching chairs. The table was littered with half-empty paper coffee cups and stacks of files, papers and books, some open. Bucky glanced at the titles of two manuals: *Surveillance Aircraft Design Analysis and Introduction to Probability and Statistics: Applications for Engineering Sciences.*

As his initial awe subsided, Bucky heard the hiss of air pumped through vents in the floor and realized that he could not detect a single scent or odor print of any sort, which was unheard of in a confined space like an aircraft. The only answer could be air filtration or scrubbers. "How many square feet do you have?" he asked.

"The fuselage is 20 by 200," Dubkova said. "I've got about 3,700 usable square feet. Know anyone else who lives in a jet aircraft?"

"No, you're certainly special."

"I have a full kitchen up front and a lab and an office in the back. The upper deck has two bedrooms."

"What's with the all security cameras?"

"Courtesy of Uncle Sam." Dubkova looked around, as if impressed by his own surroundings. "This is actually a designated DOD facility. Our drones are classified as strategic weapons by the Defense Department." He moved into the center of the room. "So you really smelled solvent that was dumped out in the desert?"

"Right."

"And how far away was it?"

"Eight or ten miles."

"Eight or ten miles away?" Dubkova regarded Bucky with doubt in his eyes. "That's hard to believe. No one can smell something that far away. At least, no human can. It wasn't a coincidence or some kind of lucky guess?"

"No."

"This has happened before? That you smell things at that kind of distance?"

"Correct. I have a highly developed sense of smell, but the wind has to be blowing toward me. Otherwise I'm blind."

"I've never heard of such a thing." Dubkova came closer to Bucky and looked at him. "Ever been tested?"

"Tested?"

"You know, by doctors and scientists. Let them find out why you can do what you do, and what your limits are?"

"No, I never wanted anything like that."

"Don't you want to *know?*"

"I'm happy the way I am." Not so happy these days, Bucky thought.

"Hold on a minute," Dubkova said. "Let's try something. I'm going back to my lab in the tail section and I'll leave all the doors open. I'll open a container of something. I want you to tell me what it is. I'll walk slowly toward you. When you smell it, give me a shout. Then see if you can identify it. OK?"

"Sure," Bucky said and watched Dubkova head toward the back of the aircraft. Bucky stood and tried to imagine living in the interior of a large aircraft. Four thousand square feet was three times the size of his own home. Bucky tilted his head up slightly, turned from side to side and inhaled. There was no information to be had, no signature odors, nothing floating around. He caught only neutral air.

Now?" Dubkova shouted.

Bucky took a deep breath through his nose. "No, nothing."

Dubkova advanced to the next doorway. Bucky saw him holding a small bottle. "Now?"

Bucky inhaled and caught the faintest whiff of a tangy, unfamiliar chemical scent. He thought it had overtones of chlorine, but shrugged his shoulders. "I barely smell it now, and I have no idea what it is."

Dubkova walked back into the work area and waved the bottle under Bucky's nose. A powerful, biting odor invaded his nasal passages, sending a jolt of pain up through his sinus. It definitely had a chlorine base to it. "Chlorine?" he said. "I don't have a clue what it is, but it has chlorine in it."

"If you have the ability you say you have, why couldn't you smell this from the other end of the plane? It has a very strong odor."

"I don't know," Bucky said. He did know but kept his mouth shut. It was because of the air filtration system on the jet. "What is that?"

"It's a new polymer glue I invented. We're using it to bond the carbon-fiber parts of one of our experimental drones. It's bisphenol-A and epichlorohydrin."

"I don't even know what bisphenol is. Epichlorohydrin is chlorine based, right?"

"Right," Dubkova said, sealing the bottle and putting it down on the pine table.

"Are you married?" Bucky asked. "Does anyone live here with you?"

Dubkova was not expecting the question. He paused for a moment. "My wife and I are divorced and she moved back to Arizona. Why are you asking? That's not any of your business. In fact, what are you doing here?"

Bucky pulled the amethyst earring and chain from his pocket and waved it in front of Dubkova. "Does this look familiar?"

Dubkova stared at it for a second and said, "No."

"This is one of a set of earrings I gave my sister years ago."

"So?"

"So, the screen saver on your laptop has a picture of a baby girl. There's a chain with an earring just like this around her neck." Bucky paused and waited for Dubkova to say something, but he remained silent. Bucky went on, "That child is my niece and I'm trying to find her. Where is she?"

"I have no idea what you're even talking about."

"You have her picture on your screen saver."

"On my screen saver?" Dubkova walked to the pine table, opened his laptop and turned it on. He booted it up and played with the keyboard. Bucky watched pictures cycle through on the screen. The picture of the baby with the necklace appeared.

"There. There it is. That's the one." Bucky got a closer look and thought the baby didn't look very healthy, but then, what did he know about how babies were supposed to look?

"What the fuck?" Dubkova said. He stared at the picture for a moment before his fingers danced over the keyboard again and the image disappeared. "Picture of a baby? What picture?" Dubkova stared at Bucky. "I didn't see any picture of a baby."

"Maybe you should be wearing your glasses."

"I don't wear—"

"That's what I thought." Bucky stood directly in front of Dubkova, looking down at the shorter man. "You know, you really are an asshole."

Dubkova relented. "My ex has been screwing with my laptop. The bitch must have added that picture to the screensaver."

"That's my sister's daughter, and I intend to find her. Is she with your former wife?"

"I think it's time for you to get out."

"I'll get the answer one way or another."

"I hope you enjoyed your visit." Dubkova escorted Bucky out onto the scaffold and gave him a hard look that didn't invite more conversation. "Don't come back."

Bucky needed the last word. He stepped toward Dubkova, grabbed him by the front of his shirt, inhaled and said, "Your soap has Verbena in it. I hate Verbena."

Dubkova took a step backward.

Without shaking hands, Bucky descended the stairs. When he reached the bottom and looked up, Dubkova had already disappeared inside and closed the hatch.

Bucky walked toward the rear of the fuselage to check out the equipment. He was certain Dubkova was watching him on the monitors, but didn't care.

The power generator, placed behind the left landing gear, was a heavy duty DAVCO, drawing diesel fuel from a large tank. Next to the diesel was a water tank outfitted with a pump. One water line ran up to the aircraft and another connected to an air conditioning compressor. Bucky looked closely and saw that it was much more than an air conditioner unit; it was also an industrial air scrubber. No wonder I couldn't smell anything in there, Bucky thought. He's cleaning his air with charcoal and HEPA filters. The test with the chlorine-based glue was just to see how well the jet's air filtration system worked.

Bucky walked past the power and air equipment to an open metal shed directly under the 747's tail. He saw Dubkova's Hummer and a Polaris Extreme OHV—a two-seater with space in back for cargo, tricked out with several halogen headlights for night driving. Bucky tried to open the door of the Hummer, to get a whiff inside, but it was locked. The open OHV had no special aroma.

What was the MIT know-it-all up to? Was he really developing a new glue and was the government funding special air filtration equipment in connection with his work, or was Dubkova covering up something else? Bucky was tempted to go back up the scaffold and ask him.

"Dawson," Dubkova's voice boomed from a speaker. "Clear out. Now! I'm calling security at Plant 42."

Bucky gave Dubkova the finger and walked to the pickup.

After Bucky closed and locked the fire access gate behind him, he swallowed two Percs and drove to Mike's office. On the way, he thought about Dubkova's air filtration system. Something about the way it was set up bothered him.

TWENTY-SIX

"I CAN'T KEEP GIVING YOU information like this," Mike said in a low voice. "It's an abuse of authority."

"I just visited Dubkova in his jet," Bucky said. "I saw the picture of the baby with the earring on his screensaver before he deleted it. He said his ex-wife must have added it. That means she must have the baby, right?" They stood in the tiny kitchen at the sheriff's station and Bucky dumped his coffee out into the sink. "Jesus, how do you drink this stuff? It tastes worse than it smells, and it smells terrible."

"Beggars can't be choosers."

"This is the last favor I need, Mike. Just find out where she lives. No one will know where the information came from. I want to go see her tomorrow. I have to find out about the kid."

"Come into my office, I've got something to tell you."

Bucky followed Mike down the hall filled with the odor of past and present cigarette and cigar smoke. "This place needs the kind of air scrubbers Dubkova has connected to his jet."

"He's got air scrubbers? Why?"

"Good question. Maybe chemical vapors. He told me he's developing a new aerospace glue. He opened a bottle of it and asked me if I could smell the chemical composition."

"That makes sense." Mike walked into his office. "You know why Fish and Game stopped the tortoise investigation?"

"Why?"

"The Department of Defense made the decision. They said it was a matter of national security."

"National security?"

"I didn't get all the details, but apparently, most of the companies out at Plant 42 are using nanoparticles to create high-strength fabric. They combine it with glue and mold it into lightweight aircraft parts. Dubkova's doing that kind of work on drones. He's supposedly developing new composites, but there's no public information—it's a black operation."

"What's that got to do with poisoning tortoises?"

"Dubkova, or someone who works for him, has been dumping liquids in the desert."

"Dubkova's doing the dumping? Shouldn't he be arrested?"

"Can you believe it? The DOD told us Dubkova's using trichloroethane as a cleaner and the residue contains trace substances of the materials he's working with. Someone curious enough, and with enough analytical capability, might find out what those substances are."

"So he's dumping it in the desert? Why doesn't the Air Force just dispose of it?"

"The story is that Dubkova doesn't trust the government to do it. He claims they could screw things up and insists on having his own people dispose of the liquids. The Air Force acquiesced because he's insistent and he's working on a top-priority project. No one ever expected desert tortoises to be poisoned." Mike shrugged his shoulders. "This must have gone right to the highest levels of the Department of the Interior and the Defense Department, and you know who won that battle. National security trumps everything, even endangered species."

"What about the lithium? I thought that was a meth lab byproduct?"

"It is, but apparently it's also used in that aerospace lubricant. Aerospec whatever."

"Are you telling me that while he was flying his drone around, he knew he was searching for himself, and was getting paid to do it? He had to be laughing at us the whole time, thinking what idiots we are."

"That's about it."

"I hate that asshole. Can't we report this to someone?"

"The DOD is someone. It's already been reported."

"You know what, Mike? I didn't like Dubkova the minute I saw him. I think he's a liar. Did you notice those thick glasses? He wasn't wearing them when I visited him in his jet. He just wants to give the impression that he's a harmless geek.

"He could have been wearing contacts."

"He told me he didn't wear glasses. He's a lowlife and he was involved somehow with my sister. I want to go see his ex-wife and find out what she knows about Brandy's daughter."

Mike sat down at his computer and signed on to a law enforcement database. "This is the last time I'm gonna do something like this," he said. He entered some information on a form, and then waited for a data search. "If we had up-to-date equipment, this wouldn't take so long." After several minutes, Mike found what he wanted. "She's using her maiden name. Jennifer Dalton. She lives in Scottsdale, 8583 Placer Drive."

Bucky scribbled the information on a pad. "Thanks Mike, I really owe you."

"Ever been to Scottsdale?"

"Nope, just Phoenix."

"Everything is upscale and expensive. It's not Lancaster. Remember, this is the last time I'm gonna do this."

TWENTY-SEVEN

C OACHELLA – CITY OF ETERNAL SUNSHINE – POPULATION 10,800.
Bucky almost passed through the tiny California desert town before he
finished reading the welcome sign. Palm Springs was behind him, along with
hundreds of 250-foot-tall wind turbines that lined the mountain ridges like a
gigantic alien army preparing to attack tiny earthlings with huge three-bladed
propellers. Ahead, toward Phoenix and Scottsdale, the highway was a straight
line of blacktop with mile after mile of sand and desert scrabble on either side.
The Sunday traffic was heavy and the old fire department pickup was happy
going 75, while Ferraris and Porsches blew past doing 125, the vacuum caused
by their speed sucking the pickup toward the center divider. A few semitrailers
that he had already left behind managed to creep past him on the occasional
downhill, only to slow to a crawl on the next climb, forcing Bucky to come
around them again.

His damaged fingers hurt too much to use his left hand on the steering
wheel. After using only his right arm for several hours without the help of
power steering, cramps and stabbing muscle pains were taking over. Bucky
tried to find a radio station, but in the no man's land between Los Angeles and
Phoenix, all he got was static. He glanced down at the passenger seat, where
his brush jacket lay. In one of the baggy pockets, designed to hold radios and
other fire gear, he had the blackened chain with the amethyst earring along
with an envelope filled with a few Percs. He thought of the comment Jack the
biker made at Mach 2, "I bet yer sister must a been a terrible mother...."

Brandy was radiant and clear-eyed, fresh from the shower, wearing a thick terry
robe. Her long brown hair gleamed. Her skin had a healthy outdoor tan. She

sipped coffee from her beloved ceramic mug and asked Schare, "Do you want Mommy to make pancakes for breakfast, honey?" Her daughter smiled and sat at the table in a bright kitchen with windows framed by red and white checked curtains. Decorative plates hung on one wall. Gleaming copper pots and pans hung over the stove. Schare wore her one-piece Doctor Denton Tinker Bell pajamas with the little feet and drank her orange juice from her favorite sippy cup. A small flat-screen TV mounted on the kitchen wall featured a cooking session from the Today Show. Brandy had a busy day ahead and didn't have time to watch. After she dropped Schare off at private school, she planned to meet friends for lunch and then go to an afternoon interview for an important job. Bucky smelled the aroma of freshly brewed coffee and something else— Bucky smelled happiness.

No.

"Eat your cereal," Brandy ordered Schare. "We don't have all day." The house trailer was small and narrow, but it was home. Brandy was beginning another empty day with a cup of bitter coffee and a cigarette, sitting at the tiny foldout table wearing jeans and a T-shirt. The small sink overflowed with yesterday's dirty dishes, cups and glasses. Brandy looked out the window at the neighbor's trailer, twenty feet across the cement. She exhaled the blue haze of her cigarette smoke. Schare played on the floor with an old doll. One of the arms was missing, but she didn't care, it was still her favorite. She drank her orange juice from a plastic cup. A milk container lay on its side on the floor, leaving a sticky white puddle from the night before. The trailer smelled of smoke and stale food.

A California Highway Patrol car that was heading west slowed, made a U-turn across the median and screamed past Bucky heading east, red and blue lights flashing.

The motel room was dark and the green shag carpet was full of mold and filth. Brandy and Schare sat on a bed covered by a stained spread, where they had slept together. "Are you hungry?" Brandy asked her daughter. "Maybe we can go out and find something to eat." Both mother and child were disheveled and dirty. Brandy sat in yellowed underpants and a torn man's undershirt.

She had dark circles under her eyes, needle tracks on her arms and her bones showed under the skin of her skinny body. Schare wore the clothes she had slept in. Her hair was tangled and her face unwashed. She had cried earlier and snot still dribbled from her nose. She wiped it away with the back of her hand and asked her mother again if she could have some orange juice. The windows of the motel room shook as trucks roared by outside on the highway. Bucky smelled the mold in the damp shag carpet.

Bucky had to stop and began looking for a rest area. At the top of a hill marked Chiriaco Summit, 1,750 feet above sea level, a small road marked the entrance to the George S. Patton Memorial Museum. Bucky turned off into the empty dirt parking lot. The museum, a forlorn and weathered white building, was closed. Two old Patton tanks, gun turrets pointed toward the highway, rested in the sand next to the museum. Bucky climbed out of the pickup and stretched his legs. He walked around one of the tanks and read an inscription about the establishment of the World War II Desert Training Center at this spot. It quoted Patton as saying: "This area is the best I have ever seen, desolate and remote enough for any kind of training exercises. It is the place God forgot."

Bucky walked around for a few more minutes, trying to ease the cramps in his right arm, then sat in the pickup and watched the traffic speed past. He thought about his upcoming visit. The anticipation of seeing his sister's child was dulled by doubts. He wasn't even certain his niece was in Scottsdale. How was Dubkova's ex-wife involved? Was Schare living with her? How old was she now, and was she healthy? Bucky wondered how he would prove his relationship. Was there some sort of legal process—another buccal swab perhaps? If his DNA matched that of the little girl, was that all that mattered? What about the father? Who was he and where was he? Bucky imagined bringing Schare home to Lancaster and more questions came to mind. What kind of home could he give her? Who would cook meals? What would she eat? He couldn't be home every night to take care of her—would he need a nanny? A housekeeper? What time would she go to sleep? What if she got sick? Was she old enough for day care and activities with other children? What would it all cost?

The questions kept coming and Bucky had no answers. He felt like his head was about to explode. He thought again of the picture of the baby with the necklace and realized he knew absolutely nothing about his niece. He began to have doubts about what he was doing. He was ill suited to take charge of a child, let alone a baby, even if she was a blood relation. He was having enough problems bringing order to his own life. Right now, it was a complete mess—he was lonely, tired, bored and worried that he might have an addiction to pain pills. Was he any better than his sister? Did it make any difference that he was using painkillers instead of methamphetamine?

He desperately needed a Percocet. Actually, he needed more than one. He had skipped his usual wake-up pills to be certain he would be alert and in control of his reflexes for the drive to Phoenix. Now it was late morning and he already felt a light sheen of sweat on his face and the beginning of rumblings in his gut. He couldn't wait any longer. Before he eased the old pickup back onto the 10 Freeway and continued his trip east to Scottsdale, he reached into the pocket of his brush jacket, extracted two Ps from the envelope and swallowed them.

TWENTY-EIGHT

BUCKY STOOD ON THE BED of the pickup, inhaled a hint of pine in the clear early-afternoon Scottsdale air and looked over the wall at 8583 Placer Drive. The street ran through a neighborhood of enormous, elaborate homes, each beautifully landscaped. Mike was right. Everything in Scottsdale looked expensive, especially this property, a two-story Spanish-style house that looked like a small hotel set back from the street. The wall around it enclosed at least four acres. In the Arizona heat, the plants, cacti and trees all looked vibrant, as though someone watered them every hour. The house was pink stucco, trimmed with weathered wood and wrought iron. It had several balconies decorated with flowering plants growing from large pots. Multicolored Spanish tile framed the windows and doors. The semicircular clay tiles that Bucky had seen on a few of the most expensive homes in Quartz Hill covered the roof. A full-sized BMW and a Cadillac Escalade, both spotless, gleamed in the sun on the driveway. The two vehicles were probably worth $175,000, more than the value of his home in Lancaster.

What did Jennifer Dalton do all day? Bucky thought she must be supremely happy. How could a person be so wealthy, live in this beautiful place, and not be happy? He wondered how divorce worked among people who had so much money. Dubkova lived in a 747. *A fucking 747*. His wife, or his ex-wife, lived in a house that had to cost several million dollars. How much money did Dubkova have and how did he get it at such a young age? When they divorced, did she extract hundreds of thousands of dollars in alimony? Did Dubkova split everything with her, write a check and say goodbye, or did they fight it out over every nickel and dime?

Bucky thought of his own pathetic bank balance and his divorce from

Patricia. It was now fourteen months since she left him. When she told him she wanted a divorce, he was surprised and wounded. A week later, she took her car and half of the $19,500 in their bank account and left for Houston. She was so anxious to leave, she didn't ask for anything else. The house belonged to Bucky, but he felt guilty and gave her $2,000 for her share of the furniture and household items. He also paid the $900 bill the lawyer sent for drawing up the divorce papers. He didn't hear from her again. Her departure left him feeling isolated and depressed.

As Bucky stood on the bed of his pickup, he realized he looked terrible. He should have brought fresh clothes. His jeans were dirty and his shirt wrinkled. His physical appearance was a disaster. He still had a bandage covering the stitches on his forehead and two of his fingers were in a splint. The hair was just starting to grow back on the side of his head and he still limped from the beating at Mach 2. Jennifer Dalton might think he was a homeless person. What if she wouldn't speak to him or called the police? Mike couldn't help him in Scottsdale. Bucky fingered the amethyst earring and chain in his pocket. He had driven all the way from Lancaster and decided this wasn't the time for doubts. He jumped down from the bed of the pickup, felt a pain shoot through his thigh, walked across the street and pressed the intercom button next to an elaborate wrought iron gate.

"Si?"

"Hello, I'm here to see Jennifer Dalton."

"Missus Dalton?"

"Yes, Missus Dalton."

"Who is?"

"My name is Bucky Dawson. I'm a firefighter from Los Angeles County."

"No fire here."

"I know there's no fire. I'm here to see Missus Dalton."

"Missus Dalton?"

"Yes, dammit. Missus Dalton."

The speaker went silent and the electronic hum of the intercom ceased. Bucky knew he was no longer connected. He waited a minute, and then rang again.

"Si?"

"I want to see Missus Dalton. Is she home?"

"Si."

"Can she come to the door, please?"

"No."

"Listen, this is important. Can you understand me?"

"Si."

"I want to talk to Missus Dalton. Yes?"

"Missus Dalton."

Bucky lost his patience. "Do you have a baby in the house? Tell Missus Dalton I'm here to talk to her about the baby."

The intercom went dead again, and Bucky waited outside the gate, outside the wall on the street where his niece lived. He paced around, trying to decide what to do next. He was about to ring a third time when the front door opened and a woman came down the long flagstone walk. She was a stunning beauty and could have stepped off the cover of a women's fashion magazine. Bucky thought she might be the most beautiful woman he had ever seen. Blond, almost white hair hung straight down to her shoulders. She was slender, wore an expensive-looking blouse; form-fitting jeans; tooled, highly polished cowboy boots and a matching belt with a silver buckle. As she approached the wrought iron gate, Bucky got a closer look. She might be in her early thirties. She wore no makeup and her flawless face was punctuated by deep brown eyes and arching eyebrows. She had slender arms and delicate hands and a bracelet with precious stones graced her left wrist. How did Dubkova find a woman like this? What did he do to lose her?

She stopped inside the gate, folded her arms in front of her chest. "Mr. Dawson. What do you want?"

"Yes, ma'am," Bucky stuttered. "I live in Lancaster, California. I'm a firefighter and recently—"

"What does this have to do with me?"

"I met your husband—uh—your ex-husband."

The expression on her face didn't change—it was a combination of annoyance and impatience. "Get to the point before I call the police."

"I saw the picture of the baby on his computer." Bucky's mouth was dry; his heart was pounding. It was now or never. "Missus Dalton, I think that child belongs to my sister. The baby is my niece." Now that he had said it aloud, it sounded ridiculous.

"Did Boris send you? Is this some kind of joke?"

"No, it's not a joke." Bucky pulled the amethyst earring and chain from his pocket and let it dangle from his hand. "This belonged to my sister, Brandy. The baby was wearing a necklace just like this in the picture on his computer."

The woman came closer to the gate and peered through the wrought iron bars at the necklace. A dry wind stirred, and Bucky caught the aroma of meat on a grill somewhere nearby. The earring on the chain swayed in his trembling hand. For the first time, Bucky noticed that the amethyst was cracked.

"Oh, yes," she said. "I recognize it." She unlatched the gate, swung it open and stepped out onto the sidewalk.

Bucky caught her delicate, beautiful bouquet. It was just a hint of a perfume he had never smelled before, interacting with the chemistry of her body. He wondered what it would be like to make love to a woman like this.

"You saw the picture on Boris' screen saver? Recently?"

"Yes."

"Before I left, I added it to all his precious drone and jet pictures, just to spite him. I'm surprised it's still there."

"He erased it yesterday."

"Brandy is your sister?"

"Brandy *was* my sister. She died a few days ago in a meth lab explosion."

"I'm sorry to hear that, Mr. Dawson." She shook her head and looked up at the sky for a moment. "I guess I'm not surprised. The last time I saw her, she was totally strung out. She was a mess."

Bucky watched a transformation in Jennifer Dalton's face. Suddenly her beauty was overshadowed by anger.

"Did you know my husband was fucking her? He had all kinds of girlfriends and the last straw was when your sister showed up and told me she had Boris's child."

Bucky was dumfounded. He thought he had already heard about every crazy and miserable thing his sister had done. Now this. The baby was Dubkova's?

"I can read Boris like a book. When I confronted him, I knew it was his child because of the way he denied it. There must have been something special about your sister, because Boris always favored pretty women. When I saw her, she looked like any other drug addict."

"I thought I could take her …." Bucky's voice faltered. "Schare? Was the baby's name Schare?"

"Yes, that sounds right." Jennifer Dalton paced around on the sidewalk in front of the gate. "Your sister said she named her after someone she knew from another planet. She said the earrings came from space. Was your sister always delusional?"

"The name comes from a story our father told us when we were kids. It's based on the people living in the Antelope Valley years ago who saw lights in the sky and thought they were aliens in flying saucers. I bought her the earrings when she was in prison in Colorado."

"Your sister must have been using meth while she was pregnant, because she passed all the drug toxins on to the fetus. The baby ... Schare ... was born with withdrawal symptoms. It was so sad. This little tiny thing had tremors, muscle spasms and seizures. They kept her in the hospital for weeks trying to detoxify and stabilize her. Your sister was frantic. She had no money and no way to take care of her baby. She went to Boris and he was true to form. He wouldn't help and threw her out, so then she came to me. Can you believe it? She came to me, and I guess I'm the biggest sucker in the world, because I felt sorry for the poor little creature and agreed to pay for some special medical care. Your sister promised me she would clean herself up and take care of her baby if I helped with some money."

"That was very kind of you. Thank you for helping."

"It didn't matter, Mr. Dawson, the baby died."

"Died?" Bucky recoiled.

"She had brain damage and so many other things wrong with her that she couldn't make it. She was in a pediatric institution. I didn't have the heart to stop paying for her care, but as it turned out, she only lived a few months. I've thought a lot about it. I think it's better that way. What kind of life could she have had?"

"Is there a grave?"

"I don't know. She died in the hospital. Your sister came back once more, a few months ago. She looked half-dead. Skinny, vacant eyes, talking nonsense. She wanted money and tried to tell me the baby was still alive. The medical bills had stopped coming and I knew it wasn't true. I told her not to come back. After that, I got out of that hellhole called Lancaster and moved back to Arizona."

Bucky felt he needed a handful of Percocets.

Jennifer Dalton looked at him and said, "You didn't know any of this?"

"Nothing, except the fact that Brandy had a daughter."

"Well, I'm sorry to be the one to give you the bad news."

"Your husband fathered a child and wouldn't help? Doesn't he have a lot of money?"

"My *ex*-husband? The brilliant MIT aerospace engineer I fell in love with? The man who was going to save the world? The man of many personalities? No, he doesn't have a lot of money."

"What about his company and his research for the government?"

"He's poured every cent into that damn drone business and it's like a sponge. I think he's almost broke now and I have no idea what he's using to keep it going. He got a huge amount of money from government contracts, but no matter how much money he took in, he spent more. For a while I stuck it out and was stupid enough to think our marriage would get better, but he was a liar, he whored around, treated me like shit and was on his way to spending my entire inheritance on unmanned aircraft. The episode with your sister was just the last event that ended it for me."

"Were there any pictures of the baby?"

"Just the one you saw. Your sister showed it to me, and I scanned it into my computer and left it on Boris' screen saver before I moved back here."

"Is there anything else you can tell me about the baby?" Bucky felt desperate to find some positive bit of information, anything that might be a memory of his short-lived niece.

Jennifer Dalton looked back at the house. "Wait just a minute."

While she walked back up the flagstone path, Bucky stood and wondered how Brandy found her way to Dubkova and remembered Jack telling him at Mach 2 that Brandy had "moved up the food chain." Jack must have been referring to Dubkova. Was he involved with the bikers? Was he at the head of their food chain, the fucking shark? Bucky became lost in his thoughts about how much he hated Dubkova and what he would like to do to him.

Jennifer Dalton returned and interrupted Bucky's daydream. "Here," she said, and reached through the gate. She held Brandy's other earring, attached to a silver chain, all in one piece and untouched by the heat and destruction of a meth lab explosion. "Your sister gave me this when she was trying to con me out of some more money. You might as well have it."

Bucky came to the gate and Jennifer Dalton dropped it into the palm of his hand.

"That's it, Mr. Dawson. It's over. I don't have anything else to tell you and don't want to hear any more about your sister or her baby, or my ex-husband and his damn drones. Please do not come here again." She gave Bucky a quick look with her dark eyes, turned and walked to her front door without looking back.

Bucky's hands were shaking so hard that he had to use the three good fingers on his injured left hand to hold the steering wheel as he drove away from Jennifer Dalton's home. His mind was in turmoil. Schare, his niece, his blood relative, was dead before he had even discovered her existence. At the same time, he realized she was Dubkova's child and at the moment, he couldn't think of anyone he despised more. His anger at Dubkova was as great as his sense of loss. He had the urge to drive straight to the spaceport and confront him. Bucky wanted to beat him to within an inch of his life, throw him out the hatch of the 747 and watch him die on the tarmac in the hot sun. A kaleidoscope of images— Dubkova, Jennifer Dalton, Jack the biker, Baby Schare, Brandy—flashed through his mind. Bucky pulled to the side of the road at the entrance to the westbound 10 Freeway and tried to regain his senses. Perhaps Jennifer Dalton was right— maybe it was all for the best. Schare would have had a terrible existence.

He swallowed three Percocets. He didn't care how long ago he had taken the last pills, how many he had taken in the last twenty-four hours or whether he would be driving back to California under the influence. He already felt as though his brain was about to explode.

Bucky kept the accelerator of the old pickup on the floor and drove west across the desert into a late afternoon sunset. He tried to occupy his mind with simple distractions. He counted telephone poles. He thought about calibrating a Draeger photo ionization meter. He recited the names of the men in his fire academy graduating class. He looked for out-of-state license plates on oncoming cars. He thought about Lexie, the young nurse with the cool hands and the pale green eyes.

After driving for two hours, Bucky needed a pit stop. He saw a sign for Wiley's Well Rest Area and pulled into a deserted spot with a dilapidated building, half a dozen weathered picnic tables and overflowing trash barrels. He wanted to splash cold water on his face, but when Bucky approached the restrooms, the odor was so disgusting that he started back to the pickup. He took a few steps, stopped, turned and walked back toward the men's room.

Two empty toilet stalls greeted him with open doors and scraps of paper on the floor. He held his breath, but the odor seeped into his nostrils. Bucky walked into the nearest cubicle, reached into his pocket with his good hand and fished out both chains and the amethyst earrings. He wrapped them in a piece of toilet paper and tossed the packet into the open toilet. Bucky pressed his boot against the flush lever and kept it there until the gushing water carried everything into the drain.

TWENTY-NINE

"**M**ORNING, BUCK." MIKE STOOD AT Bucky's front door with a man wearing a blue suit, white shirt and gray tie. He was small, lean and had the short crew cut of a law enforcement official. The lines on his face said he was at least fifty. He held a thick blue binder in one hand. "Meet Marty Phillips, he's the ASAC in the Los Angeles field office of the ATF."

"Glad to meet you," Phillips said. He smelled of drugstore-grade aftershave lotion.

"Likewise," Bucky said and glanced at his watch. It was 9:45 a.m. He felt drained and depressed after his visit with Jennifer Dalton. He wanted to go back to bed.

Phillips extended his hand. When his suit jacket swung open, Bucky saw the badge hanging from Phillips's belt and part of the leather harness that secured a pistol under his left arm.

Bucky gave him a quick handshake and asked, "What's an ASAC?"

"Assistant Special Agent in Charge," Phillips said.

"C'mon' in," Bucky said. "Want some coffee?"

"We're good," Mike said. "We just had breakfast."

"Mike told me you've taken a couple of beatings from the Vagos," Phillips said. He followed Bucky into the kitchen.

"You could say we have a troubled relationship," Bucky said, holding up his injured hand. "Have a seat. You'll have to excuse me; I'm exhausted from a round-trip drive to Scottsdale yesterday." He slumped down onto one of his kitchen chairs.

Phillips glanced at Zoll, sitting immobile on top of the rocks in her tank. "What's this?" he asked.

"That's Zoll," Bucky said, without further elaboration.

Phillips placed the blue binder on the table and got down to business. "I'm here to talk to you about an investigation we're conducting. This is an informal, off-the-record meeting." He spoke as if the conversation were being recorded. He opened the binder and pushed it toward Bucky. It contained several pages sealed in plastic, each with six mug shots. They all looked like one-percenters. "Can you tell me if you recognize anyone?"

Bucky glanced at the first two pages. "Ugly bastards, aren't they?"

"Yup," Mike said.

Bucky turned to the third page and saw a familiar face. "If you want to know what I think you want to know, this is the guy." He pointed to the picture of the big man with the strange-looking shaved head. "This is the gorilla that shot at me the night your informer was killed. He's also the one who smashed my fingers." Bucky looked through the remaining pages. "Are these guys all Vagos? A few of the other faces look familiar; I've seen some of them at Mach 2."

"It's the Lancaster chapter," Mike said.

"You sure about the big guy?" Phillips asked. "Want to take another look?"

"I'm sure," Bucky said. "He doesn't look like anyone else."

Phillips pulled the binder back. "That's great, that's what I wanted—for you to identify the Dwarf."

"The Dwarf?" Bucky said. "Yeah, that's right. One of the bikers mentioned his name, just before he arrived and started shooting. Great name for a giant."

"His real name is Edward Villanos," Phillips said. "He's the Sergeant at Arms of the Vagos Lancaster chapter. The Sergeant at Arms has to be the strongest man, because he's the enforcer, and that's the Dwarf in spades. He's seven feet tall and suffers from acromegaly, or gigantism. It has something to do with his growth hormones."

"That's why he looks so weird?" Bucky asked.

"Yeah," Phillips said. "Big forehead, protruding jaw. The hands and feet are always huge. He's a very bad guy, one scary person. Vicious, sadistic and a killer. He has a pit bull and he likes to let the dog maul his victims before he finishes them off. He's been involved in several nasty killings, even including a couple members of his own club. They were torn apart when we found them. He also carved a V on a Mexican drug dealer's forehead and stomach before he killed him."

"I was a foot away from him," Bucky said. "Right next to him at the bar when the son-of-a-bitch crushed my fingers with the bottom of a beer bottle."

"Look, Bucky," Phillips said, "here's the deal. What I'm about to tell you is confidential. Highly confidential. You tell no one. Understood?"

"You bet," Bucky said.

"The ATF has been running an investigation on the Vagos in several states for the last year and a half. We have a lot of dirt on the Lancaster chapter and we think we have enough to put several members away. The Dwarf is high on our list. We want him out of circulation and we think we can prove he shot Jack the informant at Mach 2."

"I saw him take a shot at me," Bucky said. "It was raining like crazy, but he's hard to miss."

"If you testify to that, our case is that much stronger."

"Sure, I'll testify. Why not?"

"We plan to go to a grand jury right after the first of the year." Phillips pulled a paper from his suit jacket. "Here's a list of charges. Three counts of murder and aggravated battery with a deadly weapon against the Dwarf. Against the Vagos Lancaster chapter: assault; multiple hate crimes; multiple firearms violations including felons in possession of firearms; drug deals; grand theft; perjury; payoffs; obstruction of justice and witness intimidation. There are similar charges against individuals in the Vagos chapters in Nevada and Arizona, and RICO charges against the club nationwide." Phillips closed the binder and pushed his chair back from the table. "This case is really important. Since we had the Fast and Furious fiasco—the guns we lost in Mexico—nothing but shit has been raining down on the ATF. We need some high-profile wins. Convictions here would go a long way to restoring our credibility. We especially want to take down the Dwarf."

Bucky wondered what would happen if the Vagos and the Hells Angels ever declared a truce. What if they got together and the Hells Angels convinced the Dwarf that they hadn't done the dirty deed on the Vagos' bikes? Could the Vagos ever link Bucky to the incident? Bucky imagined waking up one night to find the Dwarf, all seven feet of him, standing over his bed with his pit bull next to him. The best place for the Dwarf was in prison. "I would be glad to help," Bucky said.

"Good—that's what I needed to know," Phillips said. "I think we're done for the moment. In the next couple of months, one of our investigators and an attorney from the Justice Department will contact you to discuss the case and your testimony. I've got to go, but Mike can fill you in on some other aspects of your testimony."

"You headed back to LA?" Mike asked.

"Yeah," Phillips said, and stood up. "We got a report early this morning that the chapter president of the Hells Angels in Mesa was gunned down in front of his house at 3:00 a.m. It has to be payback for what happened at the Vagos' biker bar out here and my guess is it's just the beginning."

"I'll be in touch," Mike said. When he heard the front door slam, he leaned on the back legs of his chair. "How was your trip?"

Bucky yawned. "Exhausting. I met Jennifer Dalton. A gorgeous woman. It's true, my sister did have a daughter, but she died. Birth defects from Brandy's meth addiction."

"I'm sorry to hear that, Buck."

"The part you're not going to believe is that Dubkova was the father."

"Dubkova? You've got to be kidding. How did that happen?"

Bucky hesitated. "You know what, Mike. I feel like crap this morning. I'll tell you about it some other time."

"OK, but speaking of addiction, there is something we have to talk about now."

"What?"

"We've been friends a long time, right?"

"Forever." Bucky sighed. Mike was his best friend, but at the moment, he felt too tired to have any kind of important conversation. The two Percocets he swallowed an hour ago had done nothing to help his mood. He wanted to take another pill, or maybe two, and be alone. Bucky hadn't been able to sleep when he returned from Scottsdale. Each minute had stretched out forever while he watched the digital clock on his nightstand. He had thought all night about what Jennifer Dalton told him and had swung from sadness over the fate of Brandy's daughter to anger at Dubkova.

"I know you're taking painkillers."

"I told you I'm really tired."

"Let's talk about it now. You've done some crazy stuff lately and if you keep it up, you're gonna get yourself killed. Are you taking them because of your injuries, or is it recreational?"

Bucky thought for a moment before responding. What the hell, he decided. It didn't matter if Mike knew the truth. "Yes to both."

"What's going on Buck? Lately you seem so troubled. If you don't lay off the painkillers, it'll lead to bigger trouble. Believe me, I'm a narcotics cop, I know."

Bucky stood up and looked into Zoll's glass tank. The lizard flicked its forked tongue at him. "I'm worried about me, too. This thing with Brandy's child is just the final kick in the teeth." Bucky went to his refrigerator. "Want a pear, or some live crickets?"

"I'm good."

Bucky pulled a pear from the refrigerator and bit into it. "Mike, my life is a mess. I lost Brandy long before last week. She was on the wrong track years ago and there was nothing I could do to save her. She had a child, and now she's dead, too. My whole family's gone, except for my demented grandmother who doesn't even know who I am. In fact, sometimes I don't even know who I am. I don't feel connected to anything. I don't know what I'm supposed to be doing in life. I'm sick and tired of everything. I'm sick of living in this goddamned ghetto. I'm even getting tired of my job, and it's all I've got." Bucky took another bite out of the fruit. "My life's about as interesting as the existence of this fucking lizard. I might as well sit on a rock all day."

"Maybe you need some help. Ever thought of counseling?"

Bucky shook his head. "I know what's wrong with my life, and I don't think a shrink can fix it."

"Well, here's the immediate problem. If you're going to testify about the Vagos, you have to be an unassailable witness. If there's any hint of drug use on your part, they can't use you. A defense attorney could sink the murder charge against the Dwarf if you're shown to be unreliable. It could weaken the whole case."

Bucky scowled. "Let's just say I'm temporarily on painkillers due to my injuries and I'm about to stop."

"Yeah, but is that true? Are you about to stop? You have to be squeaky clean. I'm your friend, and I have to tell you, I think you need some help. Maybe rehab."

"Rehab? What I need is something new and interesting in my life."

"How would you like to move somewhere else?"

"How the hell am I going to do that?"

"Phillips didn't tell you everything. Why do you think they haven't convicted the Dwarf? You heard the charges of witness intimidation? People are afraid to testify in biker cases. They're being threatened and some witnesses have disappeared. The ATF can't lock up every Vagos in the nation and if you testify, someone will come looking for you. Probably sooner than later. You have to consider that. You might be eligible to go into witness protection."

"Witness protection?" Bucky laughed. "Are you serious? *Witness protection?*"

"I'm dead serious."

Bucky walked over to the glass tank again and looked at Zoll. "Scoop me up like a lizard, drop me somewhere and I start over?"

"More or less."

"How about Honolulu? That would be nice. Can I take Zoll? We'd like a beach house in Hawaii, right Zoll? Set it up for us, Mike."

"I'm not sure a beach house in Hawaii is in the cards, but you would have some choice of where you live. This could be the most important decision of your life. You have to give it some serious thought, Buck. It's not a joke."

Bucky nodded. "How does it work?"

"You sign an agreement that details your obligations as a witness and outlines the government's obligations to relocate you. There's something called WitSec—Witness Security. It's part of the U.S. Marshals Service and they create a new identity for you. Driver's license, credit cards, the whole nine yards. They're the only people who know where you are. I wouldn't even know."

"We wouldn't get to talk?"

"No. You leave behind everyone you ever knew. That might be easier for you than for other people."

"What does that mean?"

"It means you don't have a lot of friends or loved ones, people that you would miss seeing or talking to."

"What if I change my mind later?"

"You can walk away any time you want, but you would want to think long and hard about doing that."

"Could I take someone with me?"

"Yeah, but the same rules would apply. Plan on marrying the reptile?"

"Let me think about it, Mike. I think I'm in."

"First things first. Can I assume you'll stop taking the damn pills and clean up your act?"

Bucky nodded again.

"That's a yes?"

"Yes."

As soon as Mike backed off the driveway, Bucky went into his bedroom, took his pill bottle off the nightstand and dumped the contents out on the bed. Ten days ago, he had ordered two bottles, each containing thirty pills, which had cost $735, not an insignificant amount. He had already consumed over half his supply; only nineteen of the yellow beauties remained. He had increased his usage, and yet they were having less of an effect. Mike was right. Bucky knew he had to stop using the painkillers, but this just wasn't the right time to do it. He was still getting over the loss of his sister and now there was the shock of the death of her baby. There was also his loathing of Dubkova, not to mention the pain from his fingers and other injuries. If he tried, Bucky could list a dozen important reasons why it wasn't the right time to stop the painkillers. Life was just too shaky at the moment. He had time before anyone contacted him from the ATF. He didn't have to do anything right now. He could begin to reduce his intake later. In a couple of weeks, he would start cutting back. Slowly. In the meantime, it wouldn't hurt to order a reserve supply of Percs, just in case.

Bucky went back into the kitchen. Zoll was in the corner of the tank, clawing at the glass. Bucky had never seen her do that. He couldn't tell whether she was trying to climb up the side of the glass, or burrow down underneath it. Whatever she was doing, it was obvious to Bucky she was trying to get out.

He turned on his computer and logged on to *BuyDrugs.com*. When the site came up, he was shocked to see a blank page with the message: THIS WEBSITE HAS CEASED OPERATION BY ORDER OF THE ROYAL CANADIAN MOUNTED POLICE. He stared at the black letters on the empty screen, and a feeling of panic gripped him. What if the Mounties had a list of the *BuyDrugs* customers? Was he in trouble? He had just become comfortable with the idea of purchasing Percs online and now this.

He had to find another source. He had heard of people going doctor-shopping in Tijuana, where storefront medical clinics and pharmacies lined the streets. Bucky rejected that idea—that was something an addict would do. He decided to stick with the Internet. This time, when he googled "Percocet," the name that appeared at the top of the search list was *Painkillers.com*. Bucky clicked through. *Painkillers.com* claimed it was a legitimate pharmaceutical website; it required a doctor's diagnosis—guaranteed to take less than three minutes over the telephone—before processing an order. The website required a membership fee and his phone number. Bucky signed in and entered his landline number.

He sat in his kitchen, waited for the call and watched Zoll. Bucky was worried about the reptile. The poor thing wasn't born to live in a two-by-three-foot glass tank and was probably depressed. Zoll had nowhere to go and nothing to do. Who wouldn't be depressed in those circumstances? "We've got a lot in common," he told the lizard. Zoll had returned to the rock under the sunlamp. The reptile's elliptical eyes were wide open, unblinking.

Bucky's thoughts drifted to Dubkova and Brandy, and his anger ignited again. Dubkova wasn't an idiot biker. He was intelligent and there was no excuse for what he had done to Brandy, not to mention his refusal to help his own baby. Bucky decided to confront Dubkova again, which meant another visit to the 747. He thought again about the air filtration system under the tail—something about it still troubled him and he googled "HEPA industrial air purifiers." Bucky knew from HazMat training that air scrubbers were used to filter bacteria, mold, and lung-damaging particles. If Dubkova was working with space-age composites, the carbon nanoparticles—which have no scent—could be a health threat, but Dubkova seemed more intent on determining whether vapors or odors were wafting through the fuselage. What else was he trying to filter out? Bucky explored a website that outlined how to combine a HEPA system with an industrial forced–air conditioning system. A few minutes of research told him what he wanted to know.

Bucky's eyelids grew heavy after a few minutes at the computer. He lay down on his couch and dozed off. He was in a deep sleep when his landline rang.

"Mister Dahson? Hello? Is this Mister Dahson?"

The doctor had a strange accent and the connection was so bad it sounded like he was calling from the South Pole. The conversation was short—the doctor asked a couple of meaningless questions and then told Bucky he needed pain medication. He instructed Bucky to log back on to Painkillers.com and order fifty of the 10-milligram Percocets. When Bucky placed his order, the charge to his credit card was $725. Another shocking amount—one he couldn't afford—but he decided it didn't matter. After all, it was his last order.

Bucky felt relieved now that he had ordered his Percs. He went into the bathroom and stood under a cool shower, trying to shake the fatigue from the Scottsdale trip. The water roused him, but once out of the shower, he was bored and restless. It was late afternoon and Bucky felt no effect from the pills he had taken only hours before. He wanted to take two more, but decided to drop by 129s and join the men for dinner. He could kill a couple of hours and look forward to popping more Percs before he went to sleep.

THIRTY

DRIVING ACROSS TOWN, BUCKY WAS preoccupied with thoughts about Dubkova when he heard the roar of the jet. The same stubby wing craft he had seen earlier in the week passed overhead in the evening sky. It seemed to be much lower this time and Bucky thought he could almost reach up and touch it. The craft was headed toward Plant 42, or maybe Edwards.

Moments later, a muffled explosion echoed across the desert, registering as a dull thud against Bucky's eardrums. His heart began to race. He stepped on the gas pedal and said, "C'mon, c'mon," to the balky pickup as he drove toward the station. By the time he turned onto 6th Street, the equipment bay doors were already open. Engine 129 roared out and the HazMat Squad followed it, its diesel engine whining as it picked up speed. Through the big front windshield, Bucky saw B Shift Captain Swift in the passenger seat and Davis, the engineer, behind the wheel. Engine 329 followed. Bucky turned on the light bar and radio in the pickup, made a U-turn and followed the other vehicles toward Plant 42. He lowered the side window an inch and immediately smelled burning jet fuel.

Instructions from Dispatch began to stream in through his radio: *Battalion 11, Engines 129, 329, HazMat Squad, Paramedic Squad 135, Engines 117 and 134, Truck 33. Respond to Site 3 access road at Plant 42, Avenue M west of 20th Street intersection. Runway 7-25 compromised. Aircraft has impacted two structures.*

"Aircraft has impacted ..." was ominous. Bucky thought the trouble with the jet must have been catastrophic if the pilot couldn't stay in the air for the extra seconds needed to land safely on the shared runway at Plant 42 or reach the vast lakebed at Edwards. He glanced out the side window just as the red

Battalion 11 SUV passed him, lights and siren blazing, with Chief Vlasic hunched over the wheel. For the first time in months, the excitement of the incident energized Bucky and he forgot about his sister, Dubkova, and the problem of his addiction.

Rangely Composite Components building, south side of Site 3 adjacent to taxiway and adjoining Stealth Systems building are burning. ARFF team deployed to jet fire. Mutual aid protocol, unified command in effect.

A jet crash inside the perimeter of Plant 42 was a once-in-a-lifetime, full-blown emergency. Bucky anticipated an enormous IDLH—Immediate Danger to Life and Health—zone, with burning jet fuel creating a lake of flames around the aircraft and the structures it had hit. This was the chaotic, manpower-intensive type of disaster that every firefighter lived for and dreaded. The fire crew at Plant 42 would need all available outside help to cope with the situation and that was what unified command protocol was about. The chief of the Plant 42 ARFF team—Aircraft Rescue and Firefighting—and Chief Vlasic of Battalion 11 would share authority over the incident. While the ARFF team used special-ized vehicles to fight an aircraft fire, the Los Angeles County firefighters and HazMat team would battle the structure fires, monitor the HazMat risk and even provide paramedics. Dispatch had already emptied Station 129 for the initial response, but a predetermined deployment plan for an emergency at Plant 42 would also go into effect, mobilizing dozens of additional engines and support equipment from other stations in Lancaster and the surrounding communities of Santa Clarita, Palmdale and Little Rock. The computer screen in Vlasic's vehicle would already display a list of every piece of apparatus at his disposal.

Two sheriff's cars and a black SUV with no markings, its flashing blue lights mounted inside the grille, sped past in the left-hand lane. Ahead, Bucky saw boiling flames and a cloud of black smoke billowing up into the dark sky. He followed the Box and the two engines from 129s to the Site 3 Gate and was waved through by the Federal Police. Inside the restricted area, they turned right onto the aircraft taxiway that ran between the facilities and the main runway.

Bucky monitored a constant stream of radio traffic.

"This is BC Vlasic. We are responding to the Site 3 Fire at Plant 42 in Lancaster.

Vlasic was first in and had already named the incident the "Site 3 Fire."
"Dispatch requests personnel use tactical channels 49 and 50. Blue 12 is reserved for Incident Command. All other County Fire personnel clear blue 12, switch to command blue 11. HazMat communications use tactical 10."

Vlasic gave an initial size-up: *"We have a report of unspecified composite materials from the aircraft burning in the jet fuel fire, probable aerosolization and release of toxic nanoparticles. Two structures on the south side of the taxiway are also burning. I am awaiting authorization for building entry from Colonel Waters. Who is the HazMat Captain on duty?"*

"This is Captain Swift. I am right behind you in the Box. The wind is out of the east at twenty-six miles per hour. We will set up upwind on the runway."

Behind him, Bucky saw a line of flashing red lights from the engines and other emergency vehicles streaming down Avenue M toward the access road. Directly ahead, the Box and the engines following it turned in a wide arc to avoid the smoke blowing from the fireball. Bucky stayed close behind in the pickup.

"I have established Incident Command post upwind." Vlasic said, *"On the northeast side of the Rangely Composites building, in front of the Northrup-Grumman plant. This incident number is 130090."*

Reports began to come through on the tactical channel
"Engine 129 on scene."
"Engine 329 on scene."

Bucky switched to the HazMat channel and heard Swift instruct his crew.

"Set up on the main runway, upwind of the jet. I want the weather station working ASAP. We need weather values and a reading on what's in the smoke plume and where it's going."

Vlasic's report of aerosolization meant the intense heat of the fire had turned the lightweight structural material in the body of the aircraft into plasma, or atomic gas, resulting in the release of toxic particles smaller than the width of a hair. While the Air Force would never reveal what kind of composite was burning, the risk of inhalation of any kind of nanoparticle carried the risk of serious lung damage. It was the HazMat crew's responsibility to identify the toxins and develop a plume model to predict how the wind might disperse them.

Kurt Kamm

"Level C protection and air for HazMat personnel." Swift's order meant regular turnout gear and self-contained breathing equipment. The risk was heat and toxic air. The higher level suits, Level B and Level A, were good for splash and vapor protection, but could melt in the intense heat of an aircraft fire. "They're not telling us what's burning on that jet," Swift told his crew. "I want the first team out on the runway with meters to measure toxics. Set up decon on the east side of the Box."

Bucky followed the Box to its position on the runway. He could see Vlasic standing behind his SUV, dressed in soiled turnouts, but wearing a spotless white battalion chief's helmet. As Incident Commander, Vlasic had charge of every man and piece of equipment on the field from the County Fire Department. He was conferring with someone who had to be the Fire Chief of Plant 42. Vlasic held two radios in one hand and scribbled on one of the clear plastic Incident Command maps with the other. He would let the HazMat team operate separately; his job was to implement an overall action plan to deploy firefighters to the burning buildings. It occurred to Bucky that this had to be the jackpot for a control freak like Chief Vlasic.

As Bucky surveyed the scene, it appeared to him that the jet had missed the main runway, hit the taxiway at an angle, careened into the side of the Rangely plant, setting it on fire before coming to rest next to the high bay doors of Stealth Systems. He recognized the tail and one short wing of the jet amid the flames, while a white-hot inferno obscured the rest of the craft. Smoke and super-heated gases billowed upward and were pushed westward by the desert wind. Two ARFF vehicles were already close-in, starting a foam spray from their overhead nozzles. In the glow of the fire, Bucky saw the men inside the ARFF vehicles wearing proximity suits, the protective gear coated with a silvered material to reflect heat away from their bodies. There was no sign of any effort to rescue the pilot and Bucky guessed that he had no time to eject at such a low altitude. From the intensity of the burn, it was unlikely he had survived.

"Stealth Systems and Rangely have been evacuated," Vlasic announced. "Report several injuries, no casualties. Buildings are reported empty. Stealth Systems has a 'let it burn' policy and we are denied entry. Repeat, exterior attack only at Stealth Systems. Rangely will allow access."

People on the night shift at several buildings in Sites 3 and 4 had collected outside in small groups to watch the fire. Many wore white masks over their nose and mouth. Paramilitary figures wearing compact breathing gear and carrying weapons had fanned out to surround the area. Bucky looked at a surreal scene—the approaching desert night had been turned into daylight. Spotlights on rooftops and towers created halos, illuminating the area around the fire. Powerful halogen lights on hydraulic platforms, raised from underground chambers, lit up the entire perimeter of Site 3. Two helicopters made slow circles, raking the ground with intense beams. Red strobe light bars on the emergency equipment created a bright glow.

As soon as the Squad stopped, Captain Swift was on the main runway organizing his HazMat crew. Men from Engines 129 and 329 already had their breathing gear on and were running toward the Box to help set up the weather station. Bucky parked and joined the chaos on the runway. Outside, the odor of smoke, burning jet fuel and a smell of incinerated plastic hit him. He didn't linger, but went around to the far side of the Squad, where he pulled out one of the drawers and took out an extra set of gear. In the frenzy of activity on the runway, Bucky was able to put on turnouts, boots, goggles, breathing apparatus and a helmet without notice. He grabbed a purple smoke canister and a small, pointed metal cutter from a supply drawer. He took a Draeger PID—photo ionization detector—and slipped everything into the pockets of his turnout coat. The Draeger meter cost several thousand dollars and if he lost or damaged it, there would be hell to pay. Both Vlasic and Swift would be furious if they knew what Bucky was doing, but 129s would be fully engaged at the incident for several hours, maybe even until late into the following morning. Bucky only needed a couple of hours to do what he planned to do. He slipped on his right-hand glove and kept his bare hand with the splinted fingers in an empty pocket.

A constant stream of engine companies and other support equipment including a USAR—Urban Search and Rescue—team streamed through the gate and the area filled with hundreds of firefighters and other emergency personnel. Wearing their SCBA gear, they began organizing an interior attack on the fire in the Stealth Systems building and deployed with charged hoses around the exterior fire at Rangely. Paramedics set up multicolored triage tarps and prepared to treat the injured. An RIC—Rapid Intervention Crew—assembled around the safety officer in case a rescue of firefighters was necessary.

Amid the frantic mass of men and equipment, Bucky walked purposefully toward the security forces standing inside the arc of spotlights. The men were three deep, staged in a staggered pattern to prevent anyone from slipping past them. They wore uniforms made of Kevlar and carried machine pistols. As Bucky approached the cordon, he reached into his pocket with his gloved hand and pulled out the PID. He leaned in toward one of the officers and said through his air mask, "I'm going out to take a particulate reading." The man looked at Bucky, checked the Draeger and waved him through with the barrel of his gun.

Bucky proceeded to the edge of the circle of light and then on into the desert darkness. Once he was away from the glare of the spotlights and the incandescence of the fire, he dropped his mask and breathing gear, turned on his small helmet flashlight and waited for his eyes to adjust to the darkness. The spaceport and Dubkova's jet were less than a quarter-mile away. Bucky started across the sand.

THIRTY-ONE

"**O**K, DUBKOVA, YOU SON-OF-A-BITCH. Time to come out and join the fun." As he approached the 747, Bucky thought he saw him inside, a moving silhouette blocking the light coming through the fuselage windows. He checked his watch. It was 7:40 p.m., not even an hour since the disabled jet had screamed by overhead.

Low-level outdoor lighting illuminated the underside of the jet, but Bucky knew once he stepped within range of the motion detectors and surveillance equipment, the whole area would light up like midday. He took off his turnout gear and left it in a pile on the edge of the tarmac with his helmet on top. He left the PID meter in the pocket of his coat, but took the smoke bomb and metal shears.

Bucky walked a wide circle around the aircraft to the tail and stood looking at the air compressor and filtration system. Even in the low light, he realized what had troubled him about the setup. What he saw was a closed system hooked up to scrub both the air going into and coming out of the jet. There were two large metal foil vent pipes running up to the fuselage. One forced clean air into the aircraft, while the other sucked the air out and sent it back through the filters and scrubbers.

It was time to find out what odors Dubkova was covering up. First, Bucky had to force him out; there was no way of climbing the scaffold and gaining access to the 747 without setting off every alarm. From a distance, he studied the compressor and the arrangement of the two vent pipes, trying to determine which was carrying clean air up into the jet. Once he decided, he moved fast, coming out of the darkness into the security area under the 747. By the time the motion detectors registered his movements, activated the lights and alarm and sent a signal to Dubkova, Bucky had already plunged the point of the metal shears into the first vent, opening a hole the size of a quarter. He heard a high-pitched whistle as desert air was sucked in through the puncture and sent up into the jet. Bucky pulled the pin of the smoke bomb and held the nozzle to the hole. The smoke flowed directly into the opening, but Bucky's nostrils still picked up the sharp odor of potassium chlorate, the active ingredient in the device. He waited for the bomb to empty and wondered if he had chosen the right color. Maybe purple smoke wasn't a good match for the interior of Dubkova's jet. When he heard a shout from inside the 747, he dropped the empty canister and murmured, "Come to Poppa."

Bucky began to count as he walked forward toward the scaffold at the side of the jet. When he reached 13, the hatch opened, a purple cloud escaped and Dubkova staggered out coughing and choking. Bucky waited at the bottom of the steps as Dubkova struggled down, blinded by the smoke and gasping for air. His eyes were slits on his bright red face, and tears streamed down his cheeks. When he stepped onto the ground, Bucky grabbed him by the shoulders. "Hello, again," Bucky said.

Dubkova tried to clear his eyes, but succumbed to a fit of coughing. When it finally passed, he began to gag.

Bucky shook him hard by the shoulders and said, "This is payback for the way you treated my sister." He only needed one good hand to take care of Dubkova and punched him hard in the stomach. Dubkova had more core muscles than Bucky expected, but the blow still knocked the wind out of him and sent him staggering backward against the front landing gear of the 747. As Dubkova struggled to get air into his lungs, Bucky shook him again by the shoulders and slammed his head against the enormous tire. Dubkova sank to the ground. "When the smoke clears out," Bucky said, "we're going to take a little tour of your jet and see what's cooking. Then, we might take a ride to the sheriff's station." Bucky felt wonderful. Finally, Dubkova was getting what he deserved. "I hope I'm not interrupting anything important," Bucky added.

The feeling of elation didn't last long. As he watched Dubkova doubled over, trying to breathe, Bucky felt strong, vise-like arms grab him from behind and lift him off the ground.

Bucky hit the tarmac hard. The same side of his head, slammed by a shovel days earlier, bounced against the rough surface. An explosion of light passed before his eyes and pain ricocheted through his body. When the agony subsided, Bucky looked up and saw the Dwarf, all seven feet, towering over him. He was wearing khakis and a blue shirt.

"Hey, motherfucker. Nice to see ya again."

Dubkova approached, still gasping for air, rubbing his eyes and spitting, trying to rid his mouth of the taste and smell of the smoke bomb. "Dawson!" he wheezed, then turned to the Dwarf and said, "And where have you been, you moron?"

"Where have I been? I just saved yer fuckin' ass."

"If you were here on time, you wouldn't have had to save my ass."

"It took forever to get through the gate. There's some kinda security alert goin' on."

"A jet crashed on the runway at Plant 42. Did you use the SkyScan ID I gave you?"

The Dwarf nodded. "Don't I look like a space scientist?"

Dubkova wiped his eyes again and looked at his watch. "You've got to get going—it's late."

"What're we gonna do with this piece a shit?"

"This piece of shit just filled the inside of my plane with smoke."

"I'll fix him."

"Not now and not here. Take him with you and dump him after you finish."

"I think yer comin' with me. You can keep an eye on this asshole while I'm handlin' things."

"No way."

Bucky lay on the ground, listened to the two men talk and considered whether he could get up and fight. Assorted head injuries, bruises and two crushed fingers told him NO. He struggled to stand up anyway. When he got to his knees, Dubkova came over and shoved him. Bucky fell back on the ground. Pain echoed through his body.

"I will come this time," Dubkova said. "Just to see the end of this guy."

"Where's the crank?" the Dwarf said.

"In the Hummer."

"Good, you can drive."

"Alright, but we have to go now."

"Hey, ain't nobody gonna leave before we get there. We're sellin'. They're buyin'. You got anything to tie him up?"

"I have duct tape."

"Get it." The Dwarf lit a cigarette, exhaled, kneeled down and pressed one of his huge hands against Bucky's chest. On his knees, he still towered over Bucky. "Heya, bud," the Dwarf said. "This is the last time we're gonna fuck with you." He took another drag of his cigarette and blew smoke in Bucky's face.

Bucky coughed and pain coursed through his body.

"Do ya like doggies?" the Dwarf asked.

Bucky tried to clear his head.

"I said, do ya like dogs?"

Dubkova pulled up next to them in his Hummer. He jumped out and handed a roll of two-inch duct tape to the Dwarf. "Hurry."

"Just a damn minute," the Dwarf snarled. He bent over Bucky and wrapped tape around his ankles, then his wrists, binding his hands together in a position of prayer. The Dwarf lifted Bucky and dumped him on the back seat of the Hummer. "I'll be right back," he said to Dubkova.

"Where you going?" Dubkova said.

"I wanna change my clothes. I ain't goin' nowhere without my colors. Besides, Thunder's still in the truck, I gotta get him."

"Thunder? That miserable dog? He's not coming in my Hummer."

"Yeah he is."

"Well, hurry up."

THIRTY-TWO

"THUNDER AIN'T HAD DINNER YET," The Dwarf announced as the Hummer headed down Sierra Highway.

Bucky wasn't sitting on the rear seat—he was attached to it. The Dwarf had wound most of the remaining duct tape across Bucky's chest and around the back of the seat. It was so tight that Bucky could barely breathe. He wondered if any of his bones were broken. His head was pounding and his entire body ached. Bucky slowed his breathing and told himself not to be frightened. He had to stay calm and figure out what to do.

Parcels wrapped in tinfoil and sealed with plastic wrap were stacked up on the seat next to him. Bucky was certain it was meth. They were all the same size—neat rectangles—the precise work of an aerospace engineer. Behind him, Thunder strained at a chain running through an O-ring anchored to the floor. It was a short tether, with just enough play to allow the dog to get its snout and sharp teeth close to the side of Bucky's head. The Hummer reeked with the smell of the dog's foul breath.

Bucky had never met a dog he didn't like or couldn't communicate with, but Thunder might be the first. The silver-gray beast had the ugly square head and small ears of the breed. Its short, compact body was pure muscle and sinew. In the weak light, Thunder glared at Bucky through narrow, tan-colored eyes, emitted a low growl and strained to get close enough to sink his teeth into Bucky's flesh. Bucky turned his head and made direct eye contact, hoping to quiet the animal, but that only seemed to enrage him. Bucky gave up and tried to squirm away from the dog to the far side of the seat but the tape held him securely. When Thunder lunged toward his head, Bucky's heart began to pound in his chest.

"I hate being late." Dubkova said. "We should be the first ones there to check everything out."

"Nothin' to check out," the Dwarf said. "We drive up, do our business and take off."

"I like to know what I'm getting into."

"They're just comin' to buy crank."

"Do you know how many chapters the Vagos have?"

The Dwarf looked at Dubkova with a blank stare.

Dubkova answered his own question. "Twenty-four, and that's just in the states. There's ten more in Mexico. Why aren't we selling to every one of them? This could be so much bigger. I think I should talk to the Vagos national president."

"T-Bone?" The Dwarf said.

"Yeah, T-Bone. And how many different motorcycle gangs are there in California, Arizona and Nevada?" Before the Dwarf could respond, Dubkova again answered, "Eighteen or twenty, right? Why aren't we selling to all of them? Who's buying from us now? The Grim Reapers, the Mongols, the Gypsies. That's it."

"The Gypsy Jokers."

"The Gypsy Jokers. That's three gangs out of twenty. What about the Hells Angels?"

"Those fucks. What about 'em?"

"They're the biggest club. Why aren't we selling to them?"

"We're at war with them guys."

"War?"

"They destroyed a bunch of our bikes and we hit 'em back. We sure as fuck ain't selling crank to the Hells Angels."

"What about the other gangs?"

"We're workin' on it."

"Tell your biker brothers to work on it a little faster."

"Listen, bud," the Dwarf said, "we are working on it. Hear me? It takes time."

Bucky strained at the tape around his wrists and watched the Dwarf in the front seat as he glared at Dubkova. His bald head and protruding chin and forehead made him look like something out of a horror movie.

"I can't wait forever," Dubkova said. "I've got other things to do. More important things."

The Dwarf turned around to look at Bucky. "And you, you fuck, I'm gonna enjoy torching your ass." He backhanded Bucky in the face.

The blow snapped Bucky's head to the side and his brain felt like a cue ball bouncing off the side of a billiard table. Bucky knew he was in serious trouble and his fear response released a flood of adrenaline into his bloodstream. He struggled against the tape holding his wrists, but it was tough and unyielding.

"Thunder's gonna have a little fun with ya," the Dwarf said. "Then he's gonna have dinner."

The pit bull seemed to understand and strained toward Bucky, releasing a low-pitched growl inches from his ear.

Dubkova rubbed his eyes again, cleared his throat, lowered his window and spit. He glanced at Bucky in the rearview mirror. "That damned smoke is still in my lungs."

"I hope it gives you cancer," Bucky said. He watched the road as the Hummer slowed, turned onto Pearblossom Highway and headed east toward Barstow, another armpit in the high desert.

"I'll be enjoying life long after you're gone, Dawson," Dubkova said.

"If I disappear, you'll be the first person the sheriff's department comes after."

"Those idiots?" Dubkova said. He pressed down on the gas pedal and the Hummer accelerated down the empty two-lane highway. "They actually thought they could find a meth lab using a drone? They're so stupid they couldn't find a cockroach on a white table cloth." Dubkova looked at Bucky in the rearview mirror. "But I have to hand it to you, you were right. It was trichloroethane. You've got a first-class sniffer."

"I hear you're using it to clean parts for your new drones." Bucky figured he might as well keep Dubkova talking while he figured out what to do next. His options were limited and time was running out. Thunder moved around behind him. He could feel his warm breath on the back of his neck.

"Yeah?" Dubkova said, "Who told you that?"

"Who do you think?" Bucky said. "It wasn't the Marines."

"The Air Force?" Dubkova said. "They're almost as stupid as the sheriff's department. Know how you obfuscate solvent with lithium residue from a meth lab?"

"What's obfuscate?" the Dwarf asked.

"It's a verb," Dubkova said. "It means to cover up."

"How?" Bucky said.

"You add a lithium-based aerospace lubricant. I didn't go to MIT because I'm stupid. Just in case someone tried to do an analysis of what we were dumping, they'd come up with Aerospec 200, and that's exactly what happened."

"I knew you were cooking meth on your jet," Bucky said, "as soon as I realized how the air scrubbers were set up."

"I told the Air Force I was using TCE as a degreaser and it had some of my classified, proprietary chemical compounds in it along with the lubricant. I insisted I wanted my people to dispose of it, and they agreed. They couldn't care less about anything but getting a new generation of drones as fast as possible."

"Yer the man," the Dwarf said.

Bucky heard Thunder moving around behind the seat. Somehow, the pit bull managed to stretch another inch and sank his incisors into Bucky's earlobe.

"Ahh," Bucky cried out as Thunder ripped away a piece of flesh. He tried to press his hand against his ear, but with his wrists taped together, he could barely reach it. "Jesus, that hurts."

The Dwarf glanced back at Bucky, laughed and said, "I guess yer hearing ain't too good right now."

The pain in Bucky's left ear, or what was left of it, was a searing, white-hot flame. Out of the corner of his eye, he saw blood dripping down onto his shoulder.

Thunder, excited by the taste of Bucky's flesh and blood, snarled from deep in his barrel chest and pulled again at the chain.

Bucky leaned his head away.

"Dawson," Dubkova said, "you could be home watching television, or polishing your fire engine or doing whatever stupid firemen do. But no, you had to sniff solvent fumes ten miles away and then run to tell the sheriff about it. You asshole, why didn't you just mind your own business?"

"I owe you for what you did to my sister," Bucky said. The pain in his ear was becoming more intense.

"Brandy?" Dubkova said. "Hah."

"That cunt?" The Dwarf said. "She was yer sister? That fuckin' addict?"

"But a good-looking addict," Dubkova said. "You know what, Dawson? I did screw her, and at first, she was a good lay. I knew she was hot the first time I laid eyes on her. Actually, she was a terrific lay. So much better than my tight-assed wife. She was even better when she had a little meth in her—she went on for hours. She wanted drugs and she wanted sex. A great combination."

Bucky's anger at Dubkova was at the boiling point, and he was helpless. He tried again to twist his hands out of the duct tape. The pain inside of his head was unbearable.

"But he's right," Dubkova said, nodding toward the Dwarf. "Like every other miserable addict, she got to the point where she couldn't get the crank into her body fast enough, and then she was no good for anything. Who knows who else was doing her? She got pregnant and had a baby—a baby addict. Two losers. Who cares?"

"I care," Bucky said, gritting his teeth against his injury.

"Hey," the Dwarf interrupted Dubkova. "I wanna take off as soon as we're done tonight. We're not gonna hang and count cash."

"Why?" Dubkova said. "What's the rush? What if they're short?"

"They ain't gonna be short. It's a matter of honor."

"Honor among thieves?" Dubkova laughed.

"Fuck ya," the Dwarf said.

Bucky's wrists hurt from pulling against the duct tape, adding to all the other pain in his body. For the first time in his thirty-one-year life, he wondered if he would be alive when the sun rose in the morning. On duty, he had been in several dangerous situations, but even at times when his own death was possible, he somehow knew it wasn't going to happen. Tonight, sitting in the Hummer with the Dwarf towering in the front seat and Thunder growling behind him, things were different.

"No, fuck *you*," Dubkova said. "Did you go to MIT? Do you know how to cook high-grade meth? I'm the most important person you know. Fuck *you* and shut up!"

Is this the way it works, Bucky wondered. You live your life day after day, not paying much attention, and then suddenly discover you only have a few hours left? He thought of Zoll. The lizard would starve to death in its glass tank. He thought of the nurse, Lexie. He might not get to see her again.

"Yer gettin' on my nerves," the Dwarf said to Dubkova.

Bucky realized he might be about to die and that he was thinking about a lizard and about a woman he had seen once for a few minutes and hardly knew. How pathetic. Mike was right, he could go into witness protection and not leave anyone behind. Bucky hadn't accomplished much in his life. He hadn't gone anywhere, hadn't done anything exceptional and didn't have many special memories. If he died tonight, Mike would mourn his death and the brothers at the fire department would utter a prayer and keep him in their thoughts for a few weeks, but then they would forget about him and move on to the more important things in their own lives. Bucky strained against the duct tape and decided if this was the end, he would do anything possible to take Dubkova and the Dwarf with him. If he couldn't take them both, Dubkova was his first choice. He longed for a Perc. In fact, he longed for several Percs. It was possible he had already taken his last pill, and not because he had decided to go clean.

THIRTY-THREE

DUBKOVA LOOKED AT HIS WATCH. "We'll be there in a few minutes."
"Ya got a gun?" the Dwarf asked.

"Why?" Dubkova said.

"In case."

"In case what?"

"Just what I said. In case."

"I left it on the jet."

"Yer the moron."

Bucky was desperate. He wondered if Thunder was more excited by the butyric acid in his nervous sweat or by the smell and taste of his blood. It was time to find out.

The Dwarf lit another stinking cigarette and filled the inside of the Hummer with smoke.

Bucky lifted his bound wrists to the side of his head and was able to brush his fingertips across his injured ear. He almost pulled his right shoulder out of the socket, but with even his wrists bound, he managed to reach left across the seat to smear his blood on the top package of meth.

Thunder picked up the scent immediately, pulled at the slack in his chain, leaned over the top of the seat and began to lick Bucky's blood off the wrapping.

"When we get there," the Dwarf said, "get out of the car and let them see ya."

"Me?" Dubkova said. "No way. They don't know me. You're the biker wearing leathers. You get out of the car. I'll guard the meth."

"You and what fuckin' army?" the Dwarf said. "*I'll* guard the meth; I have the gun."

"I thought these were honorable brothers. Why do you need a gun?"

Bucky ran his hand across the side of his head again, collected more blood and smeared it on the meth brick.

Thunder stopped growling and concentrated on the taste of the blood. His pink tongue scoured the plastic wrap, then tore a piece of it away. He became agitated. He wanted more.

"Here's the turn," the Dwarf said, bending his head to look out the side window.

Bucky saw the green and white sign indicating Oro Grande and recognized the spot. They were now on Highway 15, part of the old Route 66. He raked the raw skin on the side of his head and the torn flesh on his ear with the metal end of his splint. It sent waves of pain through his temple, but Bucky wanted to accumulate as much blood as he could on the back of his hand.

Thunder was panting and excited. He had managed to get his paws over the top of the seat next to Bucky. As soon as Bucky smeared the sticky, sweet red substance on the torn wrapping of the package of meth, Thunder licked it clean.

Dubkova checked his watch.

The Dwarf opened the window a crack and threw out his cigarette. He pulled a chrome-plated pistol from the waistband of his oversize jeans.

Dubkova looked at the gun.

Bucky knew this location. Up the deserted road was Emma Jean's Holland Burger Café, a square, pale green building from the 1950s with an American flag in front. Across the highway, there was a parking area for dump trucks from a nearby quarry. The only other thing on this stretch of highway was Dino Land, a defunct theme park with enormous cement dinosaur statues. Bucky poked the tip of the metal splint into his flesh and collected more blood. His ear was becoming numb from the pain.

Thunder waited eagerly.

When Bucky wiped his blood on the torn foil, it only took a second for Thunder to scrub it clean with his tongue and sink his front teeth into the package, ripping it completely open.

The broken chain link fence surrounding Dino Land loomed in the headlights of the Hummer.

"So where are they?" Dubkova said. He hit his bright lights.

The Dwarf leaned forward to look through the windshield. "I dunno. Maybe they're late too."

"I got a bad feeling," Dubkova said. "It's all his fault," he said, glancing back at Bucky. "He screwed up the whole evening."

Bucky sat quietly, trying not to attract attention from the front seat. With his bound hands in his lap, he continued to struggle to twist out of the duct tape, which had now cut into the flesh on his wrists but would not give way.

Thunder lifted his head and Bucky saw white powder on his snout. He had once asked Mike if meth had any taste. Mike said sometimes it had a bitter chemical taste, sometimes it was supposed to taste like apples and sometimes it had no taste at all. Bucky hoped this batch of meth tasted like fried chicken. Thunder lowered his head and buried his muzzle in the open package again.

Dubkova slowed and stopped near the Dino Land fence.

Bucky glanced through the side window. All he could see on the other side of the chain link was a cement pad, huge claws, and the legs and belly of a predator. The sign said VELOCIRAPTOR.

The Dwarf opened his door. When he stepped out onto the pavement, headlights lit up down the road. The Dwarf held his hands to his eyes, trying to shield them from the glare.

Bucky's arms were cramping and nearly exhausted from his struggle with the duct tape. He watched Dubkova lean forward against the steering wheel, looking through the windshield to see who was approaching. Bucky expected to hear the thunder of motorcycles. He heard only a single engine.

The Dwarf came back to the open door and said to Dubkova, "They musta' come in a van." He held his pistol in one hand.

Behind the seat, Thunder's respiration had picked up. Bucky heard the dog's ragged breathing, the air rattling in his throat.

A van approached. It was almost parallel to the Hummer when Bucky saw the gun barrel appear in the van's open rear window. He heard pistol shots and the side of the velociraptor exploded. Pieces of cement ricocheted against the Hummer.

"Fuck," the Dwarf screamed. He fired a couple of shots at the van and ran toward an opening in the Dino Land fence.

The big man moved slowly and was not more than a few feet away from the Hummer when Bucky heard two long bursts of an automatic weapon.

Small red craters appeared on the Dwarf's back and he pitched face-forward on the ground. Bucky watched him struggle to crawl toward the fence until his body shook from the impact of another round of bullets and he lay still. Blood oozed into the gutter.

Dubkova's shaking hands fumbled with the key in the ignition. He started the engine, but before he could get the vehicle in gear, a biker holding a pistol jumped out of the van, smashed the driver's side window and pressed a revolver against Dubkova's temple.

Bucky watched from the back seat as Dubkova froze with fear, his hands holding the steering wheel in a death-grip.

"Open your door," the biker ordered Dubkova. "Get out."

Thunder didn't bark at the biker; he was too interested in the white powder. He leaned over the top of the seat and buried his snout in the package again.

Bucky saw several other bikers get out of the van. They all carried guns.

"No, don't shoot me," Dubkova said in a terrified voice. "I didn't do anything. I'm not a biker, I'm just a chemist."

"Ya got something against bikers?"

"Take the meth," Dubkova pleaded. "It's in the back. You can have it. You don't have to pay for it. It's top quality—take it. Please, I'm a Defense Department scientist."

"The fuck you are."

Thunder ripped apart the top package of meth and powder spilled onto the seat.

Dubkova put his palm up in front of the gun barrel "I went to MIT. Please—"

A single pistol shot exploded inside the vehicle. The bullet went through Dubkova's hand and his forehead. The bits of the backside of his skull and his MIT-trained brain splattered on the front passenger seat of the Hummer. The force of the bullet pushed his body partway onto the center console.

Bucky's ears were ringing from the pistol shot that ended Dubkova's life. Thunder was now down behind the seat where Bucky couldn't see him, but he felt the dog's body shaking against the backrest and thought he must be having seizures. Thunder began to choke and spit up, and the odor of vomit and stomach acid replaced the smell of cordite inside the vehicle.

Three bikers from the van, holding pistols and an automatic weapon, walked toward the Hummer. One of the bikers fired his pistol twice in the air.

The ensuing roar of a motorcycle army coming down the empty highway drowned out the sound of the dog retching.

One-percenters on their bikes surrounded the Hummer and one by one, their engines went silent.

THIRTY-FOUR

"**C**HECK THIS OUT."
Both rear doors of the Hummer opened, letting the dry desert air in to dispel the stench of Thunder's stomach fluids. The first thing Bucky saw was a sawed-off shotgun, the stock replaced by a pistol grip, held by a pair of rough-looking hands. A biker stuck his head inside and pushed the barrel of the gun against the side of Bucky's face.

"Who the fuck'r you?" another biker asked, then saw the packages on the adjoining seat. "Hey, brothers," he shouted, "Look a' what we got."

"Smells like crap in here," the biker with the shotgun said. He moved the barrel away from Bucky's face. "Ya shit yer pants?" He picked up the open package of meth and dipped a finger into it.

"It's the pit bull behind the seat," Bucky said. "He ate some of the magic powder." Bucky heard the rear gate of the Hummer swing open and was able to turn just enough to see several bikers, carrying guns, standing around the rear of the vehicle. They looked no different than the Vagos Bucky had seen at Mach 2, except that none of them wore green. Thunder was in no shape to growl. The only sound Bucky heard was the animal's labored breathing.

"Yer dog?" the biker with the shotgun asked.

"Not mine, no."

"Who are ya?" another biker asked.

"I'm just a firefighter. I was trying to settle a personal beef."

"With mister govermint scientist?"

Bucky nodded.

"Too late now. He's dead."

"What about the Dwarf?" Bucky asked.

"Fuckin' dead."

"Great," Bucky said. He tried to sound as happy and enthusiastic as he could, given the circumstances. "Thanks for helping me out."

"Helping ya out?" Laughter rippled through the group of bikers.

"Sure. The enemy of my enemy is …" Bucky couldn't remember what he wanted to say. He was exhausted; his brain was shutting down.

The biker with the shotgun leaned in and looked at the side of Bucky's head. "Looks like they did a number on ya. Yer bleedin'. The Dwarf do that?"

Bucky nodded again.

"Justa minute. Don't go nowhere." More laughter.

The crowd of bikers moved a few feet away and, for the first time, Bucky saw the colors on their backs. They wore winged skulls, the death's head insignia of the Hells Angels. The Hells Angels, he thought. Things were beginning to make some sense. He heard them talking in low voices.

Bucky looked at Dubkova's body slumped over the center console. He was face down and part of the back of his head was missing. Blood and gray matter covered the expensive leather trim.

One of the Angels came back to the Hummer. He was a short little guy— one of the smallest bikers Bucky had ever seen—but still nasty looking. He had a mustache, a short beard with the hair tied in small knots and a scar on his cheek. He was silent as he looked Bucky in the eye and brandished a knife.

Bucky stared back at the little biker and waited. A coyote out in the desert yelped a few times and was silent. Thunder's breathing became even more ragged. The blade of the knife reflected silver from the headlight of a Harley.

The Angel leaned in toward Bucky, holding the knife in his fist, pointing it at Bucky's stomach.

Bucky drew in a breath and held it. He imagined the blade tearing open his chest.

The Angel cut the tape binding his wrists.

"Jesus," Bucky said, and exhaled. "Thanks." He never thought he could like a Hells Angel, but now, he felt as though he loved this little guy.

The Angel said nothing, but cut through the tape holding Bucky to the seat and ripped it away, taking part of Bucky's T-shirt with it.

Bucky leaned forward and watched the knife slice through the tape around his ankles. He rubbed his wrists.

The small biker stepped back without saying anything and the Hells Angel with the shotgun reappeared. "We're taking the Hummer and ya need to clear out," he said. He waved the barrel of the shotgun at Bucky. "I'm sure ya won't remember anything that happened here. Right?"

"Damn right," Bucky said. "I have no idea what happened. Besides, I have terrible eyesight. Can't see anything without my glasses." Bucky thought of Dubkova and his fake spectacles.

One of the Angels came to the back of the Hummer with a huge red bolt cutter, sliced through the chain holding Thunder and yanked one end. Bucky heard a soft thud and a whimper as the pit bull's body hit the blacktop. A second later, a shot from a handgun ended Thunder's life. Thunder had seen his last day on earth and died without dinner.

When Bucky climbed out of the Hummer, his legs were numb and he stood waiting for his circulation to return. A Hells Angel pulled Dubkova's lifeless body out of the driver's seat and let it fall onto the highway. The biker with the shotgun jumped inside, and Bucky watched the SUV pull away, followed by the van. He looked down and saw what was left of Thunder on the pavement in a pool of blood. White saliva and foam still glistened on his muzzle.

Bucky felt unsteady as he began to walk slowly back toward Emma Jean's Holland Burger Café. He hadn't taken five steps before the remaining Hells Angels fired up their Harleys and roared past him in a cloud of exhaust. The sound of the engines echoed across the desert and died out in the darkness.

Bucky walked on in silence for a few minutes until a Burlington Northern Santa Fe freight train rumbled toward him along the track running parallel to the highway. Its headlight rotated slightly, creating a cone of light out over the track as it approached. Bucky stopped to watch the huge metal behemoth as the first of several square diesel engines lumbered past him. He listened to the click-click-click of the steel wheels as they rolled over the joints in the track while the tang of diesel fumes drifted over him. He thought it smelled wonderful. Bucky looked up into the sky. The night was clear and a million stars and planets winked at him, as if they approved of his adventure. The wind picked up and blew at his back. At that moment, even the high desert wind was his friend. Bucky thought it might scrub him clean.

He took in a lungful of air and resumed walking. It occurred to him that he wouldn't have to decide whether to participate in Witness Protection now that the Hells Angels had dispatched the Dwarf. He felt a pang of disappointment—he was starting to like the idea of moving out of Lancaster and starting over.

Now that all the excitement was over, the pain returned to his body, and especially to his torn ear. On the heels of the pain came an intense desire for a couple of Percs. How many hours had it been? He looked at his watch. It was 10:45 p.m. He had taken his last pills in the early afternoon just after Mike left the house. Bucky had expected a quick dinner with his buddies at the station and then a return home to wallow in a nightcap of painkillers. Instead, it had been a harrowing evening.

Bucky's body cried out for some Percocet now. Bucky told his body it would have to wait—he was walking down an empty highway in the middle of the high desert and his pills were miles away in the pickup, parked near the runway at Plant 42.

THIRTY-FIVE

"GOOD MORNING, MR. DAWSON."
An angel was standing on his small porch. It wasn't a Hells Angel, it was Lexie. Bucky looked at her pale green eyes. She was even more beautiful than he remembered.

She paused for a moment, looking at the bandages around his head and ear. "Your grandmother passed away last night. I just dropped my son off at a birthday party. Since I was already in Lancaster, I thought I would come and tell you in person."

Bucky stood frozen at the door.

"Mr. Dawson?"

"Come in," Bucky said, recovering from the surprise of seeing her. "I'm just Bucky, no one calls me Mr. Dawson." He held the screen door open for Lexie and inhaled her presence as she stepped into his house. He thought she smelled wonderful.

"You look terrible. Did you get hit in the head again?" She reached out to touch him. Her hand was cool on his forehead. "Are you alright?"

"Torn ear, a few new bruises and a mild concussion. Nothing serious."

"Nothing serious?"

"Thanks for coming by. It's nice to see you." Bucky thought it was very nice to see her. "How did Gram go?"

"Natural causes, in her sleep. It was peaceful."

"Well, I guess that's all you can ask for, to die quietly in your sleep." Bucky led her into the living room. "Can you stay a few minutes? I could make some coffee."

"Sure, that would be nice."

"Do you do a lot of this?"

"A lot of what?"

"Notifying families, in person."

"It's a voluntary thing. When I first started, I did it all the time, but not much anymore. It's depressing, and not everyone wants a personal notification. In fact, working at Comfort Care is becoming unbearable. Spending all my time with dementia patients is really getting to me. I don't know how much longer I can do it."

"What did you do before?"

"I was a nurse-counselor at a drug rehab center in Bakersfield. My husband and I had a nasty divorce and I needed to get away from him, so I . . ." She paused. "You sure you want to hear all this? I came to bring you a little comfort, not to recount my own problems."

"I've got nothing better to do. I'm happy to listen."

"I had to get out of Bakersfield, so I took the job at Comfort Care. It offered more money and shorter hours so I could spend more time with my son."

"How old is he?"

"He'll be five in December."

"My sister Brandy had a daughter, but she only lived a few months."

"I'm sorry to hear that."

"Brandy died a couple of weeks ago in a meth lab explosion."

"Was she an addict?"

Bucky nodded. "And her baby was born addicted, had all kinds of physical problems and didn't make it. It may be just as well. I was told she would never have been normal. Come in the kitchen."

Lexie followed and saw the empty reptile tank on the counter. "What do you keep in there, a baby alligator?"

"I had a lizard that we rescued from someone's garage. I kept it for a while, but it wasn't happy and I just couldn't imprison it in a glass tank any longer. I let it go. It may not survive, but at least it'll die naturally, doing whatever lizards do. It's better than sitting on a rock under a sunlamp, waiting for me to feed it."

Lexie sat down at the table. Bucky regarded her and thought how good she looked, sitting in his kitchen. "Would you like a piece of fruit? Maybe a pear?"

"Strange combination, coffee and a pear, but yes, I like pears."

Bucky took two pieces of the fruit from the refrigerator, washed them, cut them in quarters and placed them on a plate. "I just bought these yesterday."

"Thank you," Lexie said. "Can I ask you something? Why do you get hurt so often? Are you in some kind of trouble?"

Bucky put grounds in his coffeemaker and switched it on. He watched the little red light blink for a moment before he sat down at the table across from Lexie. "I've been through a difficult time in the past few weeks. There was this business with my sister and her baby. She was mixed up with some outlaw bikers and they beat me up twice. The second time, they smashed my fingers." He held up his injured hand. "Right now I'm on unpaid leave from the fire department. Two days ago, one of the bikers and a meth chemist took me out near Barstow and were about to kill me."

Lexie grimaced. "How frightening."

"It's strange what goes through your mind when you think you might die. One of the thoughts I had was that I wouldn't get to see you again."

She gave him a tentative smile. "You were planning on calling me?"

"I was thinking about it."

"What happened? How did you get away?"

"The Hells Angels saved me."

"The Hells Angels?" She stood up. "You're involved in drugs, aren't you?"

"My sister was. I've actually been helping the sheriff's department. I'm one of the good guys ... I think."

"Tell me you're not doing anything illegal." Lexie sat down again.

"No. I mean no, I'm not." Bucky couldn't believe this beautiful woman was sitting in his kitchen, talking to him. "Not doing anything illegal."

"Do you swear?"

"I had some personal scores to settle, but that's over. How do you take your coffee?"

"Black." She reached for a piece of pear and looked at her watch. "I have to pick up my son in half an hour."

Bucky poured two cups of coffee, pushed one across the table and sat down.

"The nurse in me says something's bothering you. What is it?"

"Well, I ... uh ... Bucky looked into her pale green eyes and decided to take the plunge. "Funny how things happen. I had no idea you were a drug counselor. I need some help. Somehow I've become addicted to Percocet. I'm taking seven or eight 10-milligram pills a day and haven't been able to stop."

"Everyone tells the same story, but not everyone really wants to stop."

"I do want to quit. I really want it out of my life," Once Bucky started, it all came spilling out. "It's terrible. Every time I decide to stop, I find a reason not to. I don't think I can get over it by myself."

"Where are you getting the painkillers?"

"I started with leftover prescriptions for back pain. Then I ordered it online." Lexie reached across the table and put her hands on his. Who's enabling you?"

"I got into this mess all by myself."

"Have you tried any treatments or rehab?"

Bucky shook his head.

"Do you have any family members or a girlfriend to help you?

"No one."

"And you really want to stop?"

"Yes."

"And stay clean?"

"Yes."

"Well, the first step is to admit that you're an addict. You seem to have accomplished that. Did you know addiction changes your brain chemistry? Some of your receptors get desensitized."

"Desensitized?"

"Yes, from the continual bombardment of the dopamine created by whatever you're taking. It's complicated. I'm not a doctor and I can't give you all the details, but the good news is that it's easier to recover from opioid addiction than from stuff like meth and cocaine."

"Would you help me get through it?"

"I don't know. I don't trust addicts." She stared at him for a moment. "You would have to go to some organized rehab program. I could give you moral support and maybe some advice." She gave him another, broader smile. "I'd have to see you on a regular basis."

"That wouldn't be so bad. I could get used to that."

"I have to warn you, one strike and you're out. I won't waste my time living through relapses and backsliding."

"I understand."

"Let me think about it."

"Thank you." Bucky was certain she had already made up her mind to help him. "I have a question for you."

"What?"

"If you could take your son and move anywhere, where would you go?"

"I don't even have to think about that; I already know. I want to move to Montana."

Bucky closed his eyes and imagined a dark blue mountain lake in a valley between majestic peaks still covered with the winter's snow. A bald eagle skimmed over the surface, caught a fish in its powerful talons and lifted off. The clear sky above, like a window into space, was the same deep blue as the water. There was no wind, no dust, no sand, only a light breeze that ruffled the pine trees on the shore. The air was cool and clear, the mountains smelled clean and pure.

"Yeah," Bucky said, "I'd like to move to Montana, too."

ACKNOWLEDGMENTS

THANKS TO MANY OLD AND new friends, who were so generous with their time and advice, and who helped make this book possible:

Los Angeles County Fire Captain Mike Brownlie, Hazardous Materials Specialist, who invited me into his HazMat classes at El Camino Fire Academy, and advised and encouraged me on this project.

Los Angeles County Fire Captain James Swift and all the men in Hazardous Materials Task Force 129 in Lancaster, California, who welcomed me to Station 129, introduced me to Zoll the lizard, helped me understand Air Force Plant 42 and told me about life in Lancaster. I will also never forget the trip we took in the HazMat Box to visit a biker bar in the Mojave Desert.

Los Angeles County Fire Captain Antonio Duran, Commander, Hazardous Materials Task Force 43 A, who took me to a training session at Del Valle, which brought to life what happens when a gasoline tanker overturns on the freeway.

Los Angeles County Fire Captain Randy Alva, Hazardous Materials Coordinator, Homeland Security Division, who helped me make contact with so many County Fire HazMat personnel.

Los Angeles City Fire Captain Jaime Lesinski, HAZMAT Task Force Commander, who allowed me to attend several HazMat technician training classes and drills.

Kurt Kamm

Members of the **Los Angeles County Sheriff's Department Bomb Squad and Narcotics Squad** who helped me understand methamphetamine addicts, their laboratories and law enforcement efforts to stop them.

Raun Burnham and **Rob Martin** for reading various drafts.

Dr. Jeffrey Titcher for expert advice on painkiller addiction.

My good friend and editor, **Denise Middlebrooks,** who consistently offers expert guidance and advice.

My long-suffering wife **Connie,** who had to hear about Bucky's addiction every day for a year.

ABOUT THE AUTHOR

Malibu resident Kurt Kamm has used his contact with CalFire, Los Angeles County Fire Department, Ventura County Fire Department and the ATF, as well as his experience in several devastating local wildfires, to write fact-based firefighter mystery novels. He has attended classes at El Camino Fire Academy and trained in wildland firefighting, arson investigation and hazardous materials response. He is also a graduate of the ATF Citizen's Academy. He is currently riding with Los Angeles County Fire Department's famed Urban Search & Rescue Task Force 2/USA-2, and is working on a USAR mystery.

One of the Malibu fires, the 60 mile-per-hour Santa Ana wind-driven Canyon Fire, burned to his front door and destroyed the homes of several neighbors. Kamm said the lessons he learned from the County Fire Department while writing his first book helped him save his home.

A graduate of Brown University and Columbia Law School, Kamm was previously a financial executive and semi-professional bicycle racer. He was also Chairman of the UCLA/Jonsson Comprehensive Cancer Center Foundation and is an avid supporter of the Wildland Firefighter Foundation.

For further information on Kurt Kamm visit his first responder/author website **www.KurtKamm.com.**